THE
HOROSCOPE
WRITER

THE
HOROSCOPE
WRITER

ASH BISHOP

CamCat
Books

CamCat Publishing, LLC
Brentwood, Tennessee 37027
camcatpublishing.com

Hardcover ISBN 9780744309294
Paperback ISBN 9780744309300
Large-Print Paperback ISBN 9780744309317
eBook ISBN 9780744309324
Audiobook ISBN 9780744309348

Library of Congress Control Number: 2022951188

Book and cover design by Maryann Appel

5   3   1   2   4

In Memory of Robert Mulgrew

Teacher Extraordinaire

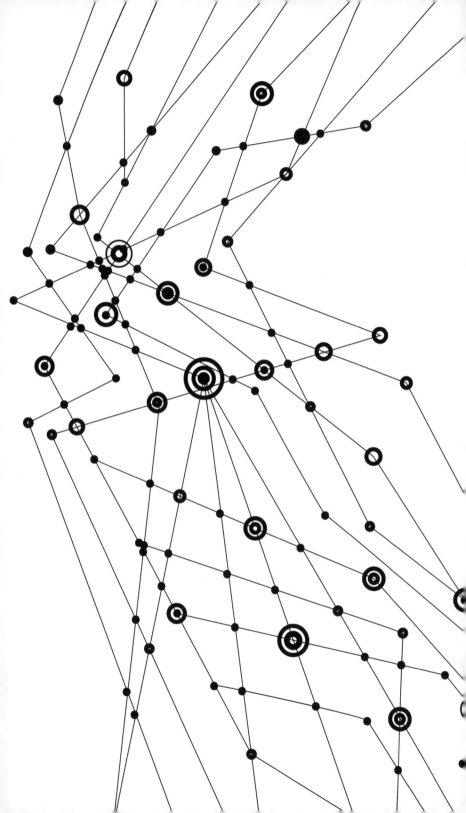

. . . and there is a Catskill eagle in some souls
That can alike dive down into the blackest gorges
And soar out of them again . . .

—*Herman Melville,* Moby-Dick

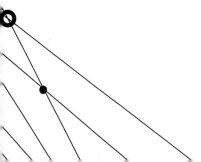

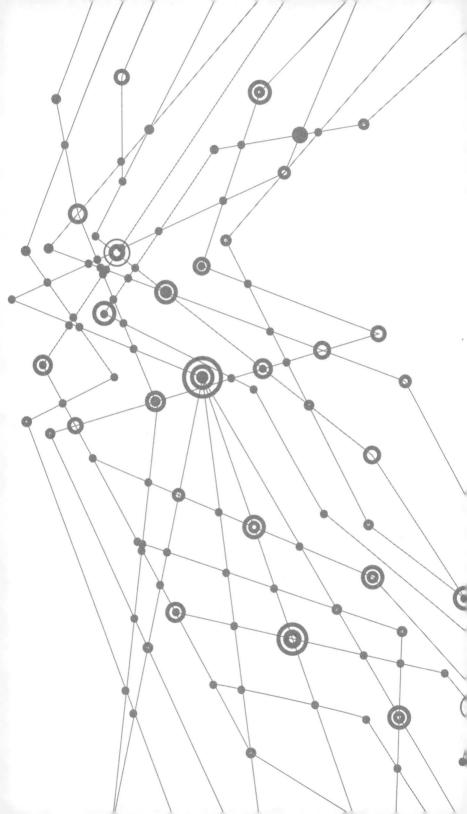

D ETECTIVE LESLIE CONSORTE didn't like being woken up in the middle of the night. In fact, he didn't like it enough to have turned off his cell phone and taken his home phone off the hook. The desk sergeant, a busybody named Roman Stevenson, had felt the situation warranted sending a unit by his house to pound on his door until he had dragged himself out from under warm sheets, grumbling, groaning, and belching out every cussword in the English language, and a few based loosely on Latin roots: *crapepsia, shitalgia, cockpluribus.*

Stevenson hadn't been wrong. Leaning on his car door and surveying the damage, Leslie dreamed of the stacks of paperwork headed his way. A fifth-year cop named Lapeyre, dressed in uniformed blues, approached, picking through the crime scene, not so much to preserve evidence as to preserve her clothes. Lapeyre was a handsome young woman, close-cropped hair of tight black curls, dark skin, driven, focused, taller than Leslie by at least a couple inches.

"It goes on for another three miles."

"This is a grisly thing here."

Leslie squinted his eyes, staring down the dilapidated Clairemont street. Clairemont was a rotten little housing project of about fourteen hundred units with dirt lawns, peeling paint, unwashed cars, rusted motor homes, and non-working boats. Most of the inhabitants had moved in decades ago when home prices were still reasonable. Now they clung desperately to their thin slice of the American Dream as their property taxes ticked higher and higher and their roads remained unrepaired.

This street was in particularly bad shape because it was smeared with blood, muscle, and bone. Someone had been dragged behind the bumper of a GMC truck. For about a mile.

"What are we looking at?" Leslie asked.

"Dispatch got a call at 12:03. A neighbor reported hearing screaming, squealing tires, and then a grinding sound. Desk jockey logged it as a domestic dispute, though I think that's a bit of an under-classification."

"That's funny, Lapeyre. Any chance we can identify the victim?"

"It's unlikely. There's only about a third of the body left. It shook loose from the car down by the mesa."

Leslie crouched in the street, running his hand over the drying blood.

"Radley found fragments of a jawbone on the next block over. We might be able to get a dental match. I also managed to extricate a patch of hair from the fender of the murder car. I've bagged it for a DNA analysis. A SID team is prepping the car for impound over on Derrick Drive. What do you want to do about this?"

"Let's knock on a door or two," Leslie suggested.

Leslie and Lapeyre walked up the nearest driveway. Leslie's suit looked like he carried it to work in a plastic bag. The top button was loose on the shirt, his tie hung low, the edges of the cuffs were frayed, and the collar was badly wrinkled. Leslie believed it was possible to machine wash and dry his dress shirts.

The collar, it seemed to him, was the only part that didn't turn out so great.

Before they reached the door, Leslie pulled Lapeyre to a stop.

"I forgot something," he said. He dug around in his pocket, finally drawing out a shiny, metallic object roughly the size of a billfold. He handed it to Lapeyre.

Lapeyre fumbled with it, trying to get it open with shaky hands. "Is this what I think it is?" she said.

"Congratulations, Detective. The captain passed word down to me as I was leaving work. I was going to tell you tomorrow, but I guess this is tomorrow."

Lapeyre didn't say anything else, but her eyes never left the badge. It reminded Leslie of his ex-wife's expression when he'd first popped open the engagement ring box. "It's a good moment, Lapeyre. You only make detective once, if you're lucky. Enjoy it." Leslie waited a moment while Lapeyre polished the badge on the front of her shirt. "Let's solve this case, huh? After you, Inspector."

"Are you going to show me how to grill a witness?"

"I will show you the ways of the master."

The nearest house was a tiny three bedroom, one bathroom with a rotting fence and a weed-strewn yard. Leslie knocked on the door. They waited a few minutes. Lapeyre pulled out her badge to look at it again, and Leslie told her to put it away. He knocked again, louder this time. No one answered. They moved to the next house, walking directly across the lawn. It was a small structure, probably close to seven hundred square feet. The roof was neglected. A Trump 2024 flag waved above the faded painting of a bald eagle, its wings stretching wide across the garage.

They knocked and waited. No one answered.

At the third house, a blonde woman in her fifties came to the door. She wore pajamas covered by a tattered robe. Her unwashed hair had a frizzy-fried texture Leslie always associated with the very poor and the chemically addicted. She smelled of recently smoked cigarettes.

"Yes?" the woman said. She was rubbing her eyes and blinking at them.

Leslie knew Lapeyre was waiting for him to speak but he didn't. After an awkward silence, Lapeyre finally said, "Sorry we woke you."

"What do you need?" the woman asked; her voice held a slight edge.

"We were hoping you saw something tonight. There's been a crime. Outside your home, all up and down the street."

"That's terrible. I'm sorry I can't help you."

Leslie was irritated by her curt response, but he tried to remain professional. He leaned in and sniffed her. In addition to the cigarettes, she smelled like very strong alcohol. Maybe 100 proof.

"What the hell are you doing?" she said.

"There was a brutal murder fifteen feet from your house," he said.

"I didn't see anything. I was sleeping."

"The murderer dragged his victim through the street. He tore the victim's body to pieces. His flesh is part of your asphalt now. It's part of your street."

"I don't know anything," the woman said. Her shoulders shook in a quick jagged motion, but she got them under control again immediately.

"You watched it from the window."

"No."

"I don't know how much you saw, but it was enough to send you back to the kitchen. A decent person calls the police. Lets us get here in time to help, maybe. But you poured yourself a shot." Leslie sniffed again. "Several shots."

"Get out of my house!" the woman barked. "I'll call the cops."

Leslie idly waved his badge. "We're not in your house."

"I'll call my brother then. He'll kick your ass right out of here."

"Go ahead and call him. We'll wait," Leslie told her.

The poor, rugged blonde took a step back and pulled her phone from her pajama pocket. Then she lurched forward and struck Leslie with her phone-clenched fist. Lapeyre moved to interfere, but Leslie called her off with a curt head shake. With her other hand the woman clawed at him for a moment, like a sick bird, then she fell to her knees, crying.

"We need to know everything you can remember. The coloring, height, and weight of the victim. The same for the killer." His voice softened. "If you tell us everything you saw, it will help you forget. I promise."

The woman remained on the floor. Leslie pulled Lapeyre aside. "Get a statement," he said. "Be as gentle as possible."

"Yeah, right. Thanks," Lapeyre said.

"I'm going to go check out the murder car. Join me when you can." Leslie moved back out of the house without looking at the crumpled form of the woman on the floor, still sobbing. He walked slowly up the street to Derrick Drive.

He had been suffering from acute lower back pain for the last thirteen years. The cause had never been completely diagnosed, but Leslie figured it to be a combination of too many nights chasing lowlifes down alleyways, too many hours behind desks perched on cheap chairs, his tendency to buy his furniture and mattresses at thrift stores, and all the collective stresses of trying to keep a city safe from itself. The mileage of life. The pinching pain caused him to shuffle his feet when he walked, and he always appeared to be leaning slightly forward.

When he reached Derrick Drive, he followed the portable lights, flares, and flashbulbs to the murder car—which was, in fact, a murder truck. He pulled on a pair of rubber gloves and pointed his belt light at the truck's bumper. A SIDs guy, short for Scientific Investigation Division, was already swabbing at it with a Q-tip. Leslie didn't recognize him, but then as all the other departments felt the pinch of deep budget cuts, the SIDs were growing like weeds.

Leslie ran his light along the left side of the truck. He noted deep, jagged scratch marks in the faux chrome of the bumper, on the right fender, and just above the tailpipe. The SID was working over his shoulder on the taillight. Leslie told him, "It looks like the victim tried to keep up with the car as long as he could. He must have been affixed to the bumper by something other than his arms. Make sure you run tests for trace elements of rope, tape, whatever the hell kind of epoxy could stick a person to a vehicle long enough to grind their bones to dust."

"Of course."

Leslie looked again at the long, snaking red swath as it disappeared down the street and around the corner. "No motive. Few witnesses. Not much left of the body. This must have made a hell of a racket, though. Make a visual record of the entire trail. Then call HAZMAT for cleanup. I don't want people waking up to find this on their street."

"You want to destroy the evidence?"

"No. Gather the evidence but do it quickly so HAZMAT can get this massacre cleaned up."

"Are you sure, sir? Whitmire's going to be pissed if we compromise—"

"You SIDs guys are supposed to facilitate our investigation, not run it. Guy gets butchered in the street, it's still a case for the homicide detective, right?"

"Yeah."

Leslie slid his hand into a rubber glove and gingerly felt around the back of the bumper. Something sticky transferred from the bumper to his index finger. He held it up to the light. It looked like candy from a toy store vending machine. He lifted it up for the pale man with the camera and the plastic baggies to see.

"Got an idea of what this is?" Leslie asked him. It wasn't quite the right texture to be brain or flesh.

The SIDs man shone a light on it, moving his face just inches from its quivering surface. Leslie turned his wrist to give him a better look, and it split, letting an inky mess free to run down onto his knuckles.

"Looks like sclera," the man said, taking it from Leslie gingerly and dropping it into one of his bags.

"I made detective because of my tenacity, not my brains."

"I'm pretty sure you found an eyeball, sir."

Eighteen Hours Earlier

THE NEWSPAPER WAS lying open on Sarah's kitchen table. It was the first thing Bobby saw after he jimmied her window, stepped a sandaled foot onto the tile of her countertop, and hopped over the sink to the floor. He slid the window closed with his palm and circled around to look. The local paper, the *San Diego Register*, had been trying to stave off extinction by delivering a free copy every Sunday. Most people just carried it right to the recycler. Sarah's was open to the same small blurb he'd noted on his copy: "Interns wanted! Apply in person or online."

Just as he had when Bobby first saw it on his porch, he became lost in the possibility. While he thought about the internship, he flipped idly to the horoscope section. He read his sign: "Libra— Your specialty is to take care of others. You always do it at your own expense, and sometime soon you're going to need to give yourself a break. A big event will change the course of your summer. Be ready for it. Your communication skills attract an admirer today. Use them to get a head start in the workplace. Those same skills will help love blossom with a Sagittarius or Capricorn."

Bobby folded the paper closed. "Sarah?" he called.

Getting no response, he opened the refrigerator and pulled out mayonnaise and butter. In her crisper he found cheddar cheese, black forest ham, and pickles. The bread was on top of the microwave. He made a sandwich.

Bobby walked over to the computer desk and pushed Sarah's laptop to life. It slowly cranked through its start-up process. Maybe he was old-fashioned, but Bobby couldn't write anything important on his phone. He hated trying to nudge at the small letters with his large fingers.

While he waited for the laptop, he took a few bites of the sandwich and looked around Sarah's apartment. It was tidy, comfortable, littered with mostly new furniture. His eyes fell on the pictures on her desk. One was of Sarah's wedding—she was kissing a bull of a man at a simple, inexpensive ceremony on the beach. His eyes moved to the second picture, her husband in full military regalia. Bobby could see that he was handsome, thick-necked, hair cut short, with just a hint of early baldness beneath the edges of his beret. He wasn't smiling, just glaring back at Bobby for sitting in his wife's office chair.

Bobby took a bite of the sandwich, licked a dab of mayonnaise from his cheek, and booted up a word processing program. He began to pick at the keyboard.

Bobby Morgan Frindley.

Age 26.

BA. Journalism. University of Southern California.

GPA: 3.72 (estimated).

Professional Experience:

The cursor blinked back at Bobby. Professional experience.

Bobby combed through his brain, reaching for any single moment when anyone had paid him money to do anything. He pictured his father slapping two dollars into his open palm for wrestling the old electric lawnmower across the family yard. Bobby leaned back in the chair, exhaling, his fingers clutched behind his head. He had done a few television interviews last August for local affiliates, just after the Olympics. Pro bono. He listed them anyway. Local 8, CBS. Fox Sports West.

A key cleaved into the front door lock. Bobby pushed Print then leaped to his feet. His sandwich landed on the bare toes of his left foot. He took two steps toward the kitchen and heard Sarah call his name. "Bobby?"

The question was slightly slurred. It was without malice. Bobby turned to see Sarah walk gingerly into her own apartment, a half smile on her pretty face, her eyes glazed. "Hey, Sarah," Bobby said.

"Hey, Bobby. Did I walk into the wrong apartment?" Her eyes roamed the room for clarification, registering her own couch, her own throw rug. "What are you doing in here? Did I call you?" Sarah said. She shoved the door closed and sat heavily in a bean bag. She was wearing a sundress and tennis shoes. Car keys dangled from her hand, and Bobby took them, gingerly.

"I wanted to borrow your laptop. I hope you don't mind."

Sarah looked straight into Bobby's eyes, flashing a bright, sloppy smile. Bobby could smell alcohol on her breath and her clothes.

"Why are you dressed like that? So fancy." She paused to tug on the lapel of his jacket.

Bobby was wearing khaki Dockers, a white dress shirt, his only suit jacket, and a pair of Rainbow flip-flops. He would put on the patent-leather shoes as late as he possibly could.

"I'm not usually drunk this early. Bad form, Bobby. I apologize. It's bad form."

"Don't be sorry." Bobby looked at the digital clock on Sarah's countertop. It was 11:13 a.m. "I was trying to write my résumé for this news media internship—"

"The *San Diego Register*? There's one on the table," Sarah said, gesturing drunkenly to her kitchen. "I saw the internship and kept it . . . to show you. Help me get to the bed. Take me to my room, my Bobby."

Bobby stood up and lifted Sarah in his arms. "My Bobby, huh?" he grunted. He carried her into her cramped bedroom and propped her in a sitting position on the edge of the bed. Her comforter was a yellow and green flower pattern. It matched the lemony blinds that hung around the only window.

Bobby pulled them shut, darkening the room. Sarah lolled around on the bed.

"It was slosh ball. Slosh ball did this. Kate Sessions Park. I'm going to take my dress off. Could you help me get in the bed and pull the sheets up to my chin?"

Bobby turned in a half circle, positioning his back to Sarah. Slosh ball. Modified self-pitch softball with a keg of cheap beer on first and third base. You have to chug a red Solo cup's worth before you can advance. A dangerous game, even for seasoned drinkers.

Sarah made small sounds of struggle as she worked the dress up her body. "Help, Bobby, help."

"What's wrong?"

"It's stuck in my bracelets."

Sarah was half lying on the bed, her hair and one arm pinned above her head by a reckless attempt to remove the dress. She kicked her legs in scissor motions and tugged fruitlessly to the left and right. Bobby pushed the dress off her wrists, her elbow, extracted both ears, and lifted the collar over her nose. When the material brushed past her eyes, they fluttered and stared up at Bobby.

"How did you get in my apartment?" she said.

"Don't worry about that," Bobby told her.

"Maybe . . . maybe you should kiss me," she slurred.

"Definitely not," Bobby said.

"Kiss me. Right now."

"I will," Bobby promised. "But I want you to close your eyes and count to ten." Bobby held Sarah's elbows tightly against the comforter. She was trying to raise herself up, her lips questing for his mouth. "One. Close your eyes. Two. Head on the pillow. I'll kiss you at ten, I promise. One. Two. Three." Bobby paused at three. He tried not to look down at her lacy white bra or her lovely legs. Sarah's eyes fluttered open again. "Four. Five. Six. Seven. Seven. Seven. Eight. Nine." Bobby waited a few more moments. Sarah made a soft mewling sound. She rolled onto her side. "Sarah? Can you hear me?"

She didn't answer.

"I would love to be your Bobby," he said. Then he lowered the comforter, slid her to the middle of the bed, and pulled the blanket up to her chin. "Also, I'm borrowing your car."

Bobby retrieved his sandwich from the kitchen floor and wolfed it down in two bites. He checked the window to be sure it was bolted tight and then used Sarah's keys to lock her front door.

Bobby crossed the street and let himself into his own apartment. He found his patent-leather shoes by the front door and kicked off his flip-flops. When he went back outside, he saw that Sarah's car was parked in the loosest sense of the word. She'd driven into the curb, threading the needle between two parallel-parked cars, leaving the tail end of her Camry sticking out into the street. Bobby slid the car seat back almost a foot and climbed in. The radio light blinked 11:45. He headed in the direction of the *San Diego Register*.

3

BOBBY PILOTED SARAH'S car out of the sleepy beach town of Crown Point, down Ingraham Street, and onto the 8 Freeway. His long frame barely fit into the early 2010s Toyota, and he found himself rolling down the window to make space. The wind whipped through the opening, sending his shaggy brown-blond hair dancing in every direction. As he drove, the grubby beach communities of San Diego gave way to the more polished homogeny of Mission Valley, which gave way to the ever-expanding bloat of San Diego University, squatting high on the hill above the freeway. Three miles farther on and he exited into a medium commercial district. He passed San Diego Unified's bus storage, a Family Fun Center miniature golf course, a tow yard, a seedy-looking sex shop, and finally turned left into the parking lot of San Diego's last surviving regional newspaper. Bobby climbed from the car, his nearly blank résumé clutched carefully between his thumb and forefinger.

The desk receptionist, a petite, ponytailed brunette, looked at him quizzically when he told her he was there for the internship. She checked his name in her appointment book and didn't find anything.

"The ad said apply in person or online."

"I think we have a lot of applications for that one," she said. "But no one has come in to apply in person."

"Kind of makes you think I might be the best person for the job, doesn't it?"

"It makes you old-fashioned," the girl said, giggling. "And a little old for an internship. I don't have any applications. If you go to the waiting room, I'll print you out a copy. Unless you just want to fill it out on your phone?"

"I'll wait," Bobby told her.

"Second door on the left. There's a bathroom to the right if you want to fix your hair. And your tie."

Bobby walked down the hall. A tall man in a brown suit with an eye patch came out of the elevator. Bobby said hi, but the man just grunted in response. Bobby passed a mirror. He ran his fingers through his hair and pulled at the wrinkles in his suit jacket.

The waiting room was stacked with rows of metal chairs, like the DMV. The art, faded in smudged plastic frames, was also DMV-esque. Bobby noted a Monet. A Dalí. A Chagall. A few more he didn't recognize, all cracked and dull from sunlight squirming in through old single-pane windows. He was the only one there. It felt ominously empty.

He wandered over to the water cooler and poured himself a cup of water. In a voice just above a whisper, he said, "God? I know I haven't prayed since July. I know I don't really deserve a favor, per se. But, uh, please help me get the job here? Amen."

A thin man entered the room and filled up his own paper cup full of water. The man was bald except for a few hairs above his ears, rallying there before final surrender. He could not have weighed more than one hundred and ten pounds on a six-foot frame, and most of his weight seemed to be carried in the huge bags under his eyes. Standing across the room from him, dwarfing him in height, structure, and general health, Bobby felt like a different species. The man offered Bobby a quick nod.

"You look familiar, son. Do I know you?" the man asked.

"I don't think so," Bobby told him.

The man offered his hand. "Milo Maslow, Sports, Calendar, and Metro, too, lately. Hey, that's a nice handshake you've got there." His speech was clipped, inflection almost an afterthought.

"Bobby Frindley."

Milo searched his pockets until he found a pack of cigarettes and, when he found them, his face briefly brightened. A subtle shift overcame Milo. He made eye contact. His shoulders straightened slightly. "That name is familiar."

"Well, I guess if you cover local spor—"

"Hot damn, you're Bobby Frindley. The Olympic athlete. We did two separate profiles on you."

It hit Bobby just as suddenly. Milo Maslow. It was on the byline of the news articles hanging on his bedroom wall in his parents' house. His mom had printed out the articles and taped them there; it didn't seem like she'd ever take them down. The *Register* had made him out to be a local hero, posting his scoring achievements for every water polo game he'd played, starting when he was first promoted to hole set his freshman year in high school. They'd nominated him as athlete of the week six times his junior and senior year. After college, when he made the Olympic squad, they'd featured him with online splash pages twice. He'd interviewed with a woman named Michelle something, but it had been Milo Maslow whose name had eventually appeared on the byline.

Milo practically jumped in place. He shook Bobby's hand again.

"That's great you've heard of me."

"Heard of you? I cheered for you! That stuff against Croatia? It was outstanding. I meet a lot of professional athletes, don't get me wrong, but it's not often you meet an Olympian. A gold medalist, right?"

"Practically."

"What the hell are you doing here?"

"I'm interested in the internship."

Milo walked over to one of the empty chairs and sat down. Bobby's words mollified him. "You shouldn't be. You should be looking somewhere else. This is a dying business, son. Have you looked around? New media has been crushing us mercilessly for the last two decades. No matter what I try to do—including a heavy focus on local sports," Milo wagged his finger in Bobby's direction, "we just can't catch up. You don't want to stake your future here."

Bobby started to say something, but Milo raised his palm and kept talking. "Do you know what we're doing? With this 'internship' program? We're replacing our admin assistants with unpaid students. We'll save on healthcare, bonuses, salaries. But there's no upward mobility. For anybody. There's no way these positions lead to jobs. In fact, they're replacing jobs. We're basically a boutique, a vanity project for our billionaire boomer board of directors. You'd be throwing your time away working here. You're what? Twenty-three?"

"Twenty-six."

"When the boomers are dead, the papers are dead. Don't hitch your wagon with us. Try and get in the bottom floor at Qualcomm."

"Really?"

"Yeah, really. This paper has been around for over one hundred fifty years. There're stories in the archives about 'Injun' attacks on wagon trains. It's as old as a damned desert tortoise, but it's dying."

"Maybe we just need a new business model."

Milo laughed nervously and then looked at Bobby, biting his lip; his eyes creased. "Well, spit it out."

Bobby patted his chest. He didn't actually have a new business model in mind. He exhaled.

Milo arched his eyebrows.

Bobby improvised.

"Think about it this way. The internet didn't just kill traditional news media. It also killed the lofty values that it was based on. These days, half-baked 'news' slingshots around the world before breakfast followed by ten thousand tweets and a hundred thousand reactions to those tweets twisting the unverified information into more and more ridiculous shapes. Politicians sipping on baby's blood in pizza parlors? Or what-have-you?" Bobby held up a finger, for emphasis. "But, I think people miss having a news source that prioritizes its own integrity and holds dear to the ideals of veracity, honesty, and truth. One that won't piss everything away in a race for more clicks or to capitulate to some pre-existing political market. What if we put investigation, authenticity, and accuracy first and foremost? As our business model we offer irrefutable, triple-sourced facts, backed by science. Without bias. We refuse to bend to the forces that have compromised the other outlets. We could build a reputation of having so much integrity that folks would know they could come to us for the real story. I'd pay money for professionally vetted information I could trust. I think a lot of people would. We stay in business and, at the same time, we sow a little faith back into the human animal."

"We should be able to pull that off by noon tomorrow," Milo said, half a smile creeping onto his face. "Is that all?"

"That's not enough?"

"Veracity, honesty, and truth." Milo chuckled. "Big Bobby Frindley. I love your youthful idealism; I love it. Sow faith in the human animal." Milo leaned forward in his chair. He had placed a cigarette in his mouth, but he hadn't lit it and it hung from his lips, smelling faintly of cloves. "What you're suggesting is totally impossible in the modern market. But I'm impressed. I am. Give me your résumé, let me take a look."

Bobby, whipped into a fervor by his own speech, had forgotten about the mostly blank sheet of paper, still clutched in his left hand. He handed it sheepishly to Milo.

Milo looked at it. "Is this a joke? It just says your name and your degree. Where's the work history?"

"Empty isn't just a void, it's a vacuum."

Milo crumpled the paper and threw it in the trash. "You're eloquent, kid. I suppose we could use you in telesales. You can cold-call consumers or advertisers; I'll give you the choice because of your Olympic achievement. It's awful work, but it'll get words on your résumé and a little bit of money in your pocket."

"I want to write."

"There's no jobs. There's nothing on your résumé. Your résumé is in the trash. My paper will be there, too, in five years. Maybe less. You should try blogging. Wait a second. Wait a second. Outstanding."

Milo scooped Bobby's résumé back out of the trash and spread it open on the top of the water cooler. From his pocket, he pulled a thick black Sharpie.

He uncapped it and wrote the following: Bobby Frindley. Horoscopist. He passed the wrinkled sheet back to Bobby, who stared, blinking.

Milo waved his arms expressively. "We do have one opening. You're getting a shot. Sixteen cents a word. Two hundred and fifty words a day, maximum. No retirement. No health insurance. Don't even ask."

Bobby stood up. He was excited. He looked at the paper again. "Horoscopist? Horoscopes?"

Milo stood up as well and shook his hand. "I'd like to welcome the newest member of our staff, Bobby Frindley."

At just that moment the receptionist came into the room, a badly photocopied application under her arm.

She handed it to Bobby.

"Horoscopes? Really?" he asked Milo.

"Yeah. Our girl, she stopped coming to work."

"That's outstanding," Bobby said.

——— ———

MILO SPENT A few minutes showing Bobby around. The building itself was large but there were almost no people anywhere. He showed Bobby the cubicles and a room with very old computers and even older printers. Before taking him back to the receptionist, Milo whispered, "Don't mention what I said about the interns."

The receptionist was named Jana, and she seemed surprised Bobby had already been given a job.

"He's great. Wait until this kid opens his mouth. It's pure silk."

"But what about Lady Ambrosia?"

"You're looking at her," he said, nodding to Bobby.

"There was a real Lady Ambrosia? I thought that was just a name you guys used," Bobby said.

Milo smiled; his strange, thin hips were leaning against Jana's circular desk. He said, "Stephanie Ambrosino. Self-righteous, kinda smart, but also flaky as hell. Like so many of your generation, she tended to think she was too good for the job. And now she's missed four days of copy in a row. I have to run three sections, so I don't have time to scramble for substitute words. The door closes on her and opens on you. You're the new Lady Ambrosia. Any complaints?"

"Well, I'll miss her," Jana said. "Do you think she's okay? Did you even try to call her?"

Milo didn't answer. He looked at Bobby with his eyebrows raised.

"No complaints, Milo. I appreciate the opportunity," Bobby said.

"The Ask Ambrosia column is linked to an email address. You answer reader emails when you can. It's part of the job. Our online presence. HR will give you the password when you get your freelance packet."

"It's nice to meet you," Jana said. "I think Hawkeye changed the password for the Ask Ambrosia account," she told Milo.

"Why? For what purpose?"

Jana just shrugged

"Find out what he changed it to and get it sent over to Bobby. No horoscopes on Mondays, so we have one day to get him warmed up." Milo grinned at Bobby. "Come in tomorrow for training. Work starts at eight a.m. We'll begin sowing faith in the human animal first thing in the morning."

4

MONDAY MORNING, BOBBY awoke and threw himself out of bed. He climbed into the shower, rinsing yesterday's chlorine out of his hair. He'd driven directly to the La Jolla YMCA after the job interview, celebrating with four thousand yards of swimming on a 1:10 per one-hundred-yard pace. His run-down apartment had seemed a little less so when he finally made it home, a *San Diego Register* human resources packet clutched under his arm. He'd knocked lightly on Sarah's door and dropped her keys in the mailbox when she didn't answer.

After the morning shower, Bobby shrugged into yesterday's slacks and pulled on a short-sleeved dark brown Dickies work shirt. He grabbed a fiber bar from the kitchen cabinet and exited his back door into the alley. He had a motorcycle, a 1973 Honda 350. It was old, weather-beaten, and wholly unreliable, but today the engine turned over on the first try. Bobby glanced at his watch, jerked on his dinged helmet, and headed down Ingraham Street. Two hundred and fifty words a day at sixteen cents a word would come to forty dollars. It barely covered gas to get to the job, but it was a start. He arrived at the *Register* building at 8:05 a.m. Jana was sitting at reception again, not yet replaced by Milo's interns. She smiled and motioned him over. "Good morning, Bobby," she said. Her voice was calm and professional. She pulled two note cards from beside her computer monitor.

"Milo's out on assignment. He left a few notes for you last night."

"Thanks," Bobby said. "Is there someplace I can go to read these?"

"Try the second floor. There are plenty of open cubicles."

Bobby found the elevator and pointed it toward the second floor. When the doors opened, a sudden, unexpected exhilaration washed over him. Only a few people were working inside, but something about the acoustics filled the room with noise. Keyboards clacked. He heard shouting, laughing, voices raised in argument, two different sources of music. They even had those oscillating table fans that you see in every newspaper movie back all the way to *All the President's Men*. Empty boxes of takeout food were stacked on archives of old newspapers stacked on oversized hardback books. Bobby slipped out of his suit jacket, already conscious of having worn it for his visit the day before. He counted six others besides himself. They were all dressed extremely casually: blue jeans, flip-flops, and T-shirts. For the first time since the whistle blew on Bobby's dreams of a gold medal, he felt like his life was going in the right direction.

He picked an empty cubicle by the window with a quarter-mile view of the 8 Freeway and unfolded Milo's notes. Inside was a number for a Star Lunes and a message indicating she was an award-winning horoscope writer for an online rag named *TheLonelyTruth.com*. Bobby dialed the number from his desk.

A voice on the other end told him Star Lunes worked from home. Bobby mentioned Milo Maslow and it was enough to get her cell number. He was surprised to see it was a 760 area code, just twenty miles to the north. Bobby dialed the new number and a luminous voice said, "Yes? Hello?"

"Hi, I'm Bobby Frindley. I'm the new horoscope writer at the *San Diego Register*. My editor, Milo Maslow, said you'd be a great person to talk to for tips."

Silence on the other end, then finally, "What happened to Lady Ambrosia?"

"I guess she left the paper in a lurch. I was lucky enough to get the gig. Now I am she. But between you and me, I don't really know what I'm doing."

"Lady Ambrosia is a friend of mine."

"I'll be your friend, too, if you can help me out."

She laughed like she talked, both loud and soft, with notes traveling across octaves. "What do you want to know, Bobby Frindley?"

"What the heck should I write?"

"You can write anything at all."

Bobby drummed his pencil. "What do you mean?"

"There's a lot of guild language. A series of catchphrases that will convince your audience you know what you're talking about. Houses, moons, cusps, and meridians. You can buy a single book at Barnes and Noble to get all the words you need to be an expert. If you can find a Barnes and Noble. As for the 'predictions,' just write whatever you want." Star continued, "The mind is a closing mechanism. It fills in blanks without being asked. I could call it our imagination, but that might be too small a word considering it's the primary governing force of our lives. It acts as a sixth sense. Whatever the five physical senses don't experience, the sixth fills in to compensate."

"I don't totally understand," Bobby admitted.

"What do I look like?"

"I've never met you."

"But your mind has already created a picture of me to compensate for what your eyes can't see. Since I said hello, you've been making subconscious judgments based on my inflections, my word choice, my vocabulary, everything. Your imagination is providing what your eyes can't. So, what do I look like?"

Bobby tried to recall what he'd been picturing during the first part of their conversation. "You're smart. Upper-middle class. Mid-to-late-twenties. College educated. There's confidence in your word choice and your tone, but not arrogance. In my mind, you're slender with long, thin hair, brown or black, and you have some fantastic feature, either a dazzling smile or beautiful eyes, something that makes people respond positively to you."

"You make me sound beautiful," Star said, flirtatiously.

"What do you think I look like?" Bobby asked her.

"Good question. Let me think. You're about six foot one. You have shaggy brown hair. Very broad shoulders. Like the shoulders of a swimmer. And a ton of abdominal muscles. Row after row."

Bobby looked around the room to see if he was being pranked. She'd gotten his height, his hair, and his shoulders just right. "I don't know about the last part but . . . how did you do that?"

"I just looked you up online. Do you ever take a picture when you're not in your swimsuit? Dang, you are fit."

It was exciting flirting with Star. Her face, the one in his imagination, was growing more beautiful as she complimented him, and for a moment he forgot all about Sarah.

Speaking into the silence, Star said, "The real lesson is to pay attention to the way we live in our heads. You made me up, completely. Your imagination supplied the missing information. It's the same trick with horoscopes. Point your reader in a certain direction, and they'll do the rest. The less educated and disciplined they are, the more their imagination will compensate."

"There's no star charts? No mysticism involved, at all?"

"People just want to believe that something governs their actions, that they are moving in synchronicity with some sort of divine—or in this case astrological—plan. Horoscopes are the small, lucrative byproduct of two thousand years of social programming. They're a playful tonic sold to a desperate and godless people."

"I'm not sure if you're helping me now or making me really sad," Bobby said.

"I kind of like you, Bobby Frindley. And these abs. Wow."

Before he could respond, Star Lunes hung up the phone. Bobby held it against his ear, listening to the silence for a minute. He wasn't any closer to writing his first horoscope.

He put the phone in his pocket and picked up a pen. He glanced around the room, watching as two men argued three cubicles away. They were talking in low urgent tones. On the desk ink blotter, Bobby wrote: "Libra—You will make significant forward progress only to find yourself suddenly lost in a strange, new land."

———

WHEN BOBBY GOT home from his evening swim, he parked his Honda in the alley. He sat on the couch by the window for a while and replayed the day in his head. Then he used his phone to research horoscope terminology. Eventually the light came on in Sarah's window, and he walked over and knocked on her door. She answered in her dental hygienist scrubs, somehow making blue polyester sexy again. She smiled at him sheepishly and rubbed her forehead. "Never let me drink again, please."

Mail overflowed from her mailbox. Bobby took it out and handed it to her. "Guess what I got?" he said.

Sarah leafed through the mail. "I don't know," she said.

"A job at the paper."

Sarah's eyes jumped up to meet Bobby's. "Seriously?"

Bobby nodded.

"Okay, one small, quick drink to celebrate that. And then let's get Mexican food. Can you? Will you come in?"

Bobby followed her into the apartment. He sat at her laptop desk.

"What's the job? Are you a sports reporter? I was thinking that would make sense because of the Olympics thing."

"Yeah, not exactly. They gave me the horoscopes."

Sarah laughed. Then she looked thoughtful. "You're not kidding? It's a start. The bottom floor, as it were. Plus, horoscopes are awesome. Do you have training though? What do you know about writing horoscopes?"

"I talked to a horoscopist today, but all she said is that it's a bunch of hokum. The professional wrestling of news media."

"Then why are my predictions always right?"

Bobby shrugged. "I just realized that I have to check the Ask Ambrosia email account. It's part of the job. Want to help me?"

Sarah walked into the kitchen area, once again leafing through the mail. A blue and white international letter appeared in her hand. She held it to her chest. Her face became deathly serious.

Bobby said, "You can go read it in your room. I know you like to read those alone."

"I just want to concentrate on every word. I'm sorry."

"Sorry? It's a happy moment to hear from a great American military hero and loving husband."

"He's just a Navy Seabee. He builds things and digs ditches. He's been trying to make the SEALs, but they tell him he's too big for recon, which doesn't seem fair. These letters take ten days to arrive, the news is old already, but . . . it's kind of more romantic than email. I'm sorry, Bobby. Get my celebration beer ready, I'll read fast."

Bobby just nodded. He got up from the desk and opened the door of her refrigerator to pull out two Pacifico beers. He watched as she retreated into her room, posture erect as if her husband had suddenly jumped into the apartment with them. Bobby was so high on his new job that he didn't feel the least bit jealous. Sarah was just a nice neighbor, with great legs, whose company he enjoyed often, platonically—and, maybe, he was just a little bit in love with her. He took a long drink from the beer and flopped back down at her desk.

The Ask Ambrosia account had one new message. Bobby looked back at the closed door of Sarah's bedroom again. Then he opened the email.

What he read was disquieting.

5

I T WAS 12:30 a.m. before Bobby managed to roll out of Sarah's beanbag and prop himself back on his feet. They had shared rolled tacos, a bottle of wine, two celebration shots of tequila, four celebration beers, and half a frozen pizza. They'd also watched two sitcoms and endless YouTube videos.

"You can't leave," Sarah said.

"I better go."

"My mind is too weakened by the YouTube commercials. Leave now and I'm going to start buying."

"I need to get some rest. It's my first real day of work tomorrow. And when I say first day, I mean first day, ever."

"You leave now, and tomorrow you'll find me riding a Total Gym, wrapped in a Sleep Pod."

"That sounds kind of hot."

Sarah walked over to her Bluetooth speaker. "Dancing will help us stay awake!" she said, as if it was the greatest idea anyone ever had. Bobby couldn't resist her drunken enthusiasm. Music filled the apartment, and they danced together on the landing just outside her small kitchen. Bobby swung his arms and elbows, grooving his feet in wild, drunken patterns. Sarah laughed and spun in a loopy circle, shuffling around the small makeshift dance floor.

When she finally collapsed next to him on the couch, they were both sweating. He thought the night was over, but Sarah struggled to her feet again and dragged Bobby by hand to the laptop. Bobby was flushed from landing the job, and the alcohol, and Sarah's attention. He wasn't quite ready for the good day to end, despite growing steadily loopier from fatigue.

Sarah opened the web browser, found the Ask Ambrosia email, and hit the Reply button. She said, "The inaugural email of the new Lady Ambrosia is ready, Captain. You dictate, I'll write."

Bobby cleared his throat and began to dictate, "Dear *Whac-a-mole* . . ."

Sarah giggled. "You want me to read you the message again? To help you organize your response?"

"Yeah. Just read the best predictions though."

Sarah peered into the glowing monitor. "Well, someone's obviously trying to do your job for you. There are twelve wonderfully imaginative predictions here. The first says: 'Aries—Mars, the planet of initiative, is your ruler and subruler.'" Sarah paused dramatically, a smile twitching onto her lips. "'As an indirect result of those energies, you will be torn apart by an endangered Indonesian tiger.'"

Sarah burst into fits of laughter.

She was drunk, Bobby reminded himself. So was he.

She continued, "The next one is: 'Taurus—You are both fierce and gentle. A white bull. But you are too young, on the cusp of the third house. Your immaturity and lack of foresight will lead you to great harm. In fact, you will be gang-raped on the property of the Theta Rho Kappa fraternity house at San Diego University.' I really don't like that one, it's not funny or anything; it sucks. I'm sorry I read it. There's a short one about a brush fire. It's the Virgo." Sarah glanced at Bobby and their eyes locked. She blushed, then looked quickly back at the screen. "Uhh, next good one is Libra. Some stuff about planets, yadda, yadda, 'you have a compelling desire to understand your own fate,' yadda, yadda, 'tragically, during a romantic dinner at the Plaza del Sol in Tijuana, you will crack a tooth biting into over-cooked lobster.'

"The only other intense prediction is Cancer. 'You're in your second decanate, the sensuous moon combines with Leo's Jupiter' et cetera, et cetera. 'A man dressed entirely in black will knock you unconscious and drag you behind the bumper of your GMC truck.'"

"All right. That's enough. They're not funny, are they? Even a little drunk, and I might be more than a little drunk, they piss me off."

"The cracked-tooth one is a little bit funny."

"You ready to type?"

Sarah poised her fingers above the keyboard. "Ready."

Bobby paced across the room, rubbing his hands together. He dictated the following. "Dear Prick-waver. Thank you for the considerate horoscope suggestions, but I think you're a little too deep in the crazies. You also missed the point of a horoscope. It works better, I suspect, if you're a little less specific. Please cease all future correspondence to this email address. Love, Lady Ambrosia."

"You sure you want to send this?"

"Why not?"

Sarah moused over to Send and pushed it, reluctantly. "I hope we didn't just jeopardize your job. It could have been some kind of test."

"Hadn't thought of that."

Bobby watched Sarah scroll back through the email. She read to herself silently. "I didn't notice this before. Look."

Bobby walked over and put his hands on her shoulders. She reached up and held his hands against her skin. He could smell the faint scent of expensive shampoo on her hair. It mixed with her perfume, making a heady combination of fruity feminine goodness. Half mesmerized, he stared down at the screen. At the very bottom of the email, just below the final prediction, was a short sentence in clear, terse language. It read, "Run these and one comes true. Ignore them and they all come true."

"That's screwed up," Bobby said.

Sarah didn't respond. She seemed to be holding her breath. Under his hands, the bare skin of her shoulders felt warm and soft.

In that moment, lost between the victories of the day, the alcohol, and the smells of her body, he forgot who he was. Leaning forward, he kissed her, lightly, just below the earlobe.

6

BOBBY FELT LIKE a monster when he awoke, late, for his first real day of work. He felt like the kind of monster that has a drumbeat in his head and a sick, churning feeling in his stomach. The kind of monster that can be killed, not with a silver bullet or a stake to the heart, but rather with noise and sunlight and guilt. He was lying in the middle of Sarah's living room, naked except for his socks and T-shirt. Sarah was nestled in his arm, fully nude, her perfect hips wedged against his belly.

He extricated himself and rose unsteadily to his feet, yanking a throw blanket from her disheveled couch. He took one last, guilt-filled look at her naked body before covering her with the soft fleece. She made a mewling sound, rolled completely onto her other side, and bunched the blanket against her chest, but thankfully remained asleep.

Their lovemaking had been frenetic, athletic, and the room was turned upside down. He had no hope of finding her car keys, especially with his head pounding, and he was reluctant to borrow them anyway, even though the clock was inching invariably close to eight a.m. Bobby forced himself to look at the picture of Sarah's husband on her desk, but it had been knocked flat, most likely when they had yanked each other's clothes off right after that first, foolish kiss.

Bobby pulled on his pants and stumbled out the door and across the street to his apartment. He kept his keys in a basket to the right of the door, and he only stepped inside long enough to scoop them up and then bend down to tie his shoes. He slipped out the back door, fixing the buttons on his shirt, and hopped onto his motorcycle. He jumped off again and ran some water from the hose and washed his hands, arms, and face. He smelled like beer, sweat, and sex. From a crouch he looked up at the sky and said aloud, "God? Please let Sarah forgive me for being an asshole. Amen."

After a long, painful ride down the 8 Freeway, Bobby turned left into the *Register* parking lot. He dreamed of disappearing into the darkness of his cubicle. Or maybe he could check in, let Milo know he'd arrived on time, then hide in the bathroom until his head stopped spinning. He pushed through the glass double doors, his helmet tucked under his arm, and was greeted by a wave of sound. People were rushing back and forth through the hallway, heeled shoes clicking on tile floors. Doors were closing, opening, and slamming shut once more. There was a muted television mounted above the lobby. It flashed bright colors and a pair of talking heads argued, gesturing to each other with exaggerated hand motions. Beneath the television, Jana smiled at Bobby, but her face was tense, and her phone was ringing.

"Hi Bobby! Can't talk now, sorry." Jana picked up the phone and said, "*San Diego Register*." The moment she did, a second line began to ring. And then a third.

Bobby ambled down the hallway staying light on his feet as reporters and other staff zipped past him heading both north and south. He sneaked into the elevator and closed his eyes for the ride to the second floor. The doors opened. His eyes opened. The second floor pulsed with life more vividly than the first. There were about twelve people buzzing around today—twice the number that had been there on Monday. Multiple televisions fought for attention, warning all who would listen of inclement weather, murder, toxic pollution along the coasts. A man screamed at a woman near the restrooms. Two cubicles to the left, a police scanner was rattling out locations and codes, 11-81, Governor and Genesee; 481, 5 North at Manchester; 10-45C, critical, Waring Road. All units.

Bobby dropped into the gray cloth chair at his cubicle. He put his head in his hands and rubbed his temple, trying to massage away the last of the guilt and the hangover. The man with the eye patch brushed past his desk and then stepped back to address Bobby.

"First day?"

Bobby looked up at the man and mustered a smile. "Second." The man was handsome, despite, or perhaps because of, the patch. He had thick, straight brown hair, brown corduroy slacks, and a white shirt, unbuttoned, to flare out at the collar.

"I've been here almost ten years. I've never seen anything like it."

"Like today?"

"It's been a wild morning. Really wild."

"What's going on?" Bobby asked.

"Everything. The city is alive today. Just yesterday we ran a piece on a guy who bowled two perfect games in a row. Today we've got multiple murders, a high-profile suicide, car chases, a brush fire, and a carjacking. That's the business, though. Sometimes you sit on your thumb, sometimes it's the book of Revelations out there. 'And he gathered them together into a place called, in the Hebrew tongue, Armageddon.'" The man paused to take a breath. "Milo's called a meeting downstairs. You should listen in."

Bobby rose to his feet, but the man was already striding away, walking between the desks and touching people on the arms or shoulders, gathering almost every able body in the room. Together they herded into the elevator and then downstairs.

The pack reached the outside of Milo's office. Bobby saw the Chagall on the wall and recognized it as the waiting room from Sunday's ad hoc interview. The other reporters grabbed seats and looked anxious. Milo rose from his desk and walked to the doorframe, where he stood, legs slightly splayed. His face was flushed red and his tiny shoulder bones were tensed.

"Twenty-five years in this business and I've seen one, maybe two days like today," Milo said. "Whatever you thought you were doing, you're about to be doing something else. At one a.m. last night, a man was mutilated in Clairemont. The corpse was in such bad condition the police can't identify the body without DNA testing. An hour later, a roof collapsed in Pacific Beach, killing a family of four. This morning, a child actor stabbed his ex-girlfriend at a bus stop. A respected judge jumped off the Balboa Park bridge this afternoon."

"Who?" a man with thick glasses asked.

"Eidelman."

"He's sitting on a multimillion-dollar patent suit. I've been in his courtroom all week. I finished the copy two hours ago."

"The copy is not finished anymore. I want you down there standing next to the police, bending over the body. I need teams on each of these." Milo addressed a man in blue jeans and a sweater. "Robert, you can take Clairemont. Bring Lane with you. Consider the hate-crime angle. Christina, I want you and Mark on the roof collapse. Be tactful. Jorge, your cousin still captain over at Station 11? There's a fire spreading through the canyon by Fashion Valley Mall. Fire chief says it looks like arson. Go check it out and get a good quote. Tell Jackson I want an aerial drone photo of the flames, especially if they get close to the mall. Something cinematic." Milo turned to the man with the eye patch who was standing beside a striking looking woman in her mid-forties. "Linda, go with Hawkeye and follow up on the stabbing. Obviously, we're playing up the child-actor angle. Everybody loves it when those little bastards grow up to be psychopaths. Move it now, move it." Milo clapped his hands, and the reporters jumped to their feet.

Once the others were gone, Milo ran out of the meeting room and down the hallway, his body gliding like a gazelle's. Bobby caught up with him at the elevator and Milo said, "Oh, hey, welcome to the paper."

"Busy news day?"

"We're finally going to sell some issues—or at least get some clicks—I can tell you that."

Milo was jabbing his finger repeatedly on the Call button when Jana ran toward him from down the other hall.

"You're not going to believe this, Milo. You're not. You're really, really not. Hi, Bobby," she said.

"Something else?" Milo asked, excited.

"Police are headed to the San Diego Zoo. A lion jumped the barrier and ate a man. Some young people were taunting it! The victim was trying to protect his son. The lion tore him to pieces."

"Is it still loose?" Milo asked, eyes huge and round.

"I—I don't know."

Milo chewed on his lip. He glanced around, spotting Linda and Hawkeye, the last two to leave, just as they passed down the hall and out of sight. He took a few steps toward them, calling to Linda when Bobby said, "I can do it. I know where the zoo is. I'll get down there and ask around."

"You're horoscopes."

"I can do it. It's not that different from water polo . . ."

"You already sold me on the Olympic thing, kid. That's how you got horoscopes. I hope you're not some kind of one-trick pony."

"Let him try it, Milo," Jana said. "It's low priority compared to the hate-crime murder and the suicide of a high-profile judge."

"Lion maulings? Low profile? That's national news. There's almost nothing people like more than lion maulings."

"Let me do it," Bobby urged.

Milo let out a long, deep sigh. Bobby could tell that he was happy, excited both by the day of news and the prospect of increased ad revenue. He looked Bobby in the eyes, and Bobby returned the gaze without flinching. The men stared at each other, saying nothing. Finally, Milo said, "Okay. You get the lion. You're just fact-finding and quote-gathering. You're a pair of legs and a notepad, not a reporter. Make sure you understand that. Someone else will write the copy and get the byline, probably me. I hope you're as tenacious out there as you have been in here. Enjoy your first field promotion. Screw this up though and you're in telesales. Understand? Sixteen cents a word."

7

THE WEATHER WAS turning foul, wind blowing strongly against Bobby's chest, but he hardly noticed as he turned his rusted-out motorcycle into the zoo's large parking lot. Jana had given him a press pass on the way out of the *Register*'s headquarters, and he had it tucked proudly into his shirt pocket. Zoo patrons were exiting en masse, and Bobby could see clusters of police vehicles, an ambulance, a fire truck, several squad cars, and an unmarked Ford Explorer wedged into a small roundabout near the ticket booths. Most of the uniforms surrounded the back of one of the ambulances where a young boy was strapped to a stretcher. Bobby approached with his press pass out, trapped between his ring and middle finger like he'd seen reporters do on TV.

Two uniformed officers stood at attention five yards from the action keeping lookie-loos back with hard stares. One of them examined Bobby's press pass. "It's not often you *Register* boys beat the AP to the scene," he said, then he waved Bobby through the perimeter. Bobby put away his pass and pulled a pen and a small notepad from his pocket. His fingers, nose, and ears were tingling from the excitement in the air and in his chest. When Bobby tried to get close to the boy on the stretcher, a gruff man in a suit jacket put his hand on Bobby's chest.

"That boy just lost his father. He doesn't need to be bothered right now."

"I'm from the *Register*," Bobby said.

"That doesn't change anything," the man said.

A female detective approached. "Leslie! Forensics says they can't be here for at least an hour. Captain wanted me to make sure you stayed to keep the area secure until they arrived. He says the SIDs teams are tied up all over the city. It's a crazy day. They're working a double on the"—the younger detective looked at Bobby, careful with her words—"situation on the Balboa Park bridge."

"Well, I'm tired too," the detective named Leslie growled back. "We've been up since what, twelve thirty?" He began and then stifled what was threatening to be an extremely long yawn. "An hour for SIDs?" Leslie's face twisted into a grimace.

"At least an hour. I guess they found something that doesn't quite support the . . ." the officer trailed off.

"The idea of suicide?" Bobby interjected. "Judge Eidelman. He was presiding over a patent case, wasn't he?"

"Which story are you covering?" Leslie snapped.

"I want to get inside. Take a look at the lion."

"Not without an escort. We've got to preserve that scene until the nerd squad arrives. This one's got liability written all over it." Leslie let out another yawn. The younger detective and Bobby waited patiently for him to close his mouth. Finally, he said, "Lapeyre, take this kid inside but no pictures, and for the love of all that is holy, don't let him touch anything. Got it?"

The second detective was much closer to Bobby's age. She took away his cell phone then led him past the ticket booths and through the turnstile. Bobby was used to women giving him their undivided attention, but Lapeyre was treating him as an inconvenience more than anything else. He hustled to catch up to her. "Do we have any ideas how the lion got out of the enclosure? I'm assuming these habitats are built to safeguard against this kind of thing."

"It wasn't a lion. It was a tiger. And it's a new habitat. It just opened last Thursday. I guess the big guy was a little worked up from those weeks spent in a kennel while they put the thing together."

"Is it possible the shelter was built poorly?"

"I didn't say that."

"It only held the tiger for . . ." Bobby looked at his watch; it was Tuesday. "Six days."

"I'm not saying anything about culpability. Only dummies go on record about that. And you should be careful to print anything about it either. It was Terry Abbattista who donated the money to build this wing. Do you know who he is? He also donated the panda enclosure. And the new elephant habitat."

"Are you saying we might have a panda mauling next?"

Lapeyre snickered. Then she outright laughed. Then she said, "Or maybe pandas riding elephants. Just stomping and clawing everything in their path."

Bobby began to laugh also. Lapeyre was finally warming up a little bit. Better yet, she seemed to be buying the notion that he was a real reporter. He was feeling good until they reached the tiger's habitat. The smell of blood, feed, and animal shit mixed into a ghastly cocktail. Bobby stood over a crimson smear zigzagging across the pavement, several benches, and a table. At the end of the trail, the body was still where the tiger had dropped it, resting partially on the walkway and partially on a greenbelt. It was a man in his forties, wearing a T-shirt and Bermuda shorts. He held a cell phone, but his hands were curled closed on it like claws. He had a huge gash in his chest and punctures in his neck. Blood had pooled beneath his body, and the wind was slowly pushing it into a wider and wider circumference.

Bobby felt his stomach churn. He turned away to collect himself.

"Still funny?" Lapeyre asked.

Bobby closed his eyes and raised his upper lip to seal off his nasal passage. He waited patiently for the nausea to subside. When it did, he said, "What's a SIDs team?"

"Scientific Investigation Division. They're our forensics unit. They get first crack at every crime scene. When I started four years ago, there were just two guys in pocket protectors; now they number twice the size of the homicide division."

"Where's the tiger?"

"It's about one hundred yards over that hill," Lapeyre said. "They tranq'd it, but it just kept rolling along, so we had to neutralize it with our weapons."

"You guys killed the tiger?"

"We had to neutralize it."

Bobby smiled his most disarming smile. "Maybe we can talk like friends instead of one of us being a reporter?"

"We had to neutralize it before it posed further risk."

Bobby wrote in his notebook. He wrote down the names of Lapeyre and Leslie Consorte and Terry Abbattista. He sketched a layout of the murder scene, made a wild estimation at the distance the tiger would have had to have jumped. He wrote down verbatim everything Lapeyre had said to him.

"There's only one tiger, right?"

"I sure hope so," Lapeyre said.

Bobby hopped the fence into the tiger enclosure.

"Get the hell out of there," Lapeyre said. "Right now!"

Bobby slid down into the channel between the enclosure and the chain-link fence. He yanked open the access door and passed under the tunnel and up into the tiger's den. There was a small trough of food, mostly full, and a pad of hay as a makeshift bed. The walls of the tiger's cave were resin, and they still smelled fresh from casting, but there was another, stronger smell. Pungent cat piss filled his nostrils. He saw dried puddles of urine on the rock walls, near the feed trough—all over everything really. How was it that the big cat fouled his cage so thoroughly, so quickly? Bobby walked out into the viewing area and spotted Lapeyre still on the other side of the enclosure, glaring at him.

"Now I hope there are two tigers," she said. "What are you doing in there? You're lucky that's not the crime scene or I'd haul you down to the station for—What the hell are you doing?" Lapeyre's voice rose.

Bobby had taken a few steps back, getting as much space between himself and the safety channel as he could. He ran toward it at a full sprint, pumping his arms wildly. At the last possible second, he planted his foot, threw his body forward, and sailed across the open space. Lapeyre flinched backward, waving her arms to keep her balance and move away from Bobby's trajectory at the same time. Bobby landed heavily against the resin slope, just managing to slip his fingers into the chain-link fence before the inertia bounced him backward. He hung perilously over the steep trench. When he looked up, Lapeyre had collected herself and was looking down at him.

"That was bananas," she decided.

Bobby hung from the fence, his legs tucked up against his bruised stomach. He slowly pulled himself to his feet and hopped over the top of the barrier. "I'm not an animal expert, but it seems odd that I was able to do that, doesn't it?"

Slightly mollified, Lapeyre looked again at the enclosure. Finally she said, "Not really. That was one damn fine jump. What sports did you play?"

"I don't think this space is wide enough to keep a tiger safely away—"

Lapeyre shook her head. "Naw. I wouldn't try the Abbattista angle. They'll take your job away. Besides, the zoo lawyers already talked to us about it. A couple of guys were here with measuring tape. It's eleven feet—like I said, one hell of a jump you made—a cool eighteen inches more than the minimum distance required by the CalWest Association of Zoos and Aquariums."

Bobby nodded, writing down a few notes. "Let's go see the tiger," he said.

Lapeyre motioned him toward the hill, and they walked over the top side by side. When they reached the corpse, Detective Leslie Consorte was standing over it talking with tired politeness to two zoo employees. All three looked pained, and one, a woman in her twenties, kept glancing down at the animal's body with a look of what had to be grief.

"The dead tourist will absolve us of any culpability. Once the tiger did that, it didn't matter if he was the last of his species or one of five hundred thousand."

Bobby walked past the conversation and crouched over the tiger. There were two feathered darts stuck in its body, one in the neck and the second on the hind flank. Less carefully placed were the bullet holes. One had entered the top left of the tiger's skull and exited just above the neck. The second, what Bobby imagined was the kill shot, had buried into the soft, wet flesh, just above the tiger's heart. There was blood everywhere, splashed across the tiger's nails and paws, blossoming like a firework from the tiger's neck and skull. Bobby could see a difference between the composition of the animal's blood and that of the man it had killed. The blood around its paws was crimson and thick, while the animal's was far thinner and a bright, almost cherry pink.

Bobby turned from the tiger in time to see Detective Consorte reluctantly hand his business card to the female zoo employee.

"They'll tell you the exact same thing," Bobby heard him say.

After the employees walked away, Bobby said, "What was that about? Were they more angry about the tiger than the father?"

"Well put," Leslie Consorte said. "And astute. They seemed to think we fired a little too enthusiastically. I'm going to be pissed if this goes to review." Leslie rubbed his forehead and let out another huge yawn. It was contagious. Lapeyre and Bobby yawned immediately after. Leslie said, "Oh, shit. I forgot I'm talking to a damn reporter. None of this goes in the paper, kid. In fact, this never happened."

"You won't be culpable no matter what the paper says—" Bobby promised.

"I'm lead; I'm not the one who shot the tiger—"

"What I mean is, no one will blame you once they read about the tourist." Bobby's eyes kept drifting back in the direction of the dead man. It was the first time he had ever seen a corpse, and it wasn't easy to get used to.

"Yeah, maybe. If those tan-suited nut jobs are to be believed, there's only a few of these tigers left in the world." Leslie scowled. "And how could they possibly know how many are left? Did they count them? Personally?"

"What did you say?" Bobby asked him.

"Nut jobs?"

"What kind of tiger is this?" Bobby thought about the email from the night before. It felt like a hundred years ago.

"An Indonesian tiger. Endangered, apparently."

"That's weird," Bobby said. He started to rub his own temple. "That's really weird."

"What is it?" Leslie asked.

"Give the kid a break. He jumped the tiger enclosure," Lapeyre said.

"No, no. It's just that we got a strange email to the *Register* last night. It declared that someone would be eaten by a rare Indonesian tiger," Bobby explained.

Leslie cocked his head. "Was it a threat?"

"It was a horoscope."

Leslie Consorte chuckled. Then he began to outright laugh. He laughed for a full thirty seconds.

"It was one of the predictions. Aries—You will be killed by a rare Indonesian tiger at the zoo."

Leslie stopped laughing. He was silent for a moment, then he said, "Should I go get my tarot deck?"

"I'm pretty sure I have a Ouija board in the trunk of the prowler," Lapeyre said.

"We were sent twelve predictions. Eight of the twelve were just fluff, and they were all highly specific, which is why I didn't take it too seriously. One was 'you'll break a crown on your tooth.' There was one about wearing the color green to ensure a job promotion." Bobby paced back and forth, his eyes occasionally drawn to where flies had gathered around the body of the dead tiger.

"If eight of the twelve were fluff, what were the other four?" Leslie asked.

"One was about a brush fire. Two were about death. The first mentioned the tiger. The other said 'you'll be dragged behind the bumper of your own car.' My friend got goose pimples when she read them because the description of that last one was so vivid. It didn't mention death, just the attack and the dragging. I'm implying death because it seems inevitable."

Lapeyre and Leslie both turned a shade ashen. Bobby looked from one to the other.

"What's going on, guys? Do you think we should take this seriously? It seemed like a joke to me."

"Don't screw us around, kid. It's unbecoming of a professional like yourself."

"Tell me what I don't know."

Leslie walked over to Bobby and put his hand on Bobby's shoulder. As he spoke, he seemed to be attempting to read Bobby's face. "Last night they pulled me out of bed at two a.m. because of a murder in Clairemont. A man was dragged behind a truck for four blocks. Death was inevitable."

"Two lucky guesses?" Bobby said. His mind drifted back to the morning meeting. There had been something about a brush fire. Near the mall.

Leslie shook his head. "I have no idea what to think."

"Give me my phone back a second," Bobby said, gesturing to Lapeyre. She looked at Leslie, who just shrugged.

"It's fine. But call the chief," Leslie told his partner. He turned back to Bobby. "Kid, what was the last prediction?"

Lapeyre tossed Bobby his phone. Then she walked fifteen feet down the path, punching at the screen of her own phone.

"Did it say anything about a judge committing suicide?" Leslie asked. Bobby scrolled through the message.

"I could look closer at the other nine, maybe one of them mentioned the suicide indirectly. There was a prediction about a man losing his life savings at the Del Mar racetrack. Something about a horse, Susie B Lassie, I think was the name. It's under Virgo. Maybe the judge bet big and . . ."

Bobby could tell Leslie was deep in thought. His eyebrows moved across his forehead, as he waved off Bobby's theory. "It's possible the writer witnesses the first murder and then makes a really lucky guess about the tiger. Stranger things have happened. The mess in Clairemont was gruesome. I can see why folks wouldn't want to get involved. Maybe it was someone's bizarre way of anonymously reporting what they saw?" Leslie had been reinflated by Bobby's information but now it was seeping back out of him. "What was the last prediction?"

"It was a rape. A gang rape at SDU. In one of the fraternity houses."

"Which one?"

"I don't remember."

"I'm way too tired for this," Leslie said.

Lapeyre came back from the call. "The chief thought I was kidding. Then he just laughed at us. He said if we try to become psychic detectives, we're fired. He said Eidelman killed himself. Said they already talked to the wife, and she confirmed it was a possibility. He'd been on heavy antidepressants but had stopped taking them a few weeks ago. He left a note."

"Anything about the horse races?" Bobby asked.

Leslie Consorte withdrew a cigarette from his chest pocket and lit it. The cigarette, smoking in his hand, emphasized his expressive arm movements. "Stop it. That wild voodoo had me going for a second. That'll tell you how tired I am."

"Shouldn't you look into the rape? Just to be sure?" Bobby urged.

"I'm going to look into getting some sleep."

"I can find out which fraternity." Bobby scrolled through his phone.

"Two out of twelve is an impressive bit of guessing. Tell your horoscope guy congratulations." Leslie stomped out his cigarette and buttoned his coat against the chill wind and encroaching clouds.

Lapeyre typed something on her cell phone and slipped it back into her pocket. They looked expectantly at Bobby.

"I write the horoscopes," he said dumbly.

"Congratulations," Leslie said.

"But I didn't write these."

Leslie handed Bobby a business card. "Send the email to me. I'll have the cyber guys look it over. Maybe the writer was involved in the first crime; even if it's just as a witness, we should try to talk to them." Impatiently, he looked at his watch. "Lapeyre, could you find out when the hell the SIDs are going to be here? Jesus."

Lapeyre walked away again, punching at her cell phone.

"I'm going to print the story," Bobby said suddenly. "I'm going to write about the horoscope and your refusal to look into it. If that rape victim comes forward—"

"You're back here, with access to the crime scene, because we let you back here. We don't let you, you're not here. You write something like that, you're never here again. Got that, kid? How long, Lapeyre?" Leslie shouted.

"They're saying at least an hour."

"Goddamn it, that's what they said an hour ago!" Leslie dropped down on a park bench, the tiger's corpse at his feet. For a moment he sat hunched into his own body, pouting like a child whose mother wouldn't let him feed the giraffes. Then he raised his head.

"You said they pulled you out of bed at two a.m.," Bobby reminded him.

"Yeah, so?"

"The time stamp on this email is ten p.m. That's got to be at least three hours before the murder occurred. That means the horoscope writer predicted both murders. Before they happened."

Leslie exhaled deeply and then looked back at Bobby. He closed his eyes. For a moment Bobby thought he might have fallen asleep. Then he opened them again and said, "Think we can get out to San Diego University and back in an hour?"

8

"WHEN YOU WRITE me into your article, I better have gleaming white teeth and a strong jaw," Leslie said. They were riding in his unmarked Ford Explorer east on the 8 Freeway toward San Diego University. Leslie turned the car off the 8 and started the long climb up Quetzalcoatl Road toward SDU's Greek community.

Bobby checked his phone and noticed three missed calls from Sarah. The Theta Rho Kappa house was located about a mile and a half from the freeway in an old Victorian model from the 1920s. Someone had blown out the back wall and built another one thousand or so square feet with a cheap shake shingle roof and stucco, at a mismatch with the wood of the original structure. Craning his neck, Bobby could see an oak patio in the backyard, and waterlogged lawn furniture.

"We should find out if the tiger victim was an Aries," Bobby said, mostly to himself.

Leslie looked at the house, and then he peered back and forth down the long street. The air was calm, and the houses appeared mostly empty, with lights dimmed and blinds drawn. In the backyard of Theta Rho Kappa, automatic sprinklers finished their timed work, grinding through the last of a *ching ching ching* rhythm Bobby hadn't even realized he'd been listening to.

"I think we're wasting our time," Leslie decided. He seemed to be considering the quiet, peaceful street. "The minute Lapeyre calls, we'll head back to the zoo."

"I disagree," Bobby said as they approached the door.

Leslie pulled his badge from his pocket and hung it in his left hand. With his right he knocked three times. No one answered.

"I can hear someone moving around inside," Bobby said.

"Me too," Leslie said. He put his hand on the doorknob, but the door wouldn't budge.

Bobby stepped back from the porch and looked down the side of the house. "There's another door over here," he said.

Leslie walked the length of the porch and around the corner. He put his hand on the second doorknob and pushed it open.

Inside was a room in total chaos. One couch was overturned, another broken in the center and collapsing in on itself. There was a wet bar covered in empty and partially crushed beer cans and a large standing speaker with an iPhone cable hanging from it like a tongue. A boy, no older than eighteen or nineteen, was lying on the floor with his head propped in one hand and the other on a video game controller. He had short, trimmed hair and a slight, thin beard sprouting from his chin.

When he rolled onto his back to greet the visitors, his eyes fell immediately to Leslie's badge. They widened and the boy climbed to his feet. His arms hung motionless at his side, the game controller suspended just below his belt line.

"Jimmy!" the boy yelled. "Jimmy!"

"We'd like to ask you a few questions," Leslie said.

The boy looked at them again and then moved quickly out of the room, yelling, "Jimmy!"

Leslie followed him; Bobby trailed a few seconds later with more trepidation. His mind kept filling with detective television show parlance where they needed "papers" and "probable cause."

Leslie caught up with the boy at the foot of the stairs leading to the next floor. He grabbed his hand and pulled him to an immediate stop. The boy opened his mouth to yell one more 'Jimmy,' but the words died on his lips.

An older boy, just a few years younger than Bobby, came walking down the steps. He was wearing a bathrobe over shorts and a T-shirt and carrying a laptop and a backpack.

"What's going on, Ronnie? Who's this?"

"San Diego PD," Leslie said, showing his badge.

"You can't come in here."

"We just want to have a conversation. I guess Ronnie is not the talkative type. Maybe you are?"

Jimmy said, "Ronnie, go upstairs and call my father. Tell him some police have broken into our house."

"We didn't do anything wrong!" Ronnie shouted.

"We just want to ask a few questions," Leslie said firmly.

"The law says you can't be in here. It says you need to wait outside. Unless you have probable cause."

Bobby heard the distinct clanking sound of workout equipment as another boy entered from a room off the kitchen. He was wearing a white tank top and the muscles on his arms were sweating and puffed. The new boy took a look at Bobby, then Leslie, then Leslie's badge, and said, "What the hell, Jimmy?"

"Ronnie's calling my dad. These two men were just about to go outside."

"Upstairs. We were just about to go upstairs." Leslie took two or three steps up the landing. A quiet tension burned in the room. Bobby could hear the creak of each step as Leslie climbed the old Victorian staircase. Another boy came out of one of the bedrooms and paused at the top. The newest boy didn't say anything, he just stared down at the intruders with his mouth pinched in a thin line.

Before Leslie could get even halfway, Ronnie reentered with a cell phone in his hand. "My dad's lawyer will be here in less than fifteen minutes. He was on the 163 Freeway." Ronnie turned to Bobby. "He said you both are legally obligated to wait outside."

"We should do that, Leslie," Bobby said.

"Why are you sweating, Jimmy?" Leslie asked the boy.

Bobby noticed it too. The boy they called Jimmy had a thin line of perspiration forming above his right temple. It pooled into a tiny teardrop and then swept down his cheek and off the edge of his chin.

Something had been bothering Bobby about the original prediction. Something that was hidden between the lines of the description. *You'll be raped on the property of the Theta Rho Kappa house*, it had said. Why make the distinction between property and house? Property distinguished from house meant backyard, or front yard, didn't it? "Let's wait outside. It would be a good idea," Bobby said.

Leslie walked heavily back down the stairs, never taking his eyes off Jimmy. When he reached the bottom, Bobby motioned him toward the backyard patio, an eyebrow conspicuously arched.

"Where the hell do you think you're going?" Jimmy asked.

"You gotta learn not to talk to a cop that way, son." Leslie stared him straight in the eyes and rolled his shoulders. Leslie couldn't have been older than forty-three or forty-four, but he was a large man with an adult's frame, gritty adult shoulders, adult biceps, thick forearms, and calloused fingers. His stomach paunched, and he had heavy lines on his face and the underside of his chin, but he was still a relatively imposing figure beside the scrawny postadolescents. Standing in the center of the room, shaking his large body and squaring off against the young man in the bathrobe, Leslie looked like Gulliver warming up to stomp the Lilliputians.

Bobby didn't wait. He let himself out of the untracked sliding door and onto the patio. The boy who had been lifting weights followed him to the door frame and glared hatefully.

Bobby scanned his eyes over everything on the patio. He spotted a nightstand in the corner, the wood warped from water exposure and beer. It, and the concrete slab around it, hosted a number of spilled red party cups. Hundreds of dried mud tracks covered the overgrown lawn, a sign of people coming and going, standing on the deck, shuffling, dancing; shoe tracks, tracks belonging to flip-flops and tracks from bare feet. Bobby studied them. They had been created over a series of days, weeks, or even months. He imagined Theta Rho Kappa didn't get around to mopping their patio too often and those auto sprinklers would cause plenty of moving muck. He noted a square of space with relatively few tracks. Moving to the edge of the square, Bobby knelt on his knees and peered at the mostly congruent corners.

"Where's your Ping-Pong table?" Bobby asked the boy at the door.

"We don't have one," the boy said gruffly.

"A fraternity house without a Ping-Pong table?" Bobby asked.

Before the boy could comment again, Leslie shouldered his way outside. "What'd you find, Bobby?"

"It's what I didn't find. See the empty space here? No mud tracks. I'm wondering where the table went that was on this patio."

Leslie just nodded his head, but he was looking at Bobby with tired admiration.

"Yeah, yeah, we did have a Ping-Pong table. You know, for beer pong and stuff. But it broke. A while ago."

"Where is it now?"

"Don't tell me a bunch of partiers like you took the time to load it in a car and drive it to the Kearny Mesa dump?" Leslie said. "A trash truck's not going to pick up something as big as a Ping-Pong table."

"I'd imagine it's still in the backyard, somewhere," Bobby said.

"I don't really know," the boy told them. "Maybe we burned it for firewood." He stepped back out of the doorway and slid the sliding door shut.

"Let's find the table," Bobby said.

They found it, hastily folded and shoved against the far south side of the room addition. Bobby tried to fold it open, but the metal frame was badly bent. There were a number of stains on the top of the table, mostly water and beer. A few dark gray stains near the back edge on one side of the table caught Bobby's attention. Maybe vomit. He crouched down and examined the legs. The table had been broken off its wheels, so cleanly that the four jagged legs stuck into the muddy ground in symmetry.

"Something with quite a bit of force must have been slammed against it, all at once, to break off each of the four wheels so cleanly," Bobby said. He ran his finger across the broken bottom of one of the legs and rust flaked off.

Leslie had been standing back to let Bobby look. He stifled a yawn into a clenched fist. His eyes burned in contrast to his yawning mouth. "You're pretty good at this. How long have you been a journalist?"

"A little less than two days. Before that I was in water polo. Do you think if we went back and studied those mud tracks, we could find some that fit the profile of a woman? Maybe in bare feet?"

The phone started vibrating in Leslie's pocket, causing both men to jump. Leslie fished it out and put it to his ear. "Yeah, Lapeyre." Bobby could hear the distant squeaking of Lapeyre's voice. "You've got to keep them company. Secure the scene. Make sure you write down everything they say to you. And then go get some sleep." Lapeyre squawked again and Leslie responded saying, "I really don't know. I'm not ready to say that, but it's pretty tense inside Theta Rho Kappa." Then he hung up.

Bobby picked up a stone and scratched at the top of the Ping-Pong table. The stain was shallow, and the waterlogged wood showed just below the surface. "We're not going back to the zoo?"

"Not quite yet. Let's go inside and talk to the kids before some douche in a suit shows up to throw around legal jargon."

Bobby rose out of a crouch, and they walked back to the porch. Once there, he looked down at the mud tracks, noting every smaller feminine arch, especially around the empty space where the Ping-Pong table had been. When he looked up again, ready to follow Leslie into the house, some douche in a suit was shouldering his way out the sliding glass door and onto the porch.

Jimmy's dad's lawyer was slick and smooth. He had thick, brown hair, combed back, and carefully maintained stubble on his cheeks and chin. He was wearing a polo and tailored blue jeans. If Theta Rho Kappa had a secret handshake, Bobby guessed he would know it. "You two can't be back here," he told them, pointing as he spoke.

"Hey there, slick," Leslie said.

Bobby took a step backward. He had only known Leslie for about two hours, but it was long enough to recognize that he wasn't going to leave without a little bit of lawyer-baiting.

"If you want to trespass on private property, you need the authorization of a judge."

"I don't understand," Leslie said.

"Then I'll say it to you nice and clear. Leave now, or I'll be forced to file a complaint with the police department and a complaint with the San Diego district court."

"Who has more power? The guy with the gavel or the guy with the gun?"

"The gavel," the lawyer said firmly. "You are only one extension of the law. If you keep up with this, any evidence you discover will be completely inadmissible in court."

"So there's evidence to discover?"

The slick lawyer shrugged. "I only know that the boy's father called to say these kids were the victims of police bullying—a charge that's been leveled at SDPD a few too many times lately in my opinion. I'm sure that—"

"My intuition tells me a crime has been committed here," Leslie said.

"These children live socially complex lives. You broke into their home. Who knows what secret trauma your intrusion could have triggered in their young psyches? It's time for you to vacate the property. Past time."

While the lawyer and Leslie continued their posturing, Bobby peered through the dirty sliding glass door of the fraternity house. Inside he could see Ronnie, the young man who had been playing video games, in an animated discussion with the boy who had been lifting weights. The gamer was clearly in a state of high agitation, thrusting his arms and jabbing his fingers in the air. Bobby wasn't sure, but it seemed possible that tears were glistening in his eyes. The other boy was attempting to keep him together. After a moment, they both turned and looked at Bobby, his hands and face pressed against the glass. The weightlifter dragged the other kid toward the stairwell and out of sight.

WHEN BOBBY MOTORCYCLED back to the *Register*'s head-quarters, he found a very angry editor waiting for him. Milo was leaning against Jana's desk, drumming his fingers on her ink blotter with ferocious intent. There was music playing from a small Bluetooth speaker. When Bobby walked through the door, Milo leaned down to power it off.

"I gave you a chance with a story and this is how you pay me back? You have no writing experience. You haven't even written a pamphlet, and I gave you not one job, but two jobs in two days. And this is what I get back? By disappearing for half the day?"

"I was just verifying some information."

"And what the hell did you find?"

"This is going to sound really strange, but I got an email last night . . ."

While Milo glared, Bobby told him the entire story.

To his credit, Milo took the ridiculous information in stride. He asked a few clarifying questions, but he mostly let Bobby speak uninterrupted. When the story finished, Milo wasn't glaring anymore. He was grinning. "'Print this or they'll all come true?'" Milo repeated.

"That's what it said."

"But do you understand what it means?" Milo asked.

"Uhh . . ." Bobby said.

"It means we're going to sell a shitload of papers."

"I want co-byline credit," Bobby told him.

"Oh, you're already off the story. Say one more thing and you're off horoscopes too. I cover this from now on. You're going to tell me every detail. And we're going to cross our fingers that another one of these deranged messages arrives tonight."

"Co-credit," Bobby said.

"Today is your last day at the *San Diego Register* because you're fired." Milo's voice was a feral growl, too deep for his thin diaphragm. "You're the horoscope writer. Not anything else."

Jana winced. She seemed on the verge of crying. It had been a stressful day for everyone.

Bobby coolly checked his watch. He had a fiber bar in his pocket. He pulled it out and slowly unpeeled the wrapper. "The last email arrived at ten p.m. That gives you about five hours before the next one comes. Do you think that's long enough to rediscover all the things I spent my day discovering?"

"Are all Olympians this ruthless? You bastards know what it takes to get to the top, don't you?"

Bobby just shrugged.

Milo silently mouthed the words "silver medal," but he seemed to be calming down. His excitement over the possibility of paper sales was outweighing his frustration over Bobby's insolence. He addressed Jana, who was scrunched into a pretty small part of her desk chair. "We run the horoscopes online, don't we?"

"Yes," she said, though she seemed uncertain.

"Let's delay when they're updated until after the paper arrives on doorsteps. Subscribers of the physical paper will get a jump on everybody else for the news. Also, reduce the number of daily free articles online from three to zero. And cut the free trial days from the subscription model entirely. Eight weeks minimum for the cheapest plan. No more free Sundays."

Jana was following Milo's words, typing notes on her computer.

"You're briefly unfired, Bobby. I'm going to take a few deep breaths in an effort to calm down, and then you're going to tell me everything you've learned."

———

AFTER MILO HAD calmed down, Bobby told him the entire story, starting with his typed response to the email, then on to the Indonesian tiger, what he overheard about the judge's suicide, and finally his and Leslie's trip to the fraternity house. When Bobby told him about sneaking around the fraternity house, he seemed impressed, just as Leslie had been. Bobby found himself not toning down any of the details. To the contrary, he was almost selling the horoscope's plausibility with his own enthusiasm.

When the story was over, Milo fell silent for a full minute. Finally he spoke. "You sent an email to a potential serial killer calling him a 'prick-waver'? I'm glad I'm not sleeping at your house tonight." He turned to Jana and told her to get Robert, Lane, Linda, and Hawkeye into his office immediately. "I don't care if you have to call them at home and drag their asses back here," he said.

Milo crossed his fingers together behind his head and exhaled a long breath. The manic energy seemed to be draining straight out of him. "There's a very good chance this is all bullshit. You understand that, right? But it might not matter if there's enough truth to run the story. People are going to love this story." Milo pointed a thin finger at Bobby. "You may have already discovered that new business model you were promising me."

"I think it might be real—" Bobby insisted.

"Okay! That's even better. I'm going to corroborate what they learned about the dragging victim in Clairemont with the details about the tiger. Then I've got to write the story." Milo shushed Bobby away. "You can go. It's just big boy work from here on out. Keep your ringer on in case I think of any more questions. But don't flap your mouth to anyone else. I'm a man of my word. You'll get your byline on the cover story. Lions and mystical serial killers." Milo rested his hands on his hips. He seemed exhausted, but happy. "Nice first scoop, kid. I guess I'm impressed."

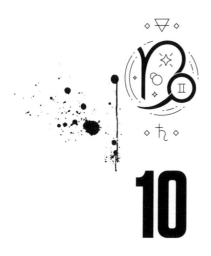

10

DRESSED, SHAVED, HAIR combed, wearing his cleanest, newest clothes, Bobby knocked on Sarah's door. It was fifteen minutes to ten p.m. Sarah peered through the window, pulling aside a set of blinds. Seeing it was him, she simply stared, unblinking and unhappy. Bobby motioned for her to open the door. Reluctantly, she did.

"Bobby, I don't know what to say to you."

"I'm really sorry, Sarah."

"I've been trying to call you all day."

"It's been a wild day. Really wild. Can I come in and tell you about it?"

Sarah remained motionless in the doorway. Bobby stood limply on her stoop. He felt like he should be doing a slow wag of his tail. "I wish you'd answered the phone. Every hour that passed made me feel more cheap. And there's something you need to know."

"I promise I wasn't avoiding you."

Sarah finally stepped aside from the door frame. Bobby walked in and sat on the couch. He wanted to get a Pacifico, but he knew it was the wrong thing to do. When he leaned against the frame of the couch, his back hit the wood. The pillows had been pulled away, and a memory burned through his head of their naked bodies intertwined, grinding against each other. He sat up again, both feet flat on the floor. "I feel awful," he said honestly.

"Yeah, me too," she said.

"I have to tell you about my first day on the job."

"Let me talk first. I'm not sure you're going to want to be my friend when I finish."

"Wait a minute. I regret last night, but I still love—I still really like spending time with you."

"Here's the thing though, Bobby. I told my husband what happened. I mean, maybe if you'd answered the phone this morning after sneaking out so quickly—I don't know, I just felt so bad about the whole business. I just wanted to talk to him for the comfort. To convince myself I hadn't already lost him. Right after he answered the phone, he told me he loved me, and it just started spilling out. I told him everything, and it just made me feel worse. And my husband—"

"You told a trained killer that I had sex with his wife?"

"Bobby, I'm so sorry. He doesn't—he said he forgives me. He said it was his fault for leaving me alone. He started to cry on the phone. He's stationed in a green zone near Yeonpyeong Island in Korea. The connection quality on the phone is terrible. There's this constant, heavy buzz, but I could still hear him snuffling and huffing on the other end of the line. His squad mates were making a bunch of noise in the background, arguing, laughing, blowing off steam, and my poor husband, in the corner on the phone with me, was weeping like a little kid. And it's our fault, Bobby."

"Oh, man."

"Well, here's the thing. He called again at five o'clock. He'd spoken to his squad commander. They're really close, and when he explained the situation, he was immediately, temporarily excused from active duty. He's flying home. He'll be here in three days." Sarah walked over to where Bobby was sitting. She hugged herself with both arms and tried to smile a comforting smile, but her mouth was tired, wane. Then she said, "He wants to talk to you when he gets here."

Bobby was silent for a long time. Finally he said, "I need to get health insurance."

"I'm going to tell him it's all my fault. That I seduced you . . ."

"No, don't do that. Tell him as close to the truth as you can. We've been growing closer. I kissed you first. We were both drinking." Bobby took a deep breath. "I hated myself when I woke up with you in my arms. I didn't sneak out to make you feel cheap. I was late for work, and I felt like a rat."

"How was your first day?" Sarah asked weakly.

"Oh, man," Bobby said again. "What time is it? Is it ten o'clock yet? I need to borrow your laptop again."

"What?"

"That horoscope, remember? Those things came true. Or they might have come true. I can't decide. There was a tiger attack."

"I saw that on the seven o'clock news, but—"

"There was a man dragged behind a car. A GMC truck!"

"No, there wasn't."

"There might have been a gang rape at that fraternity house. I went there with the police to investigate. I found clues." Bobby was growing excited again as he spoke. The entire day seemed patently impossible. But up until the very end it had been fun too.

"What you're saying is—"

"We have to check the email to see if there's another prediction!"

Sarah jumped to turn on her laptop. In her haste she tripped over her ottoman and went ass over elbows onto her back. When she landed, she laughed a laugh born of stress, excitement, and disbelief.

Bobby started laughing himself. "Why are you lying on the floor? We've got to check the email!"

Sarah bounded back to her feet, fixing her disheveled clothes as she crossed her small apartment. She clicked the laptop on, and they both waited for it to load up the desktop. Bobby was conscious of how close they were standing to each other, but tonight he made sure not to touch her. In three days, the postage would come due on last night's mistake.

With trembling fingers, Sarah logged into the email. While she did, she peppered him with questions. *How was this possible? Who was raped? Was he sure it was an Indonesian tiger?* Bobby answered the best he could, but his eyes were leveled on the email account. There was a new email, though it had been read already, likely by Milo. Sarah hastily clicked it open.

"Aries—You will have to wait for four full hours at the doctor's office. Make sure your phone is fully charged, or bring a book. Also, beware the Maiden, the Lion, and the Scarab.

"Taurus—You are strength and sexuality. Though your marriage has been sexless for several months, expect your partner to discover a sudden, unquenchable desire to be physical. Unfortunately for you, she'll be doing so by screwing a workmate, after hours, on his desk."

Sarah stopped reading aloud and began to blush. "This is silly."

"That last one's a bit of a touchy subject," Bobby said, which made Sarah blush even more. She went back to reading. Her spine straightened suddenly. "Bobby, look at Gemini."

Bobby stood over her shoulder and read it. "Gemini—Your moon is in Capricorn. The contrast between the signs gives you ambition, persistence, and excellence. You will discover a quarter of a million dollars in cash buried near the cross at the top of Presidio Park."

"Should we go check?" Sarah asked, breathless.

Bobby chewed on his bottom lip. Finally, he scanned the rest of the predictions. All except one were pretty pedestrian. The Libra prediction, which was Bobby's own sign, talked about angular houses and predicted sudden, unexpected death, due to an enlarged heart. At the end of the email came the same cryptic warning as the night before. "Run these and one comes true. Ignore these and they all come true."

"These are going in the paper tomorrow. Milo already told me. So even if it's real, only one of them will come true. I'd be very surprised if the unnamed, elusive madman chose the one that would make himself a quarter million dollars poorer."

"Let's go check. I want to go check." Sarah jumped to her feet. In her excitement, she stepped right into Bobby's arms. She stared at him, eyes frantic. Then a moment later she relaxed. She put her arm around him, her face in his neck. Bobby shook his head like a dog throwing off water. Her hair smelled like soap and heaven. Holding her there, his eyes began to close.

"I want to go to sleep," he said.

"Bobby, we can't."

"I mean by myself."

"Oh. Okay."

Bobby set Sarah down gently. He had very strong feelings about holding her longer, about keeping his body close to hers and continuing to feel her warm, soothing breath on his neck. But to stay close to her, to kiss her again, this time sober and purposeful, that was to forfeit a lot of things Bobby held dear: his labyrinthian sense of personal dignity and the simple, but elusive, higher ground. He pushed himself to arm's length and said, "There was rust on the bottom of the Ping-Pong table legs."

"What? What Ping-Pong table? What do you mean?"

"I thought someone had been raped on a Ping-Pong table. At the fraternity. I pictured a young woman being thrown onto it, roughly enough to snap off the wheels. But the wheels had to have come off days before, maybe weeks. How else could the bottom of the legs have already rusted? Someone implanted an idea in my head and my imagination started filling in the blanks, regardless of truth. I was doing the horoscope thing."

Sarah didn't say anything. She just cocked her head to the side and let him speak.

Bobby almost laughed, remembering what he'd told Milo during their first meeting, about bringing legitimacy and truth back to news media. "If enough people believe this nonsense, it will cascade outward, causing all sorts of trouble." Bobby scratched at his own cheek, deep in thought. "Tomorrow I'll figure out what's really going on, put Pandora back in her box, and we won't have to feel bad about passing up a quarter million that never existed in the first place," he promised her.

Bobby pulled Detective Leslie Consorte's card out of his pocket. He leaned over Sarah's keyboard and tapped at the keys, forwarding the email to Leslie without explanation. Then he put the card back in his pocket and moved toward the door. "Now it's Detective Consorte's problem and not mine. All I have to worry about is being killed by a Navy Seabee in three days."

"I'm so sorry."

"I'm just tired, Sarah. It's been a wild day."

Sarah gave him another hug as he stepped out the door, this one awkward and fraternal. He waited to hear the lock slide with a solid *thunk* before he walked back to his apartment and collapsed, exhausted and fully clothed, onto his unused bed.

11

LESLIE CONSORTE HAD had one foot in bed when he heard Bobby's email dinging into his inbox. That foot was attached to a leg, covered in a soft cotton robe and well-worn flannel pajamas.

The bed itself was wrapped in freshly laundered sheets, mostly untouched by his few hours of sleep the night before, still smelling like Tide detergent.

A cup of milk rested on the nightstand.

Leslie lay in bed for a few minutes, sipping the milk. Then he reluctantly lifted his phone and pushed the mail app. When he finished the milk, he settled back in his bed, his head sinking into the soft feather pillows.

His eyes half, then fully, closed.

Suddenly, he sat upright, laboriously lifting one leg out of bed, followed by the other.

And then he'd gotten dressed again.

He did not really believe that any of the predictions were true, but he knew that if the *Register* ran the story, they didn't have to be.

People would be lining up, and digging up, Presidio Park, just minutes after the first edition thumped against the first driveway.

———   ———

THERE WERE TWO crosses at the top of the park. The first was at the apex of a long, winding road that eventually led to the general use parking lot. It overlooked the 8 Freeway. The second was half a mile away, atop a grassy knoll and surrounded by brick and bush. In a state of perpetual budget crisis, the city had cut back on gardener rotations eight months prior. As a result, the refined park was slowly slipping into a more natural state. The bushes were long and gnarled, the leaves were unraked, and the grass was alternating between chunks of brown and thick green overgrowth, depending on where San Diego's light precipitation naturally channeled. In a moment of great unhappiness, Leslie discovered, eyes blurred from sleeplessness, that the porta-potties were also way overdue to be emptied. Lapeyre, still buzzing from her promotion, had volunteered to patrol the cross at the top of the hill. It was less likely to draw attention since it was surrounded by cold, dry brick. Leslie had stationed himself at the cross overlooking the freeway. When he was just settling into a seat on a nearby park bench, his radio squawked.

"Anything going on over there?" Lapeyre's electronic voice came through the walkie with robotic intensity.

"The paper won't hit its first porch until five a.m. at the earliest. We've got a couple of hours to kill up here."

"Should we dig around?" Lapeyre asked.

"I already walked the perimeter. There's no freshly dug dirt." The walkie-talkie clicked as he released the button.

There was silence and then: "Okay. So?"

"So, if our mysterious horoscope guy really planted money here, we'd see where he'd dug up the ground."

"Maybe it was there already?" Lapeyre suggested.

"You're saying two things to me right now. One, you believe the newspaper kid, Frindley, and that we really have a genius madman on the loose capable of organizing multiple crimes in a short time span. And two, he planned the crimes well enough in advance to plant a quarter of a million dollars in a park, weeks ahead of time. For no conceivable reason."

"Despite all that logic, isn't it still worth looking? Maybe the world is not as simple as we think and we're standing on a treasure trove—"

"How did it get there?" Leslie asked.

"Left by pirates a hundred years ago? Who cares how?" Lapeyre's tone had been simultaneously playful and sincere. For her next question, she left out the playfulness and asked Leslie straight, "What do we have to lose?"

"Our detective badges."

"I love my job, I really do," Lapeyre said. "Do you know what I'd love even more?"

"A quarter of a million dollars?"

"Yessir. How long have you been on the force, Leslie?"

"Seventeen years."

"Have you ever seen anything like this before?"

"No." Leslie reconsidered. "Kind of. We had a guy named Jack Madrigal about fifteen years ago. He promised to bring the city of San Diego to its knees. Sent letters made of magazine cutouts to the *Register* and everything, promising to kill specific high-profile city officials. He even had a personal beef with me. It was a lot like a movie, to be honest."

"What did he want?"

"It wasn't ever clear. He ended up setting fire to an empty library. We caught him the next day. It was one of the cases that got me bumped up to detective. The paper indicated he had lost his home the previous month to eminent domain. The city wanted to build a school or something. I don't know."

Lapeyre didn't respond.

Leslie sat in silence for a few minutes, drumming his fingers on the armrest of the park bench. Then something occurred to him. He picked up the walkie-talkie again and said, "You're digging right now, aren't you, Lapeyre?" There was silence on the other end. He said again, "Lapeyre, are you digging?"

Again, there was no answer. Leslie felt a small stir of worry start in the pit of his stomach. He clutched the radio against his mouth, "Lapeyre, what's your forty? You don't come back to me right now, I'm going to assume something happened and if it hasn't, I will bust you back to uniform before you can blink."

There was another prolonged silence and then Lapeyre said, "I wasn't digging. Not really. Just poking around a little." Her breathing was a little ragged, probably from moving bricks and *poking around*.

"Radio silence, Lapeyre."

For the next few minutes, Leslie watched the freeway. It impressed him that each car was carrying someone who thought that they had somewhere important to be. Seeing a freeway, from way up high, sometimes fought off the depression that would descend on every cop who worked the job too long. Leslie liked to think that if that many people could move in synchronicity with each other on a virtually lawless landscape then maybe, just maybe, they could also live in peace.

After he watched the freeway for a while, he walked the perimeter of the cross again.

THE FIRST PERSON appeared at exactly 5:15. It was a man in his early thirties. He strode toward the cross with purpose, a metal detector strapped to his back, a long, rusty shovel resting against his shoulder. He buried the shovel blade into the firm dirt six feet east of the cross. He was followed exactly sixty seconds later by a pair of teenagers, one still in her pajamas. They were carrying a gardening shovel and a hand trowel. Thirty seconds after they arrived, a housewife parked illegally and climbed out of her car, face red, hair bouncing in curlers. She carried her shovel across her left forearm. When the sixth, seventh, and eighth carful arrived, Leslie radioed for backup and called Lapeyre down to help him. By the time Lapeyre had hiked down the hilltop, twenty-six more cars and roughly two hundred people had gathered around the cross, many of them holding various types of metal instruments.

"Nobody takes another step closer," Leslie told them all. "We're done digging up the park today."

The young couple wearing pajamas ignored him completely, the man stabbing his hand shovel deep in the dirt. One by one, the others followed.

"Can we shoot them for digging?" Lapeyre asked Leslie.

"I don't even think it's against the law," Leslie said.

The first prowler rolled up a few minutes later. A rookie named Jeffries climbed out.

Jeffries' eyes were wide as he took in the throng of people. "What is going on here, Detective Consorte?"

"Get the tape. I want it running all the way from that big oak down across the road and onto this wall. Lapeyre, get on the radio again and tell them we want a blockade set up at the access road. We're closing the park. It won't keep everybody out, but it will help."

Leslie and the rookie centered themselves side by side right below the apex of the cross. "Follow my lead," Leslie said.

Then he addressed the throng, "You are hereby ordered by the City of San Diego Police Department to cease and desist all digging." Roughly twenty or so people stopped. The rest ignored him completely, muttered something under their breaths, or booed outright. Jeffries walked the tape around the oak, across the road, and tied it tight against the park bench Leslie had so recently been sitting on. Within a few minutes, people had stepped over, around, and through the tape. The digging was getting more fierce with each passing moment.

People were jockeying for unexplored sections. The search branched outward, its circumference widening with each fall of a shovel. A man who was digging with his young son stumbled onto a city repair horse and cone. He pulled the cone aside and discovered fresh dirt beneath.

A man standing nearby wearing AirPods saw the dirt. "There's fresh dirt here!" he shouted.

"Stupid, stupid, stupid," Leslie said under his breath. "Go get the bullhorn, Jeffries. It's in my trunk. You know what? I'll get the bullhorn; you get the shotgun."

By the time Leslie had the bullhorn in one hand and the shotgun in the other, he couldn't get anywhere near the spot where the fresh dirt had been discovered.

He rolled the siren on the bullhorn and a few people moved aside, but most were now pushing toward the fresh patch, causing small waves of humanity to crush in one direction and then push back in the other. Leslie thought of the man's small son at the center of the vortex, and he discharged the shotgun into the air. Even in the hustle and bustle of the ad hoc excavation, the echo of the shotgun blast created absolute silence. Leslie spoke loudly and firmly into the megaphone, "The digging is done for today. There's no money here. The newspaper has lied to you. Anyone who has not left this park location in ten minutes will be arrested for interfering with a felony police investigation."

Someone yelled, "You crude sonuvabitch cops just want it for yourselves."

"Now you have nine minutes," Leslie said.

Many kept digging, certain that a last fall of the shovel would strike against corrugated metal or attaché, ending their financial struggles forever. Leslie saw a man standing on the park bench with an eye patch over his eye. The man took a photograph and then lowered the camera to scribble a few notes on a notepad. When his eye met Leslie's, he flashed his press badge. The *San Diego Register*. The very paper that had started this mess. Strange they didn't send the kid who had scooped the story. Leslie wondered what had happened to Bobby Frindley.

12

WHEN THE CLOCK struck 9:30 a.m., Bobby Frindley was still asleep. Just a handful of minutes later, the relentless sun, filtering through his bent plastic blinds, beamed directly into his eyes. He rolled over onto his back, desperate to ignore the intrusion, but the roll carried him onto his cell phone, and it wedged into his ribs.

Like a warm, well-muscled cat, Bobby Frindley finally curled up into a partial sitting position. He rolled out of bed, feeling the mild euphoria that always descended on him after a long sleep. He stretched his arms again, making every muscle flex, and then a thought plunked into his head. *I slept through work.* He rolled his feet out of bed and slipped out of his clothes. He had been in the shower for exactly eleven minutes when his phone began to ring.

He ignored it.

It rang again. He ignored it again.

When it began to ring a third time, he dragged a towel off the rack and walked laboriously to the phone. Only one person alive would have the obstinacy to call three times back-to-back-to-back.

"Hello?" Bobby said.

"I hope that one day I will be able to call, and my lazy son will not be home to answer. He won't be home because he'll have an actual job with an actual income." Bobby's father's voice was cutting, without a trace of humor. In twenty-six years, Bobby had never known his father to display even a trace of self-depreciation, playfulness, or restraint.

"You called my cell phone, Dad. I'm always home for my cell phone." Bobby yawned. He knew the yawn would escalate his father's anger, and if he was being honest he'd admit that's why he did it.

"How did I spawn such a lazy, layabout piece of flotsam?"

Through the earpiece, Bobby could hear his mom's voice, speaking at a high octave. He couldn't hear her words, but his father responded to her by saying, "Yes. Yes. But when were closing ceremonies? August of last year?"

His mother said something else, but Bobby interrupted them by saying, "I got a job, Dad."

"Go on, I'm listening."

"I'm working for the paper. The *Register*."

"What, as an intern? You somebody's coffee boy?"

"No. I'm a copywriter. It's the real deal."

"I'm not sure what to say."

"Congratulations?"

"Your mother wants to speak to you."

"Thanks, Dad."

Bobby's mom's voice came over the line, buzzing in excitement. Her voice was husky, the product of thirty years of smoking cigarettes, which in and of itself was the product of having married a difficult and combative man. "What did you just tell your father?"

"I got a job, Mom."

"Nothing can stop you."

Bobby laughed out loud. It was like talking to yin and then yang. He glanced around his tiny apartment, happy to be anywhere but home with his parents.

"How are you, Bobby? We don't hear from you very often."

"I'm fine, Mom. I'm doing just fine."

"Are you getting in trouble with the girls?"

Bobby's denial caught in his throat. His mom had always had a supernatural awareness of the things going on in Bobby's life. As a kid and later as a teenager, he'd lived with the specter of her knowing what he'd fixed himself for lunch (Bobby suspected that she searched the trash for leavings, measured the cheese, counted the tortillas), her knowing what he'd done for homework (she would rummage through his book bag, pester his teachers), and her knowing who he was interested in at school (she worked with the other moms to create a sublime spy and gossip network).

If Bobby challenged her on her knowledge or her tendency to snoop, she'd claim she simply knew him so well she could predict his behavior.

It's the same way God does it, she would tell him.

"I love you, Mom."

"You love your father too."

"I have to hang up. The paper is expecting me to finish a story on that tiger attack at the zoo."

"We read about that in the morning edition. Did you write *that* story?" His mom's voice rose again, full of excitement.

"No, an editor wrote that. My name should be on the byline though. It's just supplemental copy anyway. I'm doing a full-blown investigation."

"Go, go, go. Pursue the facts. Discover the truth."

Bobby hung up the phone.

Then he called Milo Maslow.

"Where in the hell are you?" Milo said. "Where's my tiger story?"

"I'm still working on it. I'm going to try and get a quote from Ab-battista. I want his reaction. I want to know why I was able to jump the moat."

"Abbattista sits on our board of directors. He's a partial owner of the newspaper."

"Okay, then maybe I'll turn it into a human-interest story. I'll paint him as a great benefactor."

"He is. You won't. I know you already, Mr. Frindley. I already know your style. Sowing faith in the human animal, my ass. Abbattista gives a lot of money back to the community. He pays your salary. And you'll see that he's a nice guy. You treat this the wrong way, and you can kiss your promising new career 'see ya later.'"

"I just need a quote. I'll get you the whole thing in time for tomorrow's edition, I promise."

"If you don't, you're fired. You want Jana to text you his address?"

"We sold a few papers, didn't we?"

"The plant has already started on signatures for tomorrow's edition. We can't keep up with demand if we don't start early. The web traffic was ninety thousand percent higher than yesterday. You did not hear me wrong. It crashed our servers. Tell Abbattista I caused the uptick in sales. It was me."

Bobby laughed. "I will. Has any of it come true? Any of today's predictions?"

"It's hard to say. A lot of them were pedestrian and very likely came true."

"But the big ones?"

"No one found a quarter million dollars under the cross, no."

"Well, it's still selling papers, I suppose."

"Get me the rest of that tiger story, Bobby."

After getting dressed, Bobby rode his motorcycle to the Pacific Beach gym. Pacific Beach was the sister community to Crown Point, but it was a shadowy reflection of his small beach town. During the San Diego housing boom of 2000 to 2007, it had been overdeveloped in an especially cruel way. Huge block-shaped apartment complexes jockeyed for limited space on the skyline. Tattoo parlors, trendy clothing stores, and bars packed with college kids lined the main drag. Small platoons of marines on leave from nearby Camp Pendleton routinely practiced merciless scout and recon tactics on college girls migrating beachward in triangle bikinis. Bobby hated the local fitness club because it was a natural extension of the town itself: bloated, beer-soaked, and full of narcissists. However, he didn't have the time to drive all the way to the YMCA (full of nothing but old men playing racquetball, then lounging fully nude, without a hint of shame, in the locker room) and so he trudged through the turnstile and headed right to the pool.

The girl at the front desk recognized him and waved him through without checking his membership card. "Hiya, Bobby," she said, blushing.

After his swim, he dried his hair and checked the phone for Jana's text. Bobby recognized the location of Abbattista's home immediately. It was at the top of Soledad Mountain in La Jolla. Bobby didn't know much about the area except that ex-San Diego Chargers Quarterback Ricky Penn had lived there until a conflict with the general manager had led to his being unceremoniously cut from the team. He'd gone on to several AFC championships with Baltimore, savaging San Diego in the playoffs. Then the team itself had scampered up the coast to Los Angeles.

Abbattista's place wasn't too far from the gym. Three miles down a coastal highway and then straight up a winding hill. Bobby's 350cc motorcycle strained against gravity as it ground its way north at a forty-five degree angle. Halfway up the hill, the houses began to change drastically, shifting from sleepy beach cottages and retrofitted five bedrooms, to small beach castles in a Tuscan style and obscene ten-thousand-square-foot chateaus. Cresting the peak of Soledad Mountain, Bobby noted the ugly cellular towers with some satisfaction. You wanted to live up in heaven, at least you had to share it with AT&T.

Bobby found the address and parked outside a fairly innocuous home, perhaps the fourth largest on a block of only four houses. His cell phone beeped again as he swung his legs down and kicked up the kickstand. It was a text from an unknown number. It read:

Hey, it's Star. I thought of a few more things to tell you that might help. Want to meet for a late lunch?

Are you sure this isn't about my abs?

It is a little. Don't you want to see what I really look like?

Bobby stared at the text for a moment, unsure what he wanted to do. He thought of the mistake he'd just made with Sarah. And how a despicable part of him itched to swing by her apartment after work and see if he could find a way to make that same mistake again. Finally he wrote back:

Tommy-Jay's Sandwiches in Pacific Beach. 7:00. Call it a late dinner.

He pocketed the phone and rang the intercom on the Abbattista's front gate.

A woman's voice with a thick Chilean accent came back through the box.

"Yes?"

"Hi. I'm Bobby Frindley. I write for the *San Diego Register*. I was hoping to speak with Mr. Abbattista."

"Just a moment."

A few seconds later, a male voice came over the line. The voice was gruff, edged by a different and less identifiable accent, confident, but also slightly short of breath. It said, "What's this about?"

"Mr. Abbattista?"

"No. What's this about?"

"My name's Bobby, and I'm investigating the tiger mauling at the zoo yesterday for the *San Diego Register*. I had a few questions for Mr. Abbattista."

"Beat it," the voice said, and then the connection cut out.

Bobby patted his pockets.

He spotted a security camera peeking through some ivy covering a portion of the thick wooden gate. He waved to it. Then he rang the bell again.

"Yes?"

"Hi. I just have a few questions."

"I can't let you in. I'm sorry."

"Can you ask the gentleman I was just talking to, to come back to the intercom?"

"He won't change his mind."

"Just ask, please."

"Okay."

Bobby waited a few minutes but no one ever came back to the intercom. He placed both hands on the palm of Abbattista's mailbox and pulled himself into a carefully balanced standing position on top of it. Several seagulls strolling around Abbattista's roof took to the air. Bobby leaned forward and wrapped his fingers around the base of the camera. It was bolted firmly into the wood gate. He tested it with as strong a tug as he could manage. Then he swung himself upward, using the bottom of the camera for leverage. At the apex of the swing, he threw a leg over the gate, awkwardly. The motion dragged the camera inward and the fish-eyed lens stared at him as he sat astraddle the gate. He banged it back down toward the mailbox with his palm. The intercom remained silent. Bobby dropped over to the other side of the fence.

On the other side, the house kept unfolding into a larger and larger property. It was shaped like a triangle with the point of the triangle facing the street and the rest of the house branching out exponentially toward the ocean.

This wasn't the fourth smallest house on the block, it was the largest, by far. It simply appeared small from the street, designed like an iceberg. Bobby moved along a stone pathway and up to the front door. He grabbed the large silver knocker and banged it against wood. He heard a series of footfalls on the other side and, finally, a latch being thrown.

He was greeted by the sight of a young housekeeper, just a few years older than himself, and a large man, roughly his same age.

The man stepped in front of the woman and put his hands on his hips. The sleeves of his V-neck T-shirt were rolled up to reveal significant biceps, and he had a ring of sweat around his chest. He was large, but Bobby recognized that his power wasn't in his size, but rather the well-toned muscles that wrapped in bunches around each of his tensed limbs. It was a carefully constructed body, capable of great leverage. Bobby guessed he was standing in front of a professional athlete. Worse yet, the man was carrying a large bamboo shaft, roughly three inches in diameter and five feet long. He held it casually in his left hand.

The man sized up Bobby. "You don't listen too well, huh?"

"It's pretty important that I talk to Terry Abbattista."

"You're a little less scrawny than you look over the security camera. What's your sport?"

"Water polo."

The man laughed.

"Timur?" From behind the man, another older man approached. He had gray-black hair combed forward, a slight frame rounded at the belly, heavy eyelids, and a friendly, hairy Sicilian face. He was wearing a Japanese kimono and paper slippers. He was also carrying a bamboo shaft, with a little less ease than Timur. "Who's this, Timur? What's he doing inside the gate?"

"Sorry, Mr. Abbattista. He hopped the fence. I was just about to escort him out and call the police."

"I'm a reporter," Bobby said.

"That doesn't give you a right to trespass in my home. I have a dog—a very dangerous one. I can't allow just anyone to wander through my atrium; it's a liability."

"I had some questions about the tiger attack."

A look of sadness dropped over Abbattista's features. His face softened. He said, "I was deeply affected. My sister wept when she saw the news. We've already made reparations with the victim's family. Not as a sign of guilt, but as a humanitarian action toward a person in need."

"What about the enclosure? Why is it the tiger was able to escape?"

"We followed all of the CalWest Association of Zoos and Aquariums's precautionary standards. The barrier was eleven feet wide. There was a fence. You have to understand, those fences can't be so high as to obstruct the patrons' ability to see the animals."

"Mr. Abbattista, you want me to get him out of here?"

Abbattista approached Bobby and looked him over head to toe. Bobby's muscles were still puffed and tense from his swim. "You're an athlete?" he asked.

"Yes," Bobby said.

"No," Timur said. "He plays water polo."

"Water polo?" Abbattista blinked his eyes. He seemed momentarily confused. Finally, he said, "How the hell do they get the horses into the water?" Then he began to chuckle. His chuckle turned into roaring laughter, too deep and rich to be coming from his small frame. Timur laughed as well. Bobby just waited for them to catch their breath again.

"Timur here is an athlete on the Olympic level," Abbattista said.

"No kidding," Bobby said.

"Yes, he represented the Serbian national team in both gymnastics and fencing."

"It must have been tough to make the Serbian team," Bobby said.

"What the hell does that mean?" Timur said, stepping toward Bobby. In his anger, his Serbian accent thickened. He clutched his bamboo stick upright, in both hands.

Abbattista simply laughed again. "Come in, Bobby. I'll answer your questions about the tiger, but first I want to show you what we were doing."

Abbattista led Bobby through an indoor/outdoor recreation room with an indoor/outdoor pool. Diffused light filtered through the staggered wood roof and made the water sparkle.

The pool was roughly twenty yards wide everywhere except the center, which branched out another five yards to accommodate lap swimming. Above the pool was a loft full of recreational equipment. Bobby noted several frames on the wall as he passed. Abbattista's degree (in English Literature) from Princeton University; a series of horse racing pictures—one a giclée of a photo finish, the horse in focus stretching its neck for the tape; a picture of Abbattista decades younger with President Ronald Reagan at some kind of rally; a Latin phrase that read *Mensus eram coelos, nunc terrae metior umbras. Mens coelestis erat, corporis umbra iace*; and finally, a dollar bill, framed off-center in a cheap wooden frame. In the context of the other materials, Bobby thought the dollar quaint, and a little bit cheesy, but maybe Abbattista was that kind of guy. The Latin phrase was stenciled onto a small two-inch plaque.

With Abbattista and Timur walking a few steps ahead of him, Bobby took the plaque from the desk and put it in his pocket.

They continued outward, through a glass door separating the recreation room from the backyard, the lawn sloping toward the Pacific Ocean. Ahead, Bobby could see four other men standing near a chalked circle in the grass. Each of them held a bamboo shaft. Behind them a one-hundred-and-eighty-degree view of the ocean signaled the end of the property.

The men were an odd bunch. One was nearing seventy years old. He was wearing a servant's uniform, stripped down to a white tank top undershirt and black dress pants. He had sweated through his undershirt, making it transparent, and his hairy, soft, brown chest was showing. Two of the men were younger than Bobby, in their early twenties. One of them spun the bamboo stick casually in circles, his eyes never leaving Bobby's. The fourth man was enormous. He had the kind of body that could only be achieved through a careful diet, constant weightlifting, a healthy dose of powders, proteins, herbs, and vitamins, and also jabbing a syringe full of steroids into your thigh once or twice a week. His hair hung down over his eyes in tight brown ringlets, and he had circles of blood splattered on the chest and sleeve of his shirt.

Abbattista spoke to the old man in the tank top, "Tamba! Give me your stick, please."

Tamba handed his bamboo shaft to Abbattista and looked at him expectantly. "We have a new sixth; you may go back to work."

"Thank goodness," Tamba said.

Abbattista threw the shaft to Bobby who caught it instinctively.

"Are you familiar with the fourteenth century poem, *Sir Gawain and the Green Knight*?"

"I'm a little behind in my reading of fourteenth century poets."

"What poetry do you read?"

"Busta Rhymes?"

"You're even a little behind on your hip-hop," Abbattista said. "*Sir Gawain* is not a very interesting piece. It has a little bit of fun homosexual subtext. A tiny bit of chaste heterosexual eroticism. Some decent alliteration if you can get into the old English. They made a movie recently. It was . . . okay."

Bobby remained silent. He watched Abbattista, who was beaming with a great sense of satisfaction and anticipation.

"What's remarkable about the poem," Abbattista continued, "is that it gives us our first real indication of the effects of feudalism on Anglo-Norman society. The knights in *Sir Gawain* are bored. They lack the physical challenges of farming or defending the realm; they lack the instinctual struggle for survival that was characteristic of the heroes in earlier poems such as *Beowulf* and *Gilgamesh*. So, not having real problems, they begin to challenge one another to complex social and physical gaming. I can decorate my wife more beautifully than you can, or I can make a ludicrous promise and then work an entire year just to keep it, all in the name of honor. We're doing the same thing here. We're gaming."

"Are you bored, sir?" Bobby asked.

"Why don't you step into the circle, Bobby?"

Bobby looked at Abbattista. He glanced around at the other men, who were all looking back at him. Then he stepped into the chalk circle.

"Charles, get in there with him, please."

The big mass of muscles swept curly hair out of his eyes and joined Bobby in the circle. Bobby raised his bamboo shaft and held it between himself and Charles.

"Bobby, you and Charles try to stay in the circle. We'll try and get you out."

"You better be able to cover my back," Charles said in thick, clipped English.

Bobby realized he wasn't fighting Charles, but rather alongside him. He spun completely around and set himself square. From both his ten o'clock and two o'clock, the young men were advancing, bamboo held upright. Behind Bobby, Timur and Abbattista advanced on Charles.

One of the young men came in first, swinging his stick low at Bobby's feet. Bobby brought his own down fast enough to deflect the blow, but the other man stepped quickly in to level a shot at Bobby's head. Bobby got the stick just high enough to send the swing glancing harmlessly above him. The first man struck again, a quick shot at Bobby's shoulder. It connected and Bobby felt pain course through his chest and up into his throat. The second man darted in again, jabbing the end of his shaft at Bobby's neck. Charles spun in a circle to defend Bobby, deftly parrying away a weak jab by Abbattista. In a fluid motion, Charles smacked the second young man solidly on the nose, splitting it. The man stumbled back; blood appeared beneath his palm and dripped onto his chin.

"I owed you that one, Rife," Charles grumbled.

The first man advanced again on Bobby. Bobby easily parried his attack and then struck back, connecting a weak strike on the man's kneecap. The young man with the busted nose, Rife, came forward, fire in his eyes. He hit Bobby's bamboo shaft so hard it almost vibrated out of his hand. While Bobby was trying to reset himself, the other man struck him on the shoulder, sending him to his knees.

Bobby stood up again quickly and swung a wild arc; his attackers dodged backward, out of the circle. "When does this end?" Bobby said, his breath ragged.

"When you're out of the circle or we give up trying to get you out."

Charles turned his head to whisper to Bobby, "Abbattista's stick is thicker and heavier, be ready for that when he comes at you."

Bobby didn't have time to respond. Rife was advancing again. He and the other man were coming at him at the same time from different angles. He could hear the clacking of wood against wood as Timur and Abbattista struck at Charles. Bobby wanted to walk out of the circle, but he doubted he'd get his interview if he did.

Rife struck Bobby in the calf. Bobby instinctively lowered his staff to defend his legs, and the other man took advantage of the opening, swinging a berserk thrust at Bobby's head. Bobby felt the wind whoosh past his face and realized that had it connected, he'd be concussed, at best. When Rife darted in for another blow, Bobby planted his shaft in the dirt and swung himself around it. Rife's strike glanced harmlessly off Bobby's bamboo, and he wasn't positioned to protect himself from Bobby's legs. Bobby connected firmly with Rife's kneecap, and the other man crumpled to the ground.

"Well done, Bobby," Abbattista said. "We haven't seen that move, even from our Olympic fencer."

Rife lay groaning on the ground.

"Should we make sure he's okay?" Bobby asked. Abbattista lowered his shaft and walked to where Rife lay. He leaned over him and wiggled his kneecap. Rife groaned loudly in protest.

"I'll get the medic." Abbattista motioned toward the house. When Bobby turned to see where he was pointing, instead he saw Timur's bamboo shaft, winging its way directly into his face. Bobby managed only to look upward, catching the full brunt of the impact on his chin rather than his nose. The first thing he saw was an explosion of stars, then all the color drained out of the backyard, and then the grass came up fast and cradled his body. Far off in the distance, just before he blacked out, he heard Abbattista say, "Well, I guess nobody said stop, did they?"

13

WHEN BOBBY WOKE up, he was stretched out on a couch in Abbattista's great room. He blinked his eyes open, and the world swam into focus. He noted Abbattista, alone, sitting on the couch next to Bobby's legs. He was looking at Bobby tenderly, like a father would. Bobby's shirt front was covered in blood, and when he raised a hand to his chin, he felt a gauze dressing covering a one-inch gash.

"The blow split your chin. My nurse said if it stopped bleeding it wouldn't need stitches. It stopped bleeding, so I suppose you're fine. If you want to see a physician, of course I will cover the cost. I'm afraid you also have a black eye. Sometimes an impact like that can travel all the way up." Abbattista waved his hand around his own eye for emphasis.

Bobby pulled himself into a sitting position. The great room was actually a great loft. It stood twenty or so feet above the indoor half of the indoor/outdoor pool. Across from the couch was an eighty-five-inch flat-screen TV. Beside that stood a pool table and heavy-duty telescope, the telescope looking out through a picture window down onto the beach far below.

"I'm fine. I just have a few questions for you about the tiger attack."

Abbattista chuckled. "Are all my reporters this dogged? If so, you'd think my paper would be making a little money."

"Milo Maslow wanted me to tell you that sales have been up. He claimed it was all his doing."

"No surprise there. Horoscopes coming to life. Rape. Murder. A treasure trove of hidden cash. The city is beside itself today."

"No one found the cash. It was all just a hoax."

"Well, it sold some papers, didn't it? That crack addict Milo hasn't been worth much since he became default editor of just about everything. I'm a little surprised he broke the story."

Bobby didn't say anything.

"Did he break the story?"

"He helped."

"Bobby Frindley. Graduated from USC with a degree in journalism. Star hole set on the US Olympic water polo team. Earned a silver medal and scored three goals against Croatia. A hat trick. Recently taken on a position of writing horoscopes at the *San Diego Register*. Somehow jockeyed that into a full-blown national byline about a tiger attack. Maybe he was the one to actually break the story about the horoscopes? Do you know you have a Wikipedia page? Mine's a bit longer, but I'm still impressed."

Bobby laughed and it made his chin sting. "I think my mom keeps it updated."

"And I think you're purposely downplaying your accomplishments. Perhaps to put me at ease and get me to speak more freely?"

"I'm not capable of that sort of guile," Bobby assured him. Then in the same breath he said, "Why was the tiger enclosure made with only an eleven-foot moat? A tiger can jump up to twenty feet."

Abbattista leaned back against the couch. Bobby had to move his legs to avoid being sat on. "I assume that's from a dead run. I assume that's a wild tiger. You sit in a cage for a few months and you don't feel much like jumping. It was my understanding that these zoo tigers lack both the geography and the instincts of their feral brethren. Or maybe they just stare into the emptiness and it stares back? The truth is, I don't know very much about tigers or tiger habitats. You can't quote me on this, but I just pay the bill. There's a bunch of engineers and zoo planners who build the cages. It's a tax deduction for me, a little bit of local publicity also. I sign the checks and then I run around in my backyard chasing younger men with bamboo sticks."

Abbattista sighed. He looked at Bobby expectantly. Bobby did not have a question ready, but Abbattista continued talking. "I do feel quite a bit of guilt about the whole thing. A father is dead. And now the zoo feels less safe. We'll do something about it. I have the money to fix the problem as much as it can be fixed. Money can't raise the dead, but it can do just about everything else."

Abbattista stood up and walked over to the pool table. He picked up a piece of paper that was lying near the breaking rack and handed it to Bobby. "I had my secretary type up a few quotes for you. It should be enough to make getting cracked on the chin worth your while."

"A little more sanitized than I'd hoped for," Bobby said. "Do you remember the name of the architectural team that designed the habitat?"

"Everything is on file publicly with the city."

"Can you think of anyone who could have known that the enclosure wouldn't hold the tiger?"

"If someone on the team thought this tragedy was avoidable, I'm certain they would have addressed the issue immediately. I trust you're not investigating this as negligence."

"I'm not," Bobby said truthfully.

"Make sure you keep it that way." Abbattista pointed to the paper in Bobby's hand. "That's my only official statement on the matter. It's better than Milo would have gotten out of me."

"Well, thank you, Mr. Abbattista." Bobby pulled himself onto his feet. The world ran a circle around him. He blinked his eyes, trying to get his equilibrium.

"Sit down, Bobby. There's no hurry to leave." The gruffness that had edged into his voice suddenly drained back out. "Please call me Terry," the older man said.

Bobby sat back down.

"I almost forgot," Abbattista said. "When Timur knocked you unconscious, my Latin plaque fell out of your pocket."

Abbattista handed the tiny plaque back to Bobby. Bobby sheepishly placed it on the floor next to the couch. "What does it say?" Bobby asked.

"It's an epitaph. It says something to the effect of, 'Do not look to the skies for God, look for truth. When the body rests, only your mind . . .'" Abbattista struggled for the words, picking carefully through his own memory. "'Only the mind elevates'? Maybe? It's a pre-enlightenment declaration of the death of God. Kind of a creepy thing to put on a tombstone but I'm a sucker for pretty words."

"I believe in God," Bobby said.

"What? Why?" Abbattista clutched at his chest. Bobby couldn't have gotten a bigger response if he'd said he'd found Bigfoot, or a Chupacabra.

Bobby laughed. "I haven't been to church since I was thirteen. I'm not a light on the hill or anything. But I believe."

"But why?"

"The real answer? My mother and father met as counselors at a summer camp. My mother was a native of Indiana. When the summer ended, she wouldn't move to San Diego with my dad unless they were married. I'm not sure how long it was after the nuptials that they realized she was a devout Methodist and he was a raging crusader against all things holy. I've lived both realities."

"And you prefer your mom's?"

"Only a fool wouldn't."

"Bobby, the notion of God flies in the face of all practical science." Abbattista began to count on his fingers, "The universe—that's a big one, the dinosaurs, evolution, carbon dating. Do you want me to go on? You'd be just as likely to be right if you claimed you believed in Santa Claus."

"Maybe," Bobby said, nodding. "I love dinosaurs. I wouldn't want to deny them their place in history. But I do think that the longer we live with our convictions, the more they seem real. At a certain point, we close ourselves off to different ideas, and each new experience is suddenly passing through this rigid filter, one that only lets in information that supports our beliefs and ignores whatever contradicts them." Bobby almost added, "This is generally why I don't trust old people," but he managed to stop himself.

Abbattista looked at Bobby sideways. "Fact and science are not a matter of individual belief. They are the exact opposite. Fact and science make planes fly. They make bridges stay strong during earthquakes. Not prayer, not convictions. Facts. Are you ready to tell me you think the Eucharist is real?"

"I don't know what that is."

"You're a disgrace to religious zealots everywhere."

"Well, I'm not exactly an evangelical. I drink. I do a lot of reckless things, a lot of sins and so forth. Two nights ago, I had sex with a married woman."

"Why did you do that?"

"It was an accident, but I'm not sure I don't love her."

Abbattista exhaled deeply but his eyes were twinkling.

"This is a bigger conversation for bigger men than me." Bobby inched his way back onto his feet. "You've been more than decent to me considering I hopped your fence. Tell Timur I owe him one, okay?"

"You hopped my fence, stole my plaque, and you might be investigating me for negligence, in my own paper. And you believe in God.

You're very interesting. I think I like you. Come back again soon, for lunch or maybe dinner."

"Is someone going to hit me with a stick again?"

"Only if we get bored."

As he walked back out through the atrium, Bobby touched his chin lightly, feeling the wound under its dressing. He heard the dog Abbattista had talked about barking energetically behind another internal fence. Abbattista was cocky and tremendously confident in his own wealth and power, but he'd seemed to have answered Bobby's questions earnestly.

On the other hand, Bobby wasn't sure about everything he'd said to Terry Abbattista. His parents' polar opposites had dragged him in two directions at once. He'd like to think it had resulted in perfect moderation, an ability to walk between science and faith. More likely he'd accrued the terrible failings of both. He glanced at his watch. It was 7:10.

He fumbled his phone out of his pocket and saw two text messages. Both were from Star. The first, from ten minutes ago, read:

Sooo, I'm having trouble figuring out who is you. Are you the guy in the blue shirt? You look different from your pictures online.

The second, five minutes later, read:

That wasn't you and now I'm embarrassed. Are you even here?

Bobby quickly dialed Star's number. She answered, "Am I being a fool, Bobby Frindley?"

"I just woke up, Star, I'm sorry."

"You slept through our date?"

"Not exactly. I got my ass kicked. I was unconscious."

"Did that really happen?"

"I'm covered in blood. I've got bandages on my face. I can't meet you for lunch. I'm sorry you came all the way south for nothing."

"Well, I'm already in Pacific Beach and I happen to be one heck of a nurse. You want me to bring a sandwich over to your place?"

"We've never even met."

"I'm a good judge of character. C'mon, take a chance. Remember how good I looked in your imagination?" Star was practically purring now. And, in Bobby's imagination, she was getting less pretty by the second. Beautiful women rarely laid it on this thick, no matter how many abs you had.

"I don't know . . ." But Bobby did know that if he went home by himself, he'd be dialing Sarah for sympathy and because he was proud of his injury. She'd help him out of his bloody shirt, scrub his face with a warm washcloth . . .

"Large ham and cheese, on white. Mayo, lettuce, tomatoes, and pickles. I'll text you my address," Bobby said.

"I'll see you in ten minutes," Star said.

14

LESLIE CONSORTE WAS eating dinner at the Round Robin. It was a family restaurant in the mall, loud and horrible. Its signature image was a smiling bird, tremendously fat, cheese dripping from its yellow beak.

Leslie had no business being anywhere but his own bed. He'd been awake so long that he wasn't entirely aware of his own body. It seemed to sit in the booth beside him, occasionally dashing back into contact with his central nervous system just long enough to give a jagged kick to the forehead.

Leslie detested Round Robin. The food was fine, but the noise level would be grating on a man with decent sleep, much less a man clinging to his wits. Only geography placed him here. It was three minutes from his apartment, home to a blissful bed but a tragically empty fridge. When the waitress arrived with a thin smile stretched across her wooden face, Leslie tried to smile back, but his mouth refused.

He settled for ordering a patty melt. She bustled away with the menu, and Leslie put his head down on the table. With his left hand, he gently massaged the pinching pain in his lower back. Sounds erupted and clashed from all corners: clanging dishes, heartless rock 'n' roll, a balloon popping. Smaller noises formed battle lines, unifying to overthrow larger sounds. Leslie squeezed his eyes shut and slowly began to pick up thin strands of conversation. Every one of them was about the horoscope story in the *Register*. He heard the words "Libra, Sagittarius, a quarter of a million dollars, Bobby Frindley, rape, and tiger attack!" echoing from every side. "Aren't you afraid to be outside right now? I am." "What if it is true? My brother is waking up at five a.m. tomorrow. He says Allied Gardens is the first to receive delivery." ". . . cousin is coming in from Vegas. He wants to see what's up." "Mom called; she begged me to leave San Diego, just until things settle down. No way I'm leaving." "That Taurus who cheated? My wife's a Taurus, you know!"

The waitress came back with a cold beer and put it in front of Leslie. He raised his head from the table and took a long drink. In the booth to his right, a woman was trying to quiet her son. The boy looked to be about eleven. He had pale skin and a bad complexion, and he had the low, soft curve of man breasts under his black Woot shirt. *Too many hormones in the fast food*, Leslie thought. *Stop feeding it to him.*

The boy had on a sour expression but wasn't saying anything. His mother, on the other hand, was addressing him adamantly. "You need to be quiet. Be quiet. Quiet." With each new command, the boy's eyes lowered a fraction and his mouth tightened. His mother continued. "We want to enjoy our meal. Your father's coming back to the table. Calm down. Don't distract him. Don't talk out of turn."

Leslie's head pounded. Her voice had a special urgency to it. It reminded him of his ex-wife, the way she continued to demand half his paycheck, even though they'd been divorced for years. Even though she'd found another man, a lapsed ex-alcoholic on disability. She and the drunk had been living in the Consorte family home together, neither working a day since the papers were signed. "Half," his ex-wife said in her weekly calls, calls that Leslie had begun to think of as *the weekly whimper*. "Don't speak. Half. Calm down. Half."

Leslie blinked. He took another drink of his beer.

"Calm down," the woman in the next booth said again. "Your father and I want to have a pleasant supper."

"The boy isn't saying anything," Leslie told her. His voice was drawn and tired, barely audible itself over the din of the crowd. Still, she heard him.

"It's none of your business."

"It kind of is, because you're ruining my dinner with your chattering."

Both booths were silent. Leslie took a drink of his beer. As promised, the woman's husband came back to the table. He was also carrying extra pounds and he had a lot of soft flesh around his jowls. "Dad, that man threatened Mom," the boy told his father.

"Be quiet," the mother said tensely.

"Stop saying that," Leslie said.

"Don't talk to my wife that way," the man said. He stood up from the table, his hands hanging awkwardly by his sides.

"Back off, big fellow," Leslie said, without getting up from his seat.

"I think you should apologize. Please apologize."

Leslie's hand went first to his badge, but he changed his mind and instead drew the service revolver from his waist. He laid the gun on the table, conspicuously switching the safety to "off." Then he lifted his hand off it and took the last swig of his beer. The barrel pointed past the man and directly at his wife, still seated across from her doughy son. They were gone before he put the bottle down. Leslie let out a huge yawn. He didn't even turn around to see if the woman or her husband said anything to the hostess on their way out. When his patty melt arrived, he asked for a to-go box and paid in cash.

STAR BEAT BOBBY to his apartment. At least that's who he guessed was waiting on his doorstep in the flowery blouse, a cluster of books under her arm. She was much younger than he'd pictured, somewhere around twenty-three or twenty-four. She had wavy black hair tamped down by a series of barrettes and a notch on the bridge of her pierced nose. Beautifully long eyelashes framed the faintly Asian shape of her eyes. He guessed she was at least half Filipino.

"Hi."

"Hey, Star. I'm Bobby Frindley. Is that my sandwich?"

"You weren't kidding about your face. Wowsers."

"Yeah. Do you want to go inside?"

"Yes, please. That girl over there has been creeping me out since I got here. How did you get your ass kicked? Writing horoscopes?"

Bobby did a slow burn across the street. Sarah was there, standing on the sidewalk, a load of laundry in her arms. She stared unflinchingly at Bobby, an extremely hurt look on her face. Bobby gave her a weak wave and then unlocked the door to let Star into his apartment. He tried to walk in separate from Star, pausing at the doorstep to check his mailbox. When he looked back at Sarah, she was still standing on the sidewalk, still staring at him. He fought himself not to wave again. He just tucked in his tail and slunk into the apartment. Star was not in his living room. She had laid her big stack of books on the carpet next to Bobby's couch.

"Star?"

"I'm in the bathroom. How can I play nurse when you don't have any medical supplies at all? Not even a Band-Aid?"

"I think the Band-Aids are on top of the refrigerator. But they dressed me up pretty good when I got hit."

"Your Band-Aids are in the kitchen? Do you eat them?" Star asked. She came back into the room, her hands on her hips. "How did it happen? Were you pursuing this strange story, this thing about the horoscopes?"

"I was helping recreate fourteenth century chivalric ideals."

"Huh?"

"Share this sandwich with me," Bobby told her, gesturing to a spot on the couch a few feet from where he was sitting. Any desire he'd had to flirt had drained out of him when he'd seen Sarah's expression.

Star moved past the couch and sat cross-legged on the floor in front of Bobby, smoothing her skirt over her knees. She broke off half his sandwich.

"Your horoscopes sure turned the city upside down. On the news, I saw religious types are marching and chanting in front of the *Register* building. My mother called. She and all her friends are demanding I also make true predictions for my online site. They seem to think these events legitimize all astrology. Channel Five said horoscope books have been selling out of every bookstore as far north as Long Beach."

"No one ever went broke underestimating the intelligence of the American public."

"But what do you think is really happening? Is someone doing all this?"

"For what reason?" Bobby asked her. "Who benefits?"

"Figure out that second question and you'll have the answer to your first. In the meantime, you should change your shirt. It's pretty gruesome."

Bobby walked into his bedroom and stripped off his bloody shirt. He hunted around in the closet, finding a black pocket T. He smelled his armpits, found his deodorant holding, and then pulled the shirt over his head. He wanted to ask Star why she felt safe hanging out in the home of a nearly complete stranger, but he couldn't figure out how to phrase it without sounding creepy. From the other room Star said,

"Even before I saw your picture, I thought you'd look like you do. It's pretty easy to know a man's face just by the confidence in his voice."

"Is Star your real name?"

"It's my middle name."

Bobby went back into the main room and sat next to Star. She split the second sandwich and gave Bobby half. She had ordered meatballs on white. One of the few sandwiches Bobby liked hot. He felt himself relax slightly, but the image of Sarah on the curb still pulled at his brain.

"My first name is Brighton."

"Brighton Star Lunes?" Bobby asked. "Born to write horoscopes, I guess."

"My real last name is Mendoza."

They ate for a while in silence, an awkward pause in the conversation. Bobby fought the urge to peek out the window and see if Sarah was still there.

Star looked at the books on the floor. "I read these when I was starting out. They were written mostly during the big astrology push in the 1970s. A lot of the current 'experts' have been sucking on that teat for more than fifty years. Guys like Spiller and Mendelssohn. The big gimmick right now is sexual astrology." Star uncrossed her legs, extending one and pointing her toe at the indention of a phone in Bobby's pocket. "Make sure to keep notes. Use the voice app if you're driving. Creativity doesn't come from sitting around trying to be creative. You have to live your life and then take advantage when inspiration strikes. Especially if you end up doing this for five years like I have. If I'm walking on the beach or shopping at the grocery store, something will catch my interest and I'll turn it into a horoscope." Star removed her phone from where she'd tucked it into her bra and clicked open a voice recorder app. "Money will be tight this week. Now is the time to figure out that coupon app you downloaded last week."

"Would you really write that?" Bobby asked.

"No, it's far too specific. Even though everyone eats, not everyone uses coupon apps. You've got to stick with only universal possibilities, love, insecurity, hope, fear, anger, et cetera." Star pushed record again. "While shopping, you will cross paths with an attractive stranger and find yourself entertaining impulsive romantic thoughts. Trust those impulses."

"You saying everyone entertains romantic impulses in the grocery store?"

"Pretty much." Star looked him right in the eyes, but her face was expressionless.

"Do you speak Latin?" Bobby asked, changing the subject as fluidly as he could manage.

"Pig."

"Huh?"

"I only speak pig latin. It was a joke, forget it." He noticed she kept locking eyes with him. She must have known her eyes were her most dazzling feature.

"*No-skay, ought-nay hat-thay*," Bobby said. He glanced down to pull the small black plaque out of his pocket. He'd scooped it up and stuffed it back in his pants when Abbattista had turned to show him to the door. "Any idea who said this?" he asked her.

Star studied the Latin words. She pulled her phone from her pocket and typed them into it, pausing several times to check her spelling. Staring into the small screen, her face cycled through several cute expressions, and she said, "It's the epitaph of Johannes Kepler."

"The name sounds familiar. A composer, maybe?"

"Hold on." Star began to punch away at the touch screen again. "One *P* or two? I forgot already."

"I don't know."

She stared into the screen.

"Wikipedia has an entry. One *P* in Kepler. It says he's a key figure in the seventeenth century scientific revolution."

Bobby moved over to sit next to Star and stare into the tiny screen. He was conscious of where their bodies touched, at the shoulder and thigh.

Star poked a manicured finger at the screen. "Here's your plaque translated. 'I measured the skies, now the shadows I measure. Sky-bound was the mind, earthbound the body rests.'" Star took a bite of her sandwich. She was eating faster than Bobby.

"This sandwich is delicious. You are officially forgiven for standing me up."

"That's not exactly what Terry told me the words meant."

"Who's Terry?" Star punched at her cell phone screen for a few more moments. "Latin's a tricky thing. This other site, uhh, wikimonkey, translates it as the following: 'I used to measure the heavens, now I shall measure the shadows of the earth. Although my soul was from heaven, the shadow of my body lies here.'"

"That's closer to what he said."

Star was staring him in the eyes again, a small smile on her face. This time she was the one to break the gaze, spinning back to her feet and going into Bobby's kitchen. He heard her say, "Oh, hydrogen peroxide." Then she came back into the room carrying the peroxide and the box of Band-Aids.

Bobby said, "All this 'measuring the sky,' you suppose it could be referring to horoscopes?"

Star looked thoughtful. "Sure. Maybe." Then she said, "I'll look for a connection in a second. But now, sit on the couch."

Bobby sat on the couch and Star knelt in front of him. She started to work intently on his injury, peeling away the gory bandages and butterfly closures and cleaning it with wet Kleenex. Once she was satisfied that she had worked out all the gauze fibers, she soaked another Kleenex in hydrogen peroxide and poked it around his chin.

Bobby took a deep breath and ignored the sting. She tore open a Band-Aid and inched closer to him to place it carefully across the cut. When she stopped to inspect her work, her face wasn't more than three inches from Bobby's. His knees pressed against her hips and her smallish breasts pressed against his forearms, which he had been trying to keep safely folded in front of his chest.

He felt his skin heating up, his pulse quickening. "God?" he thought, trying to beam his mind toward heaven. "This isn't a good idea, right?"

Star leaned closer, and he could feel her breath on his cheek. *The trouble with women*, Bobby thought to himself, *is that they smell so good, and they manage to be both firm and soft at the same time.*

The doorbell rang. Bobby moved Star gently away so he could stand up. Though his face was flushed and his breathing a little quickened, he was glad Sarah had finally mustered the courage to come to the door. This would allow him to sort out her hurt feelings, and it would keep him from putting his hands all over Star, which he kind of wanted to do.

He opened the door and was shocked to see Detective Leslie Consorte, leaning slightly forward, his breath ragged and stinking of coffee.

There's a zombie on my doorstep, Bobby thought to himself.

Leslie's hair was flat in the front and peacocked in the back. His clothes were impossibly wrinkled. They were the same clothes he'd been wearing at the zoo the day before. His eyes were a deep bloodshot red and more than half closed.

"You don't look so good."

Leslie grunted. "It's your horoscopes. I was at Presidio Park from 12:00 a.m. until 8:30 and then—" Leslie put his hand over his mouth and only partially stifled a huge yawn, "and then my regular shift started. Lapeyre had to wake me up twice during routine investigations."

"Why didn't you go home? Call in sick?"

"No one's allowed to. The captain's not afraid of the horoscopes, but he's afraid of the people's response. We need to have a major visual presence today," he said.

Bobby laughed. "Well, I'm sorry. Where's Lapeyre?"

"Our shift's over. She went home to bed. I tried to have a relaxing dinner, but . . ."

Bobby stared at Leslie. "But . . ." *Why is he on my porch?*

"I think we should go back to Theta Rho Kappa," Leslie said.

"You need to sleep. Very badly. And none of the horoscopes came true today. It had to be in our imagination, right?" Bobby shrugged. "That's how these things work. Someone plants a seed, and our brains do the rest. I think we made up the whole vibe at Theta Rho Kappa. That Ping-Pong table had been broken for a while. It had rust on the bottom." Bobby stared at Leslie, who stared back silently. "Not that those guys weren't dicks. They were just not rapists."

From behind Bobby, Star popped into the door frame. She stood on one foot and hung from the flashing by her left hand, her body again pushed comfortably close to Bobby's.

"Hey. Hi," Leslie said. "My name's Leslie."

"I'm Star."

"Did I interrupt something?"

"I'm the horoscope writer for *TheLonelyTruth*. I was just getting ready to help Bobby with his technique."

"It seems like you were." Leslie closed his eyes and rolled his head in a slow circle. "I'll go to the fraternity alone. You'll let me know right away if you get another horoscope, right?"

"Wait." Bobby walked back into his apartment and shrugged into his jacket. He couldn't let Leslie go alone in this state. And if Bobby were honest, a couple other things were moving him forward. One was simple curiosity. Another was a small lack of conviction in his own theory about the horoscopes—how had the first set correctly predicted the dragging death and the tiger attack? Every logical explanation pulled up just short of that question. He also wanted to get away from Star. Not because he didn't like her. It just seemed like the right thing to do.

He called after Leslie, "I'll come with you." To Star he said, "My life is really chaotic right now. Obviously. I'm sorry to run out on you again."

"Bring the girl along," Leslie said. "What the hell. We're already breaking every rule in the book. What's one more?"

15

THEY DROVE DOWN the 8 Freeway back out to Quetzalcoatl Road. Bobby sat in the back deep in thought while Star and Leslie spoke in the front.

Star wanted to know everything. What did Leslie think happened? How long had it been since he slept? Who was the girl who got raped? What was it like seeing the aftermath of a tiger attack? Leslie seemed to be answering her as honestly as possible.

Bobby found himself admiring Leslie in a similar way that he'd found himself admiring Abbattista earlier in the day. Here were two older men, very different in appearance but similarly confident, powerful, and high achieving. Bobby knew he was more susceptible to the influences of males from their generation because he wanted so badly to be accepted by his own father.

Star was still pumping Leslie for information when they arrived at the front door of the Theta Rho Kappa fraternity house. Leslie answered her questions without resistance, though each truth made Star more and more unhappy. She was strongly empathetic toward a rape victim Bobby wasn't even sure existed. Star stopped speaking altogether when Leslie drew his police-issue .44 magnum and checked the chamber for bullets. Leslie slipped the gun into a holster hanging from the back end of his belt, hidden under his sports coat.

The three of them climbed out of the car and Bobby went right to the fence leading to the house's backyard.

Star walked all the way to the corner, looking up and down the whole block. It seemed like she had never seen Greek housing before.

Either that or she was trying to get away from Leslie's gun.

"Leslie, come over here," Bobby said.

Leslie walked to where Bobby was raised up on his toes to see over the fence.

"Do you see what I see?"

"I'm not as tall as you are, kid." Leslie found a broken piece of fence to see through. After a moment: "The Ping-Pong table is gone," he realized. "Three months in the backyard and just today they muster the initiative to take it and haul it out to the dump?"

"Look at the deck," Bobby told Leslie.

Leslie's eyes moved across to the deck. "It's sparkling clean. The mud tracks have been scrubbed up."

"They cleaned. Somebody worried about something?" Bobby suggested.

"Who's the girl? Where's the girl? We can't prosecute without a victim," Leslie pointed out. "I think we should try to answer those questions first."

"Well, they'll have circled the wagons in there. I doubt we'll get many answers."

"There are more eyes and ears than just those belonging to the guilty. Let's check with the neighbors," Leslie decided.

Bobby turned and looked up and down the street. Frat house. Frat house. Sorority house. Mini-dorm. Frat house. Star was standing beneath a huge poster with the words *Lambda Iota Xi*. "A girl gets raped in the backyard. Where does she go?"

Star walked the length of the fence. "What are you guys talking about?"

Bobby peered over the back fence again. On the south side, the side where the Ping-Pong table had been stored, the fence abutted a small canyon decline. At the bottom of the canyon he saw a cul-de-sac lined with houses sporting deep backyards. Bobby pointed down at the street. "Let's start there."

Leslie drove them down to the suburban cul-de-sac at the bottom of the canyon. San Diego had had two housing booms in the twentieth century, the first in late 1930s, with America just crawling out of the Great Depression. Cottages had sprung up along the coast. Developers and not a small amount of individual owners had struck ground in Pacific Beach and started to throw up adobe, plaster, and brick properties in La Jolla.

The next boom started in Orange County in 1970 and moved two hundred miles south all the way down to the border of Mexico and two hundred miles north to upper Ventura County. Most of those homes were built from a single series of blueprints, drawn up by an architect named Leo Asher, Esquire, and built by various subcontractors working under the umbrella of the Irvine Company and the O'Connor Corporation. About every third house in Southern California was of the same age and design.

Over time, each had been personalized by individual owners, but whenever Bobby entered a suburban sprawl, he still got déjà vu from the familiar slant of the rooftops, the faux brick paneling, or the identical flashing built around each driveway.

Bobby and Leslie knocked on the door of one of the tract houses that shared a back fence with the frat house high above on the top of the canyon. Not wanting to overwhelm the occupant, Star waited in the car. A boy roughly twelve years old answered the door. He was holding a box of cereal in his hand, and he had a lot of crumbs on his shirt.

"Hi," he said.

Leslie showed him his badge. "I'm a detective with the San Diego police. Are your parents home?"

"I'm here by myself," the boy said. His hand was slowly wiping away the crumbs, but his eyes never left Leslie's badge. "I can help though. What do you need to know?"

"There might have been a party at the frat house up on the hill two nights ago. We're wondering if you saw or heard anything unusual."

The boy thought for a minute. "I'm trying to remember where I was."

"You weren't home?"

"I don't remember."

Leslie looked at Bobby. This kid probably wasn't going to help them crack the case. He handed the boy his card. "Have your parents give me a call when they get home. Make sure they know that nobody is in trouble. We just want some information about the houses up on the cliffs."

The boy nodded, eagerly.

They moved to the next house. It was a ranch style, probably three bedrooms, two baths. It had a long front yard parallel to the sidewalk and a pair of mature avocado trees, well-trimmed. A man in his mid-forties answered the door. He was wearing slacks, a white undershirt, and a robe. His feet were bare.

"I'm not sure what you gentlemen want, but I'm right in the middle of dinner."

Leslie showed him his badge. "I'm with the San Diego Police Department. This is Bobby Frindley from the *San Diego Register*."

"Come in, come in." The man stepped aside and waved them past. "This is about the rape, isn't it?"

"Did you witness a rape?" Leslie asked.

"No, no. I would have called right away. But I read the paper this morning, and I just knew that the rape—in the horoscope case—I knew that that rape had to have happened at the frat house on the hill. It's Theta Rho Kappa right at the top, isn't it? I drove my car by to double check on my way home from work."

Leslie and Bobby walked into the man's living room. He gestured for them to sit down, and they took spots side by side on his black leather couch.

Bobby noticed that the man did have dinner on the table. It looked like a bowl of soup. He was eating alone.

"You live here by yourself?" Bobby asked.

"I do. My wife moved out last March."

"So why do you think there was a rape?"

"Well, I read about it in the paper. I mean, there was no specific report of a rape, but the paper included all the horoscopes' predictions, so it wasn't hard to figure it out. But there's only so many blocks with clusters of frat houses. I knew, right when I read the prediction—"

"What's your name, sir?"

"Why?"

"I'm Detective Leslie Consorte. I just wanted to call you by your name."

"I'm Ethan."

"Ethan, what I want to know is, did anything happen Friday night that made you think a rape might have been occurring in the home on the top of the hill? Anything concrete. Disturbing sounds or something you saw?"

"It was very loud. There was a lot of heavy music. Lots of cheering. To be honest, it sounded like they were playing some kind of drinking game."

"But no screaming or cries for help?"

Ethan looked pained. It was clear to Bobby that he wanted to have heard screaming, that if he thought about it long enough, he would eventually remember having heard screaming, but that he had heard no actual screaming. Finally, he said, "I'm not sure. I did hear girls' voices."

"Do you mind if we take a look around your backyard?"

"No, please do."

Ethan led them out to the backyard. The canyon sloped down into Ethan's yard. There was a small pool on the north side at the bottom of the slope and a flower garden on the south side. It was getting dark, and Ethan went back into the house to turn on the porch light. When he came out again, he looked at the garden. "That's weird," he said.

"What?" Leslie asked.

"Look at my garden."

The three men approached the flower garden, and Leslie and Bobby both saw what Ethan was pointing at. On the back side of the garden there was a long ten-by-ten-foot box of perennials and all the flowers on the slope side were impressed into the ground. With a little imagination, Bobby could make out the shape of an arm, a leg, a torso. Leslie bent down and touched a flower stalk; it was sheared in half.

Ethan turned white as a sheet. He was imagining the same thing they were. "She rolled down this hill. She landed right here in my garden," Ethan gasped.

"You didn't see anything Friday night? Anything moving back here? Maybe Saturday morning even?"

"I-I didn't."

"We're going to get a forensics team out here in about an hour. Can you stay inside until they arrive?" Leslie said.

"I'll stay inside. I'll accommodate them however I can," Ethan promised.

Leslie looked up at the top of the long slope. "So they gang-rape the girl, and then roll her body off the side of the canyon, or maybe she flees her attackers and plunges off the side. Either way, she comes to a stop all the way down here. Maybe she lies here in shock, shivering, or maybe she's knocked out and regains consciousness in the morning. But then she goes . . . where?"

Bobby looked at the fence the neighbors shared. The boy next door had a basketball hoop, the rear of the backstop abutting Ethan's yard.

Bobby and Leslie walked quickly back to the car. Bobby asked, "Do you think that impression would have looked human shaped if we hadn't been looking for a human shape? It could have been a coyote lying back there. Or maybe the kid next door, stomping around retrieving a basketball?"

"Not now with that stuff, Bobby."

"I have to report the truth. I just want to make sure this isn't all in our imaginations."

"I don't think it was our imagination the first time."

When they reached the car, Leslie radioed police headquarters for a SIDs team. Bobby sat in the back seat with Star.

She whispered to Bobby, "I think we should head home soon. Something's weird. The vibe is weird. The detective . . . I didn't like when he unholstered his weapon. I don't trust him."

"Leslie?" Bobby asked. "He's been totally aboveboard with me."

"Why did he bring two horoscopists along on his investigation? What does he gain from us being here? It's not all adding up. Did you notice that he didn't even mention the huge bandage on your face? How do you not ask about something like that? He's acting weird, and we have to be careful."

"It's a tough job. And he hasn't slept."

"It's more than that. I feel like we're being set up somehow, and I want to be left out of it."

Bobby did not share Star's concerns. Leslie had been unconventional from the get-go, but he didn't seem sinister.

Just exhausted.

Leslie climbed back into the driver's seat and retrieved a camera. Bobby and Star walked with him into the backyard, with Bobby still thinking about Star's words.

Leslie took photographs of the flower bed from three angles. They walked through the side gate. Leslie found tire tracks in the mud, just beyond the driveway. He snapped another series of pictures. "Forensics said it'll be at least an hour before they can get here. They're backlogged. Do you think we can trust Ethan to sit tight?"

"He will definitely come out and poke around. He's ready to solve the case all by himself," Bobby pointed out.

Leslie scratched the back of his neck. "Screw it," he said. "Thinking about that girl getting raped then rolled down a hill like so much trash. It makes me want to have another word with our frat boys."

LESLIE WALKED UP to the door of the frat house and pounded on it with a clenched fist.

He motioned for Bobby to stand back from the porch. Bobby took another long look at Leslie. He still appeared mostly average—his hairline receding in the front and peacocked in the back, a slight paunch around his belly, yellow sweat stains sneaking out from the edges of his armpits.

But something in his posture, or the tension in his shoulders, something there seemed to hold great energy.

Star climbed out of the car and stood next to Bobby. "I don't think that man should have a gun. Not right now, anyway," she whispered. "Let's stay in the car."

"Maybe you're right," Bobby told her.

The boy who'd been lifting weights during their first visit answered the door. He was wearing wristbands and a headband and had sweat lined around his collar. Leslie shucked his gun out of its holster and pointed it directly at the boy's forehead. They walked together in slow lockstep backward into the fraternity house.

"Oh no!" Bobby said.

"Oh no," Star echoed, breathless.

Bobby followed Leslie, cautiously. He sensed Star a few steps behind.

Leslie had backed the boy all the way into the widescreen TV. He was pushing him against it with the tip of the gun.

"Who's the girl you raped? Where is she?"

The boy seemed about to open his mouth.

"I swear if you call out to Jimmy or any other douchebag in this house, I swear I will blow your brains onto the TV."

The boy shut his mouth again.

"Where's the girl you raped?"

"I-I didn't rape anyone," the boy whispered.

"Where is the raped girl? How many others are in this house?"

The boy began to stutter. Bobby watched a trickle of urine glide down his leg, mixing with sweat in the tops of his tube socks.

"How many others are in this house?" Leslie said again, more slowly.

"Why didn't you stay outside?" Bobby whispered to Star.

"Because you didn't either. And somebody needs to make sure you stay safe," Star whispered.

Bobby spoke to Leslie with words chosen carefully. "Leslie, you have two reporters here with you. Are you sure you want to do this?"

"You have a sister, Bobby?"

"I'm an only child."

"I have a sister. And I know whoever's sister got rolled down the hill into that garden, I know that guy can't be here right now doing what I'm doing, but I know he wishes he was." Leslie smiled at the boy pressed against the TV. The boy began to groan. "I don't want to let that guy down."

There were sounds from the other side of the door. It swung open and a boy Bobby had never seen before strolled into the room drinking a beer. Leslie swung the gun and pointed it directly at him. The first boy slid along the TV to the ground, still whimpering. The newcomer raised his hands in the air, dropping his beer to the carpet with a muffled thud. Without a word he lowered himself to his stomach and put his hands behind his head.

Leslie slapped handcuffs on him. "This guy knows the drill," he said. Then he spun the gun back onto the original boy. For a third time he asked, "How many people are in this house right now?"

"T-there are four more upstairs. One more downstairs in the game room. Or the kitchen."

Leslie pushed his way through the door and into the main portion of the house.

The minute Leslie left the room, the first boy jumped to his feet and raced for the door. Bobby shouldered him into the wall, and he spun to the ground, whimpering, his arms curled forward like a spider.

"Please. Please. We didn't do anything! We didn't touch her!"

From the floor, the handcuffed boy shouted, "Alex, you dumbass! Don't say a word."

Alex struggled to his feet again and raced once more for the door, this time reaching it and tearing it open. He stopped in the doorway and turned back toward them. The wind was picking up outside, tunneling through the opening. The boy's hair whipped around his face, the parts of his clothes not plastered to his body by sweat and urine danced.

"I'm sorry I didn't call the police," he said, "I'm so sorry. I don't understand why I didn't help her. I can still see her face. Please tell me she's okay."

"You're asking if she's okay!" Star said, incredulous.

"We don't know where she is. Or who she is," Bobby said.

"I hope she's okay!" Alex cried as he disappeared into the street. The door shut with a loud thump, cutting the wind and bringing a strange stillness to the room.

Bobby heard the sound of a revolver discharging upstairs.

16

SOMETHING HEAVY SLAPPED against the upstairs floor, spitting dust out of the plaster above Bobby's head. Star didn't say anything, but she looked at Bobby with eyes as round as saucers. He grabbed her by the bicep and pulled her through the door in the direction Leslie had gone. They reached the stairs, but Bobby pulled Star the other way.

"He could be shot," Star said in protest.

"I don't think so. He has the element of surprise and the training. The worst thing that could have happened is if he shot one of them."

"After hearing what that boy said . . ." Star didn't finish her sentence.

She didn't have to. It wasn't all a bunch of nonsense. The boy had confirmed there was a girl and that something had happened to her that no one wanted to talk about. Bobby's imagination was going wild, and it made him kind of feel like opening fire himself. He dragged Star into the addition off the main house. They found themselves in a room with a series of weightlifting equipment, a bench with chapped, fading leather, a curl bar, and a weight stand. Beyond the gear was a ratty couch sitting in front of an older, smaller

LED TV screen. The television was playing *SpongeBob SquarePants* with the volume off. There were two closed windows and a closet, but no other exits besides the door they'd just used.

"He must be in the kitchen," Star said.

Bobby shushed her. He slipped past the workout equipment, stepped over the couch, and looked behind the TV. It was empty besides a mess of wires. He went over to the closet.

His ears picked up a faint, unrecognizable sound. He gave Star a look that said *pay attention*. It was unnecessary; she was staring at the closet door. He yanked it open, and Ronnie leaped out, moving like a frightened quail.

Bobby lunged after him, but Ronnie moved so fast that Bobby bounced off the pads of the couch, arms empty.

Star squared her feet as he raced toward her. It seemed to Bobby that she was steadying herself, trying to get out of Ronnie's way before he bowled into her. That wasn't an altogether correct observation. Star did step aside to let Ronnie race past, but before he was completely out the door, she slugged him, snapping his head backward and knocking him off course into a clumsy pirouette.

Ronnie hit the weight bench and somersaulted into the weight stand. The center of the stand struck him right in the spine, and he yelped like a dog. His inertia took him even farther, weights spilling everywhere. He rolled to a stop against the west wall, whimpering in pain.

Star was grimacing, opening and closing her right fist.

"Your hand okay?"

"If not, it was worth it."

Bobby picked his way through the spilled equipment and stood over Ronnie. Ronnie was somewhere between terrified and hysterical.

He looked up at Bobby from his prone position. Snot was dripping down his nose and into his mouth, and his lip was split and reddening. His right arm was pinned under his body, but his left arm was free, and he used it to feel around his spine, under his T-shirt. "She could have paralyzed me."

"The angels are crying," Bobby said. "Where is the girl you raped?"

"We told you before. We didn't rape anyone."

Bobby curled his fingers through a twenty-five-pound weight and lifted it above Ronnie's head.

"Bobby, don't do that," Star said.

"Oh, crap," Ronnie said, his voice breaking.

"We had a little talk with Alex. He confessed to the rape. He said it was your idea. That you orchestrated the whole thing. That Jimmy tried to stop you, but you threw yourself on the poor girl."

Bobby hated how easy lying was coming to him lately. He didn't mind what the lie did to Ronnie, but he hated to compromise himself for a house full of pasty-faced, tiny-pricked monsters.

"Please put the weight down."

"Alex said you threatened to kill everyone if they talked."

"Put the weight down and I'll tell you the truth."

Bobby lowered the weight.

Ronnie continued speaking, the words spilling out of his mouth. "I know you're lying because it's not like you said. Not anything like you said. But it's been hell. I haven't slept. And then the horoscope thing in the paper . . . Everybody is looking at us like we're predators. I can't live with it. I'll tell you the whole story. I can't hold it inside any longer."

Star fumbled into her pocket for her cell phone, quickly opening the recording app.

"Talk," Bobby said.

"We were partying. It was just a normal, small, house party. These two girls from Delta were here and they were dancing around, rubbing their bodies in everyone's face. I got kind of turned on. I think everyone else did too. One of them kept saying if she had another beer, she'd flash her tits, but we kept getting beers and she never did. Eventually she puked on the Ping-Pong table, and the other girl took her home. Right after they left, I was getting ready to play *Call of Duty* online, but the doorbell rang. I answered. If I'd known what was going to happen, I swear to you I would have locked the door and never opened it. I swear it to God."

"Who was she? Why was she there?"

"Nobody knows. I opened the door and there's a girl on the steps. One of the most beautiful girls you've ever seen. Long, blond hair, blue eyes, incredible body, everything. She's completely naked on our doorstep. Her hair is all styled up, pinned back like she was going to the prom or something, but she was really drunk. Her eyes were glassy, and she swayed, you know, back and forth. I'm surprised she even managed to ring the bell, to be honest.

"I should have helped her, right then. I should have covered her in a blanket and rushed her home, wherever that was. I was going to. It was my first instinct. I swear to God it was. But then Jimmy yells from the other room, 'Who the hell is at the door, Ronnie?' and I was proud of my discovery in a twisted way. Like if I'd found a wallet full of cash on the ground. I wanted to show it off. Brag. 'Some drunk chick. Totally hot. Naked.' I shouted back. Jimmy didn't believe me, and he said something about my mom."

Bobby took a deep breath. He heard angry voices shouting from upstairs, then the sound of something thumping against a wall. "Keep talking," he said.

"Jimmy eventually came into the room, and he started hooting and hollering. The other guys heard the noise, and they came down. A few of them took pictures—but it wasn't pervy. They were just shocked at what was happening and that's what you do when you're shocked. Still, it felt gross, all of us circling around her, when she could barely stand. Nobody could figure out exactly what to do, though. Jimmy always has to show off, so he slapped her on the ass. He swears he did it just to wake her up a little. And it worked. She stumbled back through the door and out onto the lawn. I can't really say what happened after that . . ."

"You raped her."

"What? No!" Ronnie insisted.

"What do you mean, no?"

"We didn't touch her. No one did. I mean other than the slap. And I'm sick to my stomach about that. Do you know what kind of trouble we could get in even having a strange naked girl here? Drunk? Surrounded? I don't know if she came to our house on purpose or if it was some kind of setup, but she put us in terrible danger just being here. I've been shitting bricks and I'm not even the one who touched her butt. I'm so, so, sorry we didn't help her. You have to believe me. I've been worried about her, nonstop."

"No one else touched her?" Star said in disbelief.

"Alex and Steven S. took the pictures, but Jimmy made them delete them. It was like, their first instinct, but they feel bad about it too."

Bobby scrunched up his face. He looked down at Ronnie. Ronnie had seemed dangerous before, a hardened rapist surrounded by weights used to sharpen his insidious craft. Now he just looked like a scared little boy.

"I can't say what happened to her because she just disappeared into the darkness. She headed out to the edge of the property, and she was gone."

"You let a drunk, naked girl go without helping her?"

"That's why I feel bad, man. But we couldn't help. We couldn't let her stay. What if she wakes up and thinks we messed with her? What if some doorbell camera catches us loading her into one of our cars? It was a setup. Someone was trying to set us up. We're the bad guys now. Everyone is coming after us because we're straight white males and we like to party."

"Give that a rest," Bobby said.

"We're being sacrificed to something! By somebody!" Ronnie started to cry. "A naked girl comes to the door, like an Amazon delivery. Then a day later a cop and a news reporter show up—then our fraternity name is plastered all over the news. That's a setup, man. That's a setup. The only thing is—we didn't do anything to her. She just ran off..."

Star looked at Bobby.

"How old are you?" Bobby asked Ronnie.

"I'm nineteen. An adult. An adult in the eyes of the law," Ronnie whimpered.

Was I this young and stupid just seven years ago? Probably, Bobby decided.

During the course of the story, Ronnie hadn't climbed to his feet, or even rolled off his back. He just lay on his side, looking up at Bobby and Star. "We slammed the door on her. We left her out there, alone. I swear I feel so bad. We just didn't want to get involved."

Just as Ronnie finished talking there was a large thumping sound from upstairs. It sounded like a body hitting the floor, hard.

"Uh oh," Star said.

"You're involved," Bobby told Ronnie.

By the time they reached the main room, Leslie was walking down the stairs slowly, a huge Rottweiler cradled in his arms. Its head lolled with each step Leslie took.

"They had a rotty upstairs in one of the rooms. It almost chewed my arm off. Open the slider."

Bobby opened the sliding door and Leslie spilled the dog out onto the deck. It landed with a meaty thud. Star screamed when it hit.

"Is it dead?" Star gasped.

Leslie shook his head. "I just pistol-whipped it. Not the dog's fault its owner is a dick. My gun discharged, though. Put a hole in the roof and scared me half to death." Leslie patted his pockets. "Somebody should call a vet."

Bobby looked at the injured dog nervously. Its chest rose and fell in shallow, ragged breaths. "We might have a problem," he said.

The three of them walked out the front door. At the end of the street a police car was screeching toward them, sirens blazing. Leslie drew the badge from his waist and held it open toward the approaching car, his other hand empty and raised in the air. "I already know," he said. "The kid upstairs told me everything. After I shot his roof, he was too scared to lie." Leslie shrugged. "They didn't help her either. Makes them criminals in my book. Kid told me he watched from the window as she tumbled down into the canyon. She couldn't even walk straight. Either really drunk or high on something like GHB."

"But how'd she get here?" Star asked.

"I think a more important question is who brought her here," Leslie said.

The policeman was exiting his car. He had his gun drawn but he was holding it down by his leg, not aiming at anybody. From a distance he peered carefully at Leslie's badge.

"I have to stay and take care of this," Leslie said, handing his keys to Bobby. "Get the pretty lady to a happier place."

Bobby looked at Leslie, a huge question hanging from his lips. Another prowler blew around the corner, tires screeching. "Leslie, I have to write the story tonight. The predictions are true, or, at least, someone is trying to make them true. I have to tell San Diego about everything I've seen. What are they going to do if I write that you burst into the frat house gun drawn? That you put a hole in the roof?"

"You write the truth. Everything that happened."

"But your career? Did you just throw it away?"

"Write the whole truth, no matter the consequence," he said. "And get the lady home; she's shivering."

BOBBY AND STAR didn't drive Leslie's car directly home. They
went to the twenty-four-hour FedEx Office Center on Garnet
Avenue, and Bobby bought two hours behind a computer screen. He
simply had too much to write to be plunking away at his cell phone
screen with fat fingers.

He wrote about the dragging death in Clairemont, jumping the
tiger enclosure, the mud footprints, and the broken Ping-Pong table.
He wrote about what he'd learned of the pandemonium at the Presidio Cross. About returning to the fraternity house and finding the
impression of a body pressed into Ethan's backyard. He wrote about
Detective Leslie Consorte forcing himself into the frat house, gun
drawn. With careful adjective selection, he tried to make Leslie's
actions seem as heroic and necessary as possible, though he hated
himself for it. *So much for putting authenticity and accuracy first and
foremost*, he thought, shaking his head. He wrote about, and quoted
from, Ronnie's version of the events. He played the digital recording
back again and again, until other late-night FedEx patrons began to
listen, ears cocked his way, work temporarily paused. When it was all
finished, he emailed it to Milo Maslow and then he sent Milo a text

message telling him to check his email. He sat back in his chair and exhaled deeply, his hands covering his eyes.

"You sure know how to show a girl a memorable first date," Star said. She had been busy for the first hour writing her own horoscopes, but then she'd taken Abbattista's small Latin plaque and spent an hour searching the internet.

Bobby just grunted.

"Suspected rape, breaking and entering, canine savagery. I'm going to live my whole life and never have another night as eventful as this one."

"I hope that's true," Bobby said.

"The horoscopes were right again. Kind of."

"The stars are controlling our destiny," Bobby told her.

"Perhaps," Star said with a half smile. "More likely, we get online right now and find that Theta Rho Kappa has a history of sexual transgressions. Somebody wants to cause a rape, so they drop a drugged, naked girl on the doorstep and ring the bell. It's not a guarantee she'll be raped, obviously, but the entire history of mankind suggests she might."

"You think someone out there is insidious enough to orchestrate all this?"

"Generally, I don't believe in grand conspiracies. People aren't even organized enough to make sense of their individual lives much less pull off something like this. But I can't think of any other explanation," Star said.

"I'm afraid I might agree with you. On both counts. The question is, who is smart enough to put all this together?" Bobby took the little plaque out of Star's hands and spun it in his palm. Abbattista was an obvious possibility, but he hadn't struck Bobby as psychotic enough to kill, much less in such a gruesome way as dragging a person behind his car. Furthermore, how did he get the tiger to jump out of its enclosure?

Bobby was keenly aware of not letting his imagination get the best of him. Just four hours ago, he thought it was all a bunch of nonsense. Two hours after that, he would have bet a million dollars that the frat boys had raped the girl. Half an hour after that, he was pretty convinced they hadn't laid a finger on her. The spinning in circles was making him dizzy.

He was also exhausted. Leslie Consorte might have been the only person in San Diego County more tired than ace reporter Bobby Frindley.

Star glanced at her phone. "It's past ten! The new predictions!" she reminded him.

Bobby pulled himself back into an upright position and logged into the *Register*'s Ask Ambrosia email. The excitement of past evenings had been replaced by a lingering dread. It felt awful being able to see the future in this small, terrible way.

It was waiting, an otherwise innocuous line of gray text.

One new message.

Bobby clicked.

He read aloud to Star. "Aries—You've overindulged in food and drink, and now you're as heavy as a Thanksgiving turkey. You will spend time working hard in the local gymnasium, but when you get on the scale afterward, you will have gained weight. Don't fight it; you're fat."

Bobby took a deep breath and kept reading. "Taurus—You'll spend several hours poring over the personals on Craigslist, but you'll once again find yourself drawn to the erotic massage advertisements. There will be no narrow escape for you this time, however; the police will burst through the door while the masseuse has her hands all over your private parts. Prepare a careful explanation for the court, your wife, and your mother, but don't be ashamed of your actions. It was a married Jupiter who seduced Europa in the guise of a bull, thus forming your sign, the Taurus.

"Cancer—You will stub a toe walking on the beach. Don't dig through the sand to see what you stubbed it on, however. The answer to that question is disgusting, and you're better off not knowing.

"Nothing too frightening in the first three," Bobby said. He pushed print on the email and an ancient laser printer sprang to life.

"Listen to the Leo," Star said. "Pluto in your Eastern hemisphere makes you unusually consistent. You will awake tomorrow and eat a normal breakfast, take a normal shower, and dress in your normal work clothes. You'll read the paper and have a cup of coffee, and then you'll step out the door, prepared for a normal day. But you'll never reach your workplace. You will vanish, without a trace."

"That one's a little scary."

"A lot of people are going to be working from home tomorrow."

They sat together and read the last of the predictions. Bobby started to shut down the computer and gather up his notes.

Star picked up the small Kepler plaque and stared at it. "While you were writing, I read some interesting things online about Kepler. Turns out he discovered the ellipse. The geometrical shape, not the three dots at the end of a sentence. His most famous work is a treatise called the *Mysterium Cosmographicum*."

"He was a scientist? Or a mathematician?"

"Yes, but no, but yes. He was an astrologer," Star explained.

"Huh? How do you mean? Kepler was a horoscope writer?"

"A member of our tribe," Star said. "From what I can understand, he was using math to look for the secret language of God, a posteriori, meaning based on deductive knowledge and not just blind faith. He'd felt he'd found it in a mathematical study of the distances between, and the motions of, the planets. Think about it. If God exists, why else would he have created the solar system?"

Bobby nodded. "It had to be up there for a reason. Its existence alone must have already destabilized folks who were fully onboard with Adam and Eve up until that point."

"Kepler reasoned that God created the solar system so the planets could pull on our strings, like nine elliptical puppeteers. He was charting their movements to divine God's plans for mankind."

Star swung her chair around, so she was no longer facing Bobby. She put her head on his shoulder, which was a good thing because she wasn't able to see Bobby's confused expression as she said, "Obviously Kepler wasn't the first. He was just the first hypereducated white dude to have that idea. And one of the first to incorporate all of Galileo's discoveries. Astrology as a general concept dates all the way back to the Greeks. *Astron* is the Greek word for star."

"Astron Lunes," Bobby said. "I should probably mention that I spent a good bit of my classics classes thinking about how I could lower my one-hundred-meter swim intervals. Did Kepler pull it off? Did he figure out how to read God's language in the skies?"

"I only had, like, an hour to research him. But it seems he felt geometry was the best approach to combining teleology and theology. The orbit of Mars could be reexamined as a tetrahedron. Earth's orbit could be traced as a twenty-sided icosahedron. Just drop a few isosceles triangles on the distance between the two, and all God's secrets would be revealed. Heck, you could predict the next attack of the Huns." Star shrugged. "Kepler himself was a bit of a Venn diagram—a moment in history where math, God, and mysticism all came together."

Bobby took the plaque back and ran his fingers along the edges. "Today I met a billionaire with a love of gaming and an interest in astrology. An interest he lied about," Bobby said. "That's why he pretended to not remember the Latin translation. 'I used to measure the heavens . . .'"

"The guy who hit you with a stick?"

Bobby rubbed his chin. "Yeah."

Star shook her head. "It's a lead, but don't get too excited. There are three million people in San Diego, so the chance that you hopped the fence of the killer is pretty slim. It would be one hell of a coincidence. What do you have for evidence?"

Bobby pointed to the tiny, engraved plaque.

"I doubt a real reporter would think this is enough."

"Good thing we're just horoscope writers," Bobby said. He yawned, deeply. "But let's save that for tomorrow. We have to return Leslie's car. And I want to get some sleep." Bobby started to stand up, but Star kept her hand on his own, pinning it against the armrest. He lowered himself back into the chair.

"Was she your girlfriend?" Star asked.

Bobby knew immediately who she was asking about, the forlorn girl who had glared at her from across the street when they'd met at his apartment. She was asking about Sarah. He said, "No. She's married. There was just some romantic energy between us . . ."

"Unrealized romantic energy?" Star asked.

"What did you see in her face?"

"I saw a jilted lover."

"Maybe that was only your imagination?"

"Why don't you just tell me?"

"Because you already figured it out."

"You screwed her even though she's married?" Star tried to mask it, but her face dropped slightly. "I think I'll head home. I'm ready to get some sleep too," she said.

18

THE NEXT MORNING, Leslie Consorte awoke at eleven fifteen. It was his first night of good sleep in four days, and he felt like a million dollars. He'd dreamed of swimming in a vast ocean; he hadn't needed to breathe, and he'd simply drifted from one large school of fish to another, occasionally resting his tired feet in on a bed of kelp or rubbing them on a sea anemone.

He'd been slightly cognizant of the phone ringing. It had begun ringing around 5:03 a.m., right when the first edition of the paper hit driveways, and it hadn't stopped. He hadn't risen, or even awoken to answer. A brief glance at his cellphone showed nine new messages, and a "Mailbox Full" warning.

He imagined one message was from his ex-wife, berating him for his behavior at the fraternity house, while also managing to sound smugly satisfied that now the courts would see his true character. He knew at least two would be from his police chief, Grunden, the first asking for an explanation, the second demanding an immediate response, maybe even raising questions about his behavior at the local Round Robin. He even figured one would be from Milo Maslow, asking him to go on record about the kid's story. He guessed all this, but he didn't listen to a single message. Instead, he took a nice, long shower, rotating slowly under the showerhead until the water beat the last of the stress from his body.

He walked out to the driveway and picked up the *Register*. It was so thin and light but carrying such heavy news. A lot of his neighbors were subscribers now, too, the younger ones seeing a paper for the first time in their lives.

Returning to the kitchen, he boiled two three-minute eggs using his favorite pan and sat at the small kitchen table. It was odd to be reading the paper with such bright light filtering through the small window on the east wall. He promised himself he would sleep in more often. He opened the paper to a large photograph of his own face. It was an archive photo. He was standing at a police shooting range, legs spread apart, slowly squeezing the trigger of his revolver. Beside that picture was another shot of the dead man at the zoo, and beside that was a picture of Jimmy from Theta Rho Kappa, a violent sneer stretched across his face as he pointed an accusatory finger off camera.

Leslie read the article carefully and found he was impressed by Bobby's writing skill. *Not bad for an ex-athlete*, he thought. He got up and fixed a cup of coffee. Then he went back and read the horoscopes. Leslie reached Leo. "You'll read the paper and have a cup of coffee, and then you'll step out the door, prepared for a normal day." He looked at the paper before him, the coffee in his left hand, and he chuckled to himself. "But you'll never reach your workplace. You will vanish, without a trace."

Leslie closed the paper without reading Virgo through Pisces. He went back into his bedroom and got dressed in a white long-sleeve button-down shirt, brown corduroy slacks, and loafers. He pulled his revolver out of the top drawer of his bureau, slipped it into a shoulder harness. He dropped his spare set of car keys into his pocket and combed his hair with his fingers.

Satisfied with what he saw in the mirror, Detective Leslie Consorte went out his front door, locking it behind him.

He never made it to work. In fact, no one there, including his friend, newly minted detective Therese Lapeyre, would ever see him again.

———

BOBBY AWOKE TO the ringing of the phone. He gathered himself out of bed, scratching an itchy thigh, and stumbled to the receiver on his desk. He fell to one knee in the process, and when he answered, his hello had extra breath behind it.

"Hello?"

"Hello?" Bobby said again.

"Hi, is this Bobby Frindley?"

"Yes, it is."

"This is Terry Abbattista."

The voice snapped into focus for Bobby. "How did you get my number? Wikipedia?"

Abbattista laughed. "I called Milo Maslow. Technically you're an employee of mine, and in a losing business I might add."

"Not lately," Bobby said, massaging his knee. "What can I do for you, Terry? Are you upset I mentioned you in my article?"

"Not at all. Some of my high society friends are absolutely thrilled that I'm involved even in the small way that I am. Did you hear that gruesome horoscope predictions were sent to a newspaper in Spokane, Washington, and another set to a radio station in Duluth? It's all the rage now, I guess. I'm throwing a horoscope-themed masquerade party next Saturday. Is that too uncouth? Everyone wants me to be Taurus, the bull, but I think a lion is more accurate."

Bobby said nothing, he just stood up then sat down again on the top of his unmade bed.

"Bobby, the reason I'm calling is twofold. One, I wanted to congratulate you on the article. It was terrific, a real powerhouse entry into the business. You should really consider moving to one of the bigger, online rags. Or at least the Associated Press. You've got the momentum now to do it."

"And the second reason you're calling?"

"We want to have a little congratulations dinner for you tonight at my place. I've been working on a new twist for the game with the bamboo sticks. I think you'll be a great part in it."

Bobby's hand went up to his chin. The gauze was loose, and the skin still felt tender underneath. "Not so sure about that, Terry. I still haven't healed from the last version."

"I don't take no for an answer. Seven. Bring a date."

AFTER HE SHOWERED and dressed, Bobby walked across the street to Sarah's apartment. He knocked on the door. There was no answer, no sound of movement inside. He called her cell phone, but it rang endlessly, without going to voicemail. He pulled a pen out of his pocket and slipped a piece of junk mail out of her mailbox. On it, he wrote the following:

Dear Sarah, please call me as soon as you can. I can't reach you on your cell and I'd really like to talk. Bobby.

He wedged the envelope under her door, and when he turned to leave a man was standing on the sidewalk directly beside him. The man looked at Bobby, then shifted his eyes to the note.

"Is she your girlfriend?" the man asked. "The girl who lives here?"

Bobby sized the newcomer up. It looked like he lifted weights every day, but that's about all he must have done to take care of himself. His clothes were wrinkled and about fifteen years out of fashion.

He had curly brown hair that hung in clumps on his forehead. His arms were covered in tattoos and crusted with dirt.

"Can I help you?" Bobby asked.

"Are you Bobby Frindley?" he asked.

"Who wants to know?"

"Me."

"Sorry," Bobby said, and shouldered past him toward his own apartment. He was used to seeing homeless guys in Pacific Beach. He knew, and liked, most of the ones who bunked down in the area. But something about this guy seemed disconnected. Unnervingly so. The fact that he knew Bobby's name didn't help. When Bobby reached his own porch, he looked back at the man who was still standing on Sarah's walkway. His eyes were locked on the letter Bobby had left under her doormat.

Bobby shouted back at the man, "Don't touch anything. Just move along."

The man turned and looked at him, then shuffled down the street. Bobby watched his slow progress all the way to Lamont Avenue. He stopped there at the edge of the sidewalk and turned to look at Bobby again, his eyes lingering. Bobby shook his head, walked into his apartment, and bolted the door behind him.

19

DETECTIVE THERESE LAPEYRE sat at her desk, waiting patiently for her partner to arrive. The station was almost empty. Most of the other officers were either working their shifts or home asleep, enjoying brief respites from mandatory double and triple overtime. Therese herself was working a double today. She'd make the rounds with Leslie, then at six o'clock move over to one of the newly formed horoscope tactical squads, under the auspicious eye of Special Agent Randy Michaels. The FBI had sent Michaels out from Washington two days ago.

He had already ruffled Grunden's feathers as the two men sparred over control of an investigation that had reached the headlines of every news site in the nation.

Tonight, Therese was the second shift of two teams working the Scorpio prediction. She picked up the wrinkled photocopy from her desktop. It read: "Scorpio—It is a good day to solve problems and make important decisions. In fact, consider making the decision to finally kill the pesky customs agent working at Dock 44 downtown. You were born Sagittarius Ascendant, giving you a steady hand and a cogent eye. Tonight you will use both."

It bothered her that the Scorpio prediction was the first placing the reader in the position of killer. For the last three days, all the predictions, even those that did not actually come true, painted the reader as victim: murdered, raped, cuckolded. But with this, the reader was committing the crime. It made her think that either every lunatic in San Diego would be out with murder in their eyes, or, more likely, her task force would be in for a long, boring night while others chased more legitimate possibilities. There was already buzz surrounding the Cancer prediction. Earlier that morning, a retired nurse had pierced the bottom of her foot while walking at Windansea Beach. The wound was bad enough to need a stitch. When lifeguards retraced her path, they'd found a hypodermic needle half sticking out of the sand, its barrel caked with dried vomit.

Still, Therese's eyes drifted to the Leo. "You'll read the paper and have a cup of coffee, and then you'll step out the door, prepared for a normal day. But you'll never reach your workplace. You will vanish, without a trace." She checked her watch and then called Leslie Consorte's cell phone. When it rang for the ninth time, she hung up and walked the thirty yards to Captain Grunden's office.

Grunden was on the phone, arguing with someone.

Naomi Strauss, a girl from legal, was sitting in one of his office chairs waiting with an open yellow legal pad on her knee. When Grunden saw Therese slide through the office door, he motioned for her to sit down next to Naomi, and he continued to talk animatedly into the phone. Whenever he would pause, the person on the other line would respond in a pitch high enough for Therese to hear. Grunden held the phone away from his own ear and frowned.

Therese glanced down at Naomi's legal pad; it read, "Maslow. Legal Action? Check the books." There were two more sentences beneath that one, but when Naomi caught Therese reading, she held the pad tight against her chest.

"You guys going after the *Register*?" Therese asked.

"We're not allowed to discuss legal action," Naomi told her.

"You think we can get them to foot the bill for all this increased police traffic?"

Naomi just looked at Therese, her mouth pursed into a tight line. Finally she said, "Your partner Consorte is in a lot of hot water. Grunden's talking about him now, probably to internal affairs."

"He'll be fine."

"How can you say he'll be fine? He broke into a high-profile home, compromised a crime scene, and discharged his firearm."

"He'll be fine."

"How can you say that?"

"I read about this study once. It determined that if someone speaks with confidence, people will accept what they say as truth unless someone else contradicts it within seven seconds."

"That sounds like something you just made up," Naomi said.

"I watched a guy parlay the trick all the way to the presidency," Therese said.

Naomi shook her head. "What's the study? Which university? That might be something men can get away with. Rich, white men. But not me or you." Naomi tapped her pen against her legal pad. She looked at Therese with a mixture of appreciation and amusement.

Therese waited until the sixth second had passed. Smiling, she said, "It's a real study. By scientists. At an Ivy League school."

Grunden spoke again into the phone, his voice rising. This time when he paused to hear a response, he covered the receiver completely. Therese could still hear the other voice shouting into the earpiece.

"Where's Consorte?" Grunden demanded.

"He's still not here," Therese said with a shrug.

"Why the hell not?"

"I was thinking of going to his house. See if I can rouse him out of bed. It's not something I haven't done before," she said.

"Not under these circumstances you haven't," Grunden said. With his free hand, he tapped the newspaper sitting on his desk. Therese could see Leslie's face on the front cover. "Go after him, but when you find him, bring him directly here. Michaels wants to talk to him, but I want to talk to him first. Do you understand? I'm not sure why one of my best detectives decided to become a loose cannon, but this wasn't the time to do it."

Grunden returned his attention to his phone call.

"I'll find him and bring him back," Therese said.

When she was halfway out the door, Grunden covered the mouthpiece again. "Lapeyre!"

Therese stopped, her hand resting on the edge of the door frame. Grunden handed her a file. Affixed to the front was the picture of a greasy-looking Italian with high, arching cheekbones and thick eyebrows.

"Does the name Jack Madrigal mean anything to you?"

"Leslie mentioned him. Said he played games with the newspaper and the police department about a decade and a half ago. Something about eminent domain."

"Madrigal paroled two weeks ago," Grunden said.

"Curious," Therese said, studying the picture. The man was thick, well-muscled, with wavy brown-blond hair and a shadow of unshaven scruff on his upper lip and chin. She handed the file back to Grunden.

"There's something else about Madrigal, Lapeyre. In '09, when the whole business was going down, he took a personal interest in Consorte. He threatened Consorte's wife. Broke into his home while Consorte was on the job. It's part of the reason his marriage failed."

"Really?"

"Ask any of the older guys about it."

Into his cell phone Grunden said, "Of course I'm still listening." Then he said to Therese, "If Madrigal can cross that line with Leslie, he can do it with any of us, with any high-profile figure on the case. Lock your door at night. Keep your gun close. And find Consorte."

"You think Madrigal's the guy?"

"He's a person of interest. The timing adds up."

"Did we get anything on the email address? The one that's been sending the messages? What about the photos of the naked girl from the frat guy's phones?"

"I wouldn't ask Cybercrimes to tell me what they had for lunch. They'd couch it in a whole bunch of techno-jargon. They read me some bullshit about firewalls and proxies and Aruba or some garbage like that. We're still pursuing that angle, but I wouldn't hold your breath. Nothing on the phones either. At least not yet. Remember when you could see clues and put your hands on them, Lapeyre?"

"Not really," Therese said.

Grunden simply waved her out of the room and went back to barking into the phone.

EVER SINCE HIS divorce, Leslie had rented the bottom half of a duplex in Tierrasanta, a suburban region of San Diego that skewed family but was run-down enough to keep the rent low. His building bordered a busy street. The paint was faded blue and chipping. When Therese arrived, she found two cops squished together on a small, three-step "porch" that led up to Leslie's front door. She flashed her detective badge.

She still loved doing that.

"Detective Therese Lapeyre," she said.

One cop was male, the other female. The woman was well-groomed, her hair styled short like Therese's, her clothes ironed, crisp shirt tucked into pants cinched high around her belly. She stood to greet Therese, shaking her hand with a firm grip. The man remained seated. He wore a faded blazer, picking at his teeth with his index finger. Therese didn't recognize either officer.

"Reyna Nakamura," the woman said. "This is my partner Jake Pierce. We're from internal affairs."

Therese groaned. "You guys really interested in a bullet hole in a fraternity roof, or does your boss just want a piece of the publicity hanging around this thing?"

Pierce remained sitting. Nakamura started to blush. Therese tagged her as the smarter of the two. Nakamura said, "I assure you every case is held to the same strict guidelines."

Therese shushed Pierce off the step and fished around in her pocket for the set of keys Leslie had given her.

"I recognize the name. You're his partner, right? Just recently promoted? We'd like to ask you a few questions about Detective Consorte," Nakamura said.

"Leslie's our best cop. He's innocent of any wrongdoing."

"Members of the press, and multiple other eyewitnesses, have him forcing himself into a private residence. Discharging a firearm. One report even indicates he physically assaulted a tenant of that residence. That he threw the young man up against a television and attacked a dog."

Therese slipped Leslie's key into the lock and pulled the door open. She knew seven seconds were ticking down, so she quickly said, "In the years I've been working with him, Leslie has always observed the very letter of the law. He slows down at yellow lights."

She stepped through Leslie's door and started to close it behind her. "Leslie?" she half yelled. The door bounced back open, and she looked down to find Nakamura was blocking it with her foot. "You want to come in?" Therese asked her.

She nodded.

"Not without a warrant," Therese said, nudging the other woman's foot back and closing the door. She hoped they would sit outside and let her words about Leslie sink into their brains. She had lied by painting Leslie as a Boy Scout, but truth wasn't a factor with the seven-second rule.

"Leslie?" Therese yelled again. She pulled her gun out of her holster and moved into the bedroom. The bed was made, the floor of the room was picked up, and there was no sign of a struggle.

Therese reholstered her gun. *What in the hell is going on?* She wandered into the bathroom and poked her finger into the bristles of Leslie's toothbrush. They were damp. Water was still drying on the floor of the shower. She went into the kitchen and found the remains of breakfast in the trash. There were no signs of a struggle there, either. *Leslie must be fine*, she thought to herself. *Or at least he was when he walked out the door this morning.*

Therese headed back out of the house. She wanted a look at the carport. If someone jacked Leslie as he climbed into his car, the clues would be there.

Nakamura and Pierce were waiting at the door like domesticated ducks. She let them in, stepping aside while they pushed past, eager for answers, promotion. Therese pulled the door shut and walked down to Leslie's carport.

The carport was made of old wood, laden with termites and splotchy paint. A small storage unit hung above where a parked car's hood would be. Therese poked around, looking through the bushes beside the carport. She pulled at the storage container door, which gave just enough for her to see it was empty. She searched the planter box atop the center divider. She walked a few steps and inspected the oblong box holding the neighbor's mail.

Therese found herself growing increasingly worried. Coming from an impoverished town called El Centro two hours to the east of San Diego, Therese had moved to the coast to attend Southwestern Community College, working multiple jobs and sharing a two-bedroom apartment with four other girls. The girls had thrown a party for her when she'd earned her associate's degree and another when she had been accepted into the police academy. But her first few years on the force had been undeniably unsuccessful. She had trouble bonding with her mostly male colleagues, and when she interacted with the public she felt like she could never find the right balance between gruff and kind.

The first time she met Leslie, she had just been assigned to two weeks in the equipment room even though the regular rotation was only supposed to be one week. Alone in the break room, she was choking back tears, considering a complete career change, when Leslie had ambled in looking for a cup of coffee. Seeing her distress, he put his hand on her shoulder and said, "We all feel like that on the inside. At least once a day, if not more. Absolutely no shame in showing it." Then he'd ambled back out of the room, giving her a goofy smile between sips of coffee. It had been a small moment, but it was what she needed. After that she had started to notice him all around the station. He began introducing her to the other officers as his friend, and it changed how they treated her. Less preoccupied with social failures, she was able to pay closer attention to the world around her, and slowly claw her way up the ladder. Leslie had been the first one waiting to greet her at the top.

Therese was just about to walk back to her car when she had the idea to lie down and look under the car parked beside Leslie's spot. Stomach resting on rough gravel, her face inches from a black, fetid patch of oil, she saw something gleaming just beneath the car's exhaust manifold. She pressed her head against the ground and reached, suddenly anxious that Pierce and Nakamura might reappear through Leslie's door. The tips of her fingers hooked the object.

It was Leslie's cell phone, the LED screen shattered by deep, jagged cracks as if someone had smashed down on it hard with the heel of their boot.

20

BOBBY WASN'T SURE what to expect when he walked through the door of the *Register*'s headquarters. It was considerably quieter than it had been two days prior. Jana was sitting at her desk leafing through some papers, one hand resting on the receiver of her desk phone. She smiled broadly when she saw him, waving him over to her. "I've been here four years, Bobby, and I've never seen anything like you." She handed him a sealed envelope.

Bobby tore into the envelope and withdrew a check. The amount read $10,526.43. "This is more than sixteen cents a word," he said.

"Your story got picked up by the AP, no surprise. You got paid for every website that bought it. And that was pretty much all of them."

"Well, that's something," Bobby said, folding the check into his wallet. *Maybe I will get a laptop, finally. And a new, used motorcycle.* "Is Milo around?"

"I don't think he's in. He had a lunch meeting with members of the board of directors. There's a lot going on, a lot you missed by not coming in yesterday. Stuff involving the police force. Hawkeye is pissed that they ran your story instead of his. Milo is suing, like, sixty-eight different websites to keep them from publishing the predictions. If we can't stop them, we lose a huge income stream."

"Veracity, honesty, and truth," Bobby said.

"What?" Jana's phone made a beeping sound. She recoiled from the receiver. "I totally forgot. I have someone on hold. Who do you think is doing this? You don't really think it's the work of a legitimate psychic, do you?"

"Answer the phone." Bobby picked up the receiver and held it to Jana's ear. She smiled and took it from him, but she let her hand linger on his longer than necessary.

Women were always responding positively to Bobby. He suspected it had to do with the height, or the build, or the shaggy hair, or the Olympic achievement. He tried to enjoy it, but it was consistent enough to lose a little bit of its charm. On his way to the elevator, he reminded himself it wouldn't last forever. Someday he'd have his dad's anger, Milo's baggy eyes, Leslie's paunch.

The elevator took Bobby up to the second floor. His desk, previously sitting innocuous in the corner, was now piled high with copies of the newspaper containing his article. Beside the stacks of papers was a bottle of champagne and a note reading, "I thought you'd like a few copies for your relatives—MM."

His phone was blinking 19. He sat down with a pad of paper and a pen and listened to every message. Most of the messages were regarding his story. One message was from his mother, proudly calling his 'office' in near hysterics from happiness about the front page. Several messages were from the AP and Reuters, two were hang-ups from an extension within the office—he guessed either Milo or Hawkeye—and one was from a WSK Literary Management in New York asking about story rights.

Messages four and thirteen were from the same man, Sonny Ambrosino, Lady Ambrosia's father. He was growing worried about her. He'd filed a missing person's report with the police. He'd seen that the Ask Ambrosia articles were still running, and the reception-ist had patched him through to this extension. Could Bobby help him? Did he know anything?

Messages sixteen, seventeen, and eighteen were hang-ups; Bobby guessed it was Mr. Ambrosino again, growing desperate for answers. Bobby jotted down his number, but he hesitated to call. It was a police matter. There was very little Bobby could do about it.

Message nineteen was Terry Abbattista reissuing his invitation to the night's dinner. Bobby guessed he'd left it before reaching Bobby on his cell.

Abbattista again insisted he bring a date, and when Bobby hung up the phone, he started wondering who that would be. The thought brought his mood crashing down.

There were many reasons to believe that this would be Bobby's last night as a whole man. Sarah's husband would arrive from the waters of the Yellow Sea tomorrow, and Bobby imagined him stepping off the plane, fully automatic weapon cocked and loaded, the words *Kill Bobby* etched onto its wicked barrel.

The worst part was Bobby probably deserved death. He had screwed the man's wife, enjoyed the pleasures of her company and her body while her husband was knee deep in artillery fire and IED shrapnel.

No, the worst part was Bobby still couldn't stop thinking about Sarah. He ached to see her, to take her to the Abbattista party tonight and snoop for clues together. He ached to tell her how he felt. He tapped his fingers on his phone screen, stared at it blankly for a moment, and then called Star Lunes.

"Yes?" she answered. Her voice was silky smooth and full of confidence, like it had been the first time he had called her for advice.

"Star? It's Bobby."

"Oh, hi, Bobby. How are you?"

"I'm fine."

"I liked your story. Not bad for being spaced out at a FedEx Office Center with only Mountain Dew and AMPM hot dogs. I especially liked the parts that mentioned me."

"Terry invited me to dinner tonight."

"Terry Abbattista?"

"Want to come help me pursue the Kepler angle?"

"Oh, Bobby Frindley," she said, her voice purring again with that strange inflection. "I will absolutely be your date. When should I pick you up?"

"Six thirty?"

"I'll wear something nice."

"Looking forward to it."

Bobby's phone rang again but he didn't answer. After the caller gave up and left a message, Bobby listened to it while he jotted down notes for himself: Consorte. Eidelman. Kepler. Abbattista. Donations to the zoo? The message was from Sonny Ambrosino again, talking for five or six minutes about his daughter and how worried he was. Bobby called Milo and told him about Sonny's messages.

"I've been getting calls from Sonny for the last three days. I'm not sure it's a story, Bobby. Stephanie is probably out getting drunk in Mexico somewhere, having a hell of a time and too far south for cell phone range," Milo said.

"I don't like not helping," Bobby said. "And we've got a missing girl in our story too. The one that rolled down the canyon and disappeared."

"They're definitely not the same person—" Milo began.

"How do we know for sure?" Bobby asked.

"The art of journalism isn't to discover all the things that could be possible. It's to gather facts and uncover what's real."

"Two of the kids took pictures of our mysterious nude girl. They deleted them, but nothing digital is ever really deleted, right? Do we know if the police were able to recover the images?"

Milo tsked on the other end of the line, but Bobby could tell he was thinking about what Bobby had said. "For the record, I think you're a little off course here, but at least you're talking facts now. I'll follow up. I have a few contacts at the department. I'll call them."

"Thanks, Milo."

As soon as Bobby hung up the phone, it began to ring again.

21

WHEN HE GOT home, Bobby took a quick shower and shave to prepare for the Abbattista dinner party. During the shower, he thought of his own father with some venom. Sonny's voice had been cracking with emotion as he spoke into Bobby's answering service. Would Arthur Frindley reveal such an intimate display of pain if Bobby were to go missing? He highly doubted it.

At six thirty sharp, Star was on Bobby's porch, knocking on his door. He let her in quickly, trying to see if Sarah saw her arrive without letting Star see what he was trying to see. Star was wearing a beautiful summer dress bedecked in canary yellow and purple flowers. She was carrying a bottle of red wine. Bobby kissed her on the cheek as he hustled her through the door.

"Do I look beautiful?" Star asked slyly.

"You look like a million dollars," Bobby said.

Star rolled her eyes and laughed. "Where we're going, I'm not sure that's enough."

"I won't sell you tonight even if Abbattista offers twice that."

"Very sweet," Star said.

Something had shifted between them.

Even though she had learned of his affair with Sarah, even though this was only his second time seeing her, the odyssey of the previous night had bonded them quickly. Bobby noticed her eyes—framed in long, natural eyelashes—looked even more beautiful than the day before.

"Now if he offers three million . . ." Bobby said after a pause.

"You'll still say no."

"Everyone has a price."

"Not the heroic Bobby Frindley."

Star leaned into Bobby and put her arms around his neck. It was a bold move, even with the new closeness they seemed to have. She rested her head on his shoulder and Bobby enjoyed the warmth of her body. They hung together silently for a few moments before Bobby glanced out the window again. Sarah's apartment was dark, but the sight of it still stabbed him with guilt.

"C'mon, Astron. Let's go to the show," he told Star.

———

HIS GLIB, SIMPLE rhyme proved prophetic. When they were buzzed past the gate leading to Abbattista's long driveway, the home appeared to be under heavy construction. Piles of lumber were stacked by the garage next to six-foot lengths of heavy Styrofoam tubing. A smaller security door was propped open, and men in red vests and hard hats were walking out, toolboxes tucked under arms, jeans coated with dirt and grease.

Bobby had just finished telling Star about how Abbattista lived in a demure palace. "It appeared almost a normal house," he told her, "until you got inside and it unfolded into triangular majesty."

"This is not what I was expecting," Bobby said when they arrived.

They moved through the garden gate and into the garden proper, crossing the small wooden bridge to the front door. The door was propped open by a cinder block, but neither Bobby nor Star felt comfortable pushing their way in. Bobby rang the bell and they waited, his arm around her shoulders. After three minutes and a short debate regarding the civility of ringing again, a young woman came to the door.

"I heard the doorbell; has anyone answered?" she asked. Her voice was thick with an accent that Bobby couldn't place. Bobby must have been looking down because the first thing he saw was her blood-red heels, which added at least three inches to her height. They matched her tight, designer skirt. Her tailored blouse was cut liberally, giving the world a generous view of impossible breasts surging toward freedom like the bald heads of twin newborns. Bobby's eyes crawled up to her face and found a delicate jaw and surgically fattened lips.

Star carefully removed his arm from her shoulder, and he realized that he must be gawking. If Star was jealous, she had misunderstood his gaze. The young woman was a facsimile of beauty, a clever replication of a thousand matching Instagram posts. Technically beautiful, but also grotesque.

"We haven't been invited inside yet. Are you one of Terry's daughters?" Bobby asked.

The girl tittered a moment at the question, "No. I am ... errr ..." She searched for the right word, her accent making even the words she found hard to understand, "I am Timur's girlfriend. My name is Rhona."

"I'm Bobby and this is Star. It's nice to meet you."

"Yeah," Star said.

"Please come in. Ignore all the mess." The girl stood aside. She seemed relieved not to have to struggle any longer to speak. Bobby remembered that Timur was from Serbia, and he guessed that's where he'd found Rhona.

Before walking away, she turned to face them.

"Uhm . . . Terry has a feral dog. I'm not sure why he loves it; it could kill someone. Stay out of the . . ." she struggled a moment to find the word, "upstairs of the house."

Bobby laughed, but Rhona's face stayed serious.

Once Rhona had walked down into the foyer, Star leaned into Bobby's ear and said, "That's probably not what she looked like, originally."

"Agreed. I'm not a big fan of the needle and the scalpel," Bobby said, honestly.

"Is that why you were gawking at her? From uncontrolled disgust?"

"I was impressed by her dedication to the façade." Bobby pulled Star out of the main walkway. They huddled together in the middle of the huge foyer, surrounded by large white vases bedecked with Japanese dragons, three-foot-wide sculptures made of sea glass, and an entire wall of commedia dell'arte theater masks. "The dog is going to be a problem. How are we going to poke around the house for clues when there's a savage animal loose somewhere?"

"We may have to stay on the bottom floor," Star realized.

Terry Abbattista strolled into the hallway leading to the foyer. He was whistling a tune that Bobby faintly recognized, and he clutched an appletini in a fancy martini glass with his left hand. When he saw Bobby and Star, a look of displeasure crossed his face.

"Rats, Bobby! I was hoping to get this mess cleaned up before you arrived. The construction company guaranteed they'd be done by seven, but then the workers started making noise about the, uhh, unique nature of my blueprints."

"Mr. Abbattista, this is Star."

"Please, call me Terry. Is this the young lady you told me about yesterday?"

"Yes," Bobby lied. Abbattista took Star's hand and kissed it. Halfway into the bow, Bobby caught him looking at Star's hand to see if it had a wedding ring.

"You're twice as lovely as he described," Abbattista told her.

Star looked from Abbattista to Bobby and then back again. In the transition between glances, Bobby saw her eyes register the lie. Bobby hadn't yet met her in person when he'd visited Abbattista's house. Bobby began to blush, but as smart as Star was, she was also civilized. She took the false compliment graciously. "You're much more handsome than he described," she told Abbattista.

It was Abbattista's turn to blush. "Splendid," he said. "Come inside, well, outside really, I've got to show you something." He led them into the foyer, and they took a left turn into the great room where Bobby had recuperated from his smack on the face the day before. He noticed that several members of the construction crew were repairing a banister that ran along the loft above the indoor/outdoor pool.

"Are you remodeling?" Bobby asked.

"That? No, the idiots broke that unloading the construction materials. One of them carried a wooden log straight into it, smashed up the whole railing. My housekeeper was not pleased, and she let them know it. She also let me know it. No, the work being done is right there." Abbattista pointed out the large picture windows to the backyard.

Bobby could see the corner of some kind of platform. It was big, maybe ten feet high, and another eight or nine feet long.

"What is that?" he asked.

"Go see for yourself," Abbattista said. He walked over to the men working on the railing and said something in a stern voice. One of them wiped down the railing with a cloth hanging from his belt. They hadn't finished the job. Bobby could see where the wood had been replaced but not sanded, matched, or anchored. Still, the men began to pack up their tools. "Go check out the backyard," Abbattista said again. His voice was full of excitement now. "I'm having a number of things built for the horoscope party, but this one is the main piece."

Bobby walked down the steps of the loft and moved carefully past the indoor pool. The smell of chlorine wafted up to his nostrils, filling his mind with a thousand happy memories.

He pulled open the door and stared at Abbattista's new construction. It was a single wooden platform running across the center of the pool, elevated two body lengths above the surface of the water. The sides of the beam were etched with some kind of Celtic runes, or maybe Sanskrit. Bobby wasn't exactly a scholar.

Timur was standing on the pool deck staring at him.

"Bobby, I'm glad you're here. Terry asked me to apologize for hitting you in the face. I wouldn't have done it if I had known you'd be a regular guest."

"Apology accepted, I guess."

"I would usually only hit someone like that if they were a weasel. The way you broke into Terry's home, tried to steal his possessions—"

"Imagine all the things I'd have missed if I hadn't. We met Rhona at the door. Is she your girlfriend?"

Timur got a strange look on his face. His voice, already distorted by a Serbian accent, took on a tone of gravelly menace. "She is my girl-friend, yes. Be careful not to get too interested in her. Right, Bobby?"

"Right, Timur. And you don't have to worry anyway, I brought my own lady." Bobby motioned to the long, thin beam. "What is this thing?"

"Climb on and I will show you," Timur said. Timur walked to the south side of the platform, pulled himself up onto it, and strode effortlessly to the center. He set his feet and motioned for Bobby to follow him. Bobby climbed the north side, crossing to meet Timur on wobbly feet. Ten feet under their heels, the pool water was calm.

"Has anyone tested this yet?" Bobby asked.

Timur didn't answer. Star and Abbattista pushed through the door, into the backyard.

"We were watching you from inside," Star said. "Terry told me all about this device. It's based on a design by an Egyptian architect named, Pet—uhm."

"Petosiris," Abbattista said. "But he was not the architect. He was an Egyptian high priest. His necropolis was discovered in 1919. His body was entombed atop a dais just like the one you're balancing on."

"Petosiris, the high priest," Star said, correcting herself.

"Egyptians had mastered the art of preserving the body, but they also wanted to preserve the metaphysical knowledge a person had accrued in their lifetime. How do we keep the memories intact?" Abbattista pointed to his head. "The mind is far more important than the body, is it not? The Egyptians' solution was geometry. They believed that after death, metaphysical energy would slowly seep from the corpse. Those hieratic inscriptions on the sides, even the flat, simple elegance of the dais itself, were so shaped to redirect that energy back into the body of the deceased. To trap it there."

Star and Bobby glanced at each other. Star arched her eyebrows. They were at the intersection of geometry and mysticism again. Bobby hoped Abbattista hadn't noticed their nonverbal exchange.

"Can you read these hieroglyphs?" Star asked, peering at the laser-carved etchings on the side of the wood.

Abbattista walked to the beam and ran his hand along the writing next to Timur's heel. "This one here says, 'A man is revived when his name is pronounced.'"

Bobby looked down at the unfinished wood structure beneath his feet. More than anything else, it reminded him of a child's playground structure hastily built to stretch the length of a billionaire's pool. "Why is it so wobbly?" he asked.

"Well, that's part of the game," Abbattista told him. "Hold on."

Abbattista disappeared around the side of the house. When he returned, he was carrying two of the long bamboo shafts. Their ends were wrapped in cloth and padded by foam lining. He threw one to Bobby and one to Timur.

"Again? Really?" Bobby said.

Timur swung the bamboo shaft, thwacking Bobby hard on the shoulder.

22

LESLIE CONSORTE WAS missing. When Therese had returned to the station and reported her findings to Captain Grunden, Grunden issued an APB on Leslie's car, and made a special call to the border patrols at Santa Ynez and Yuma to keep their eyes peeled. Leslie was driving a tan Ford Crown Victoria, a car he'd purchased at a police auction seven years ago.

Grunden had become particularly agitated when Therese brought up the possibility that Leslie's disappearance was the work of the horoscopes. "That prediction was for a Leo. Consorte's a Gemini," Grunden had rationalized. Therese found little solace in that line of reasoning.

To add to her misery, right this minute, Detective Therese Lapeyre was freezing. She was on Dock 44 in the port district of San Diego. The sun was near the horizon, and what little remained was blocked by thirty-foot stacks of metal shipping containers.

Dock 44 was in a peculiar spot. It jutted west partially under the 5 Freeway. SDPD had police stationed in clusters on four points across the dock, including a SWAT team holed up in one of the large metal storage bins. They had coned off the far right lane of the freeway for a mile in either direction and had stopped just short of shutting down the entire freeway, as it was the main travel corridor through all of San Diego and further south into Mexico.

Therese was dressed as a dock worker, leather jacket—complete with extra padding in the shoulders that she did not think she needed—blue jeans, work boots, and a knit beanie. Under her jacket and stained black T-shirt, she wore a standard police-issue Type II bulletproof vest. Despite all those layers, the wind was tearing right through her clothes and chilling her bones. Working helped keep her warm, and once she'd shaken off her lingering thoughts about Consorte, she hefted an empty wooden crate onto a jack-loader and signaled for Special Agent Randy Michaels to haul it away. Instead, Michaels leaned out of the cab and said, "You look cold, Detective. Would you have preferred a position on the periphery?"

"I'm doing fine, Randy."

"Why did you volunteer to join me as the bait? Don't get me wrong, it's heroic. It's also a job for older, single types. The ones without so many good years ahead of them."

"Wouldn't it seem suspicious if all the dock workers were over forty?" Therese countered.

"It's suspicious to have a woman disguised as a man." Michaels blinked his eyes. He seemed to immediately regret his choice of words. "Sorry. I shouldn't be mentioning gender at all, should I? I swear I took those classes. When you're with the Bureau, there are so many sensitivity classes."

Therese leveled her gaze at the man on the jack-loader. Randy Michaels was middle-aged. His brown hair was peppered with gray. He had a boyish face, but it was in contrast to the deep battle lines etched into his forehead and temple. "The reason I signed up to be bait is I'm not worried," Therese said, effortlessly changing the subject. "If there is a grand horoscope conspiracy, if someone is truly going to kill a dock worker tonight and has orchestrated all the other events of the week—and that's a big if—if they've done all that, then they're smart enough to know what we're up to. And they're smart enough to know this whole dock is swarming with cops and SWAT. I figure they either accept the challenge of trying to outmaneuver us, or we're out here freezing for nothing."

"That's a comforting thought," Michaels said. His knit cap was starting to ride up to the top of his head. "Except that the horoscope mentioned 'a steady hand and a cogent eye.' To me that means we could have our chests in the viewfinder of a sniper rifle this very second."

Therese put a hand on her own knit cap, holding it in place. "In this strong coastal wind—this terrible, freezing wind—a sniper shot from almost any distance would be close to impossible."

Therese had another reason for being confident. Leslie had left for work, without his cell phone, and had never arrived. Only one horoscope came true per day, that was Bobby and Milo's rationalization for printing them. If Leslie was gone—she hoped to hell he wasn't—but if he was gone, then the horoscopes were satisfied, and both Therese and Michaels were in for a cold, quiet night on the docks.

And there was another reason she'd volunteered for the most dangerous job. Therese had made detective just two nights before. She was out of the equipment room, but a long way from being established. She knew a major shake-up like this horoscope thing could help her earn a useful reputation. Michaels had picked a nice word to describe it, *heroic*.

Therese didn't offer any of these explanations aloud, and Michaels didn't ask for them. He rolled the knob of the jack-loader until the cargo was lifted six feet into the air, and then he piloted it down the long dock toward the loading bay. Once Michaels had puttered away, Therese sat down on a box of Chiquita bananas. She scanned the ocean for any signs of a boat. The Coast Guard was stationed in an umbrella pattern, every nautical mile. Even knowing all those boats were out there in the darkness, Therese couldn't see or hear any sign of them. A feeling of stark isolation washed over her. Despite being surrounded by the combined forces of the SDPD, the FBI, and the Department of Defense, she felt abjectly alone.

———

STAR HAD SLIPPED out of her skirt and was unbuttoning her blouse. Bobby could see that she had worn a blue silk bra and matching panties. He wondered if it was for his sake that she'd chosen such a nice pair. Though Timur had already whacked Bobby with the bamboo once, Abbattista had stopped the contest before it could continue, insisting they "dress appropriately first." What he'd failed to mention was that dressing appropriately was just undressing.

Star had to be freezing, nearly nude against the offshore breezes that were blowing up the cliff face and across the long lawn of Terry Abbattista's backyard. She held the empty glass from her second dry martini, pinched between the finger and thumb of her left hand. "I can't believe I'm doing this. I can't believe I'm doing this," she whispered.

Bobby took a deep breath and then slipped off his own pants, revealing not quite as carefully selected brown and gray plaid cotton boxers. He began to unbutton his shirt.

"Hey Terry," he said, "I didn't invite the lovely lady here to let you exploit her."

Terry laughed. He gestured to the bottle of beer at Bobby's feet. "You drink that drink," he said. Then, after a moment, "This is America, Bobby. Do we have any form of entertainment that doesn't somehow relieve our repressed sexuality?"

Bobby thought for a minute. "I guess not," he said. "But why do you get to wear swim trunks?"

"Because it's my house!" Abbattista roared. He stood beside the platform in a red bathing suit. The legs were cut long, stopping just above his knobby knees. "And nobody wants to see my wrinkly old rear end," he added.

"Don't be so sure," Star said, laughing. She took another sip of her cocktail.

Timur walked through the sliding glass door with his arm around Rhona's shoulders. Rhona was biting her lip nervously. "She's changed her mind. She'll play," Timur said.

Rhona turned away from the group and shimmied out of her dress. Her back was slender and muscled, her shoulders petite. Her panties were dark blue, the same color as Star's, but cut much less conservatively across the back.

Standing next to Rhona, Timur looked at Bobby, his head cocked at a threatening angle. Bobby quickly shifted his gaze to Star, but her expression was only slightly less antagonistic.

Abbattista turned back to Bobby. "I didn't even think about getting our dinner clothes wet when I built this. I placed the Petosiris dais over the pool so that no one had to worry about concussions."

"Just drowning," Star said wryly.

"Not even that. We have an Olympic-level water poloist among us, don't we, Bobby? Why are you still wearing your shirt?"

Bobby took off his shirt and rubbed his biceps and forearms. Rhona was watching him carefully, arms crossed over her cantilever chest. She wasn't the only one.

Abbattista said, "Look at you, Bobby. Your physique is fantastic, the product of years of hard work. The pool exercises eighty-nine percent of the body's muscles, doesn't it? No other sport can match that."

Timur stripped off his clothes and let out a series of aggressive grunting sounds. He was loaded with biceps and triceps, all the glamour muscles worked into puffy glory. But he'd neglected to develop his legs, and with his shirt off he looked like an apple on stilts. He still possessed the grace of an Olympian, though. His motions were angular and fluid, with the certainty of a dancer, or, Bobby supposed, the world-class fencer that he was.

Abbattista kept speaking, "The body is our most sacred geometry. More true than the planetary alignments of astrology, more pious than the mysticism of Petosiris. Da Vinci was obsessed with it, Heraclitus, Michelangelo, Whitman too; it is math, theology, history, and it should be worshipped. Or at least displayed whenever possible."

While Terry was speaking, Bobby took a step closer to Star and put his arms around her naked shoulders and torso. She was covered in goosebumps and welcomed the warmth of his body without complaint.

"Do you think the pool is heated? I might fall in on purpose," she whispered.

"Star, you and Rhona go first!" Terry said.

Star was quick, pulling herself onto the beam and shuffling across to the center. Rhona struggled up the other side, inching slowly along the thin wood.

Bobby's eyes shifted back to Star, who had a big goofy smile on her face. "Being around you sure isn't boring," she said from across the wheel.

Abbattista misunderstood who she was talking to. "You haven't seen anything yet," he told her. "Here's one for each of you." He leaned over the edge of the water, giving each a padded shaft of bamboo.

Rhona shuffled forward to take the bamboo from Abbattista, and for a moment Bobby thought she would fall off before the game began.

"Don't worry," Bobby said. "If you die, the machine will preserve your memories forever."

"Everyone ready?" Abbattista asked. Without waiting for an answer he shouted, "Go!"

THERESE WAS STILL sitting on the box of Chiquita bananas at the end of Dock 44 when her phone rang. She fumbled it out of her pocket, thinking for a minute that it was Leslie's ancient iPhone 8. Leslie's phone was silent. Disappointed, she placed it on the crate next to her. When she fished out her own faded blue department-issue Samsung Galaxy, she saw Grunden's name flashing on the LED screen.

"Yeah," Therese said.

"Lapeyre? Where the hell are you?"

"I'm on Dock 44, disguised as a worker."

"No kidding? You're playing the decoy? Good for you."

"Thanks."

"I have some bad news though. Strange news, anyway."

"Something about Leslie?" Therese asked.

"We pulled the archival footage from the San Ysidro, Otay Mesa, and Yuma border crossings for this morning. We got a hit in Otay Mesa. Leslie's Crown Vic passed a camera at nine a.m. piloted by a lone male driver. No sign of distress or injury. I'm looking at it now."

"Nobody's in the back seat?"

"The footage is grainy. The back is covered in shadows. Even so, a person, Madrigal even, could be there, lying down, a pistol pressed against Leslie's gut. I don't know, Lapeyre. It might not even be Consorte driving, but it could be."

"I'll head into Mexico tomorrow, see what I can find out."

"I can't spare you, not even on unpaid leave. I'm giving Nakamura and Pierce the green light to go after him," Grunden said.

"Those clowns from internal affairs?"

"I thought you'd want to know."

"Nakamura and Pierce couldn't find a book in a library," Therese said.

"I can't spare you," Grunden said again.

Therese had to lean to the side to get the phone back into her pocket, and as she did it, something just over her left ear exploded. The crate she was leaning against absorbed most of the impact and most of the sound, just a cracking of splintered wood and the shifting of boxes. The second snapping sound burst just over the top of her knit beanie.

Therese pulled her revolver free from her belt. "Sniper!" she yelled, firing three shots into the air. She had intended to shoot only once, but adrenaline wrenched her finger down on the trigger. She was standing, leaping, rolling, before she had the chance to give it a second thought. Another explosion split the wood of the dock, right where her feet had been.

At the sound of Therese's gunfire, the entire Scorpio team started moving. In her periphery, Therese could see SWAT piling out of the storage bin, the noses of their rifles sniffing the air for signs of the shooter. Therese reached the edge of the dock. Every sense she had was heightened, but she was grasping mostly for a sense of ESP: *When would the next bullet strike? What direction to jump? Where to hide?* Having fled from the boxes, she'd moved herself away from any reasonable cover. Panicked, she made the quickest choice, flinging her body off the end of the dock. She hung in the air for what seemed like forever, hyperconscious of her stretched out back, her exposed neck. Even as she dropped toward the icy-blue ocean, she was still expecting that last fateful bullet to tear through her tendons and snap her spinal column. It didn't come, and she splashed, ungracefully, into the cold waters of the Pacific Ocean.

BOBBY PITCHED BACKWARD off the platform, Timur's bamboo staff wedged between his chest and his neck. The other man was too quick. Too graceful. He had dropped to a knee, ducking under Bobby's attack, and then sprung forward with a vicious slash.

The stick was padded, so it was mostly Bobby's pride that hurt as he dropped through the air and into the warm pool with a giant splash.

Star crested the surface like a mermaid two feet to Bobby's left, giving him a radiant smile. He grabbed at her, but she deftly maneuvered away. Bobby pursued, chasing her all the way to the western edge of the pool. She surfaced again, and they both took in the view of the ocean below, the darkening sand, the gentle crashing of waves, and the incandescent lights dotting the hillside. Star rolled onto her back, propping one foot on the metal handrail near the steps, and resting her head against the blue tile. She kicked her other foot and her breasts surfaced, the thin, wet material of her bra clinging for its life. Bobby put his hand on her stomach and pulled her next to him. She floated there, half on his lap, half propped on the handrail, staring up at the gray sky.

A servant appeared behind Bobby with a new Pacifico beer and a fresh margarita on a salver. Bobby took the Pacifico and handed the margarita to Star. She held it idly in her left hand, the edge of the glass dipping dangerously close to the pool water.

"Not a bad life here," Star admitted.

"If you don't mind the big Petosiris thingy."

"More sacred geometry," Star said. "Seems to line up with his interest in Kepler. Suspicious. But it doesn't mean he's the horoscope writer," she reminded Bobby.

Bobby let himself drift; his eyes cast upward. The bottom half of his sandy-blond hair swirled around in the water. His ears slipped above and below the surface as the waves lapped. One minute he'd hear the submerged hum of the pool filter, then when the small ripples rolled away, he'd hear Terry and Timur arguing playfully on the other side of the pool. He put the beer to his lips and took a long drink, enjoying the sour taste of Mexican brew, lime, and a dash of chlorine.

The mystery of the horoscope writer seemed less important in this moment.

"That cloud is shaped like a walrus," Star said. "See the tusks?"

"Nope," Bobby said, his hand now on her waist.

"What do you see up there, Bobby?"

"Night clouds," he said. He took another drink, languidly.

His hand had traveled all the way down to her hips. He could feel the smooth, wet silk of the edge of her panties. Star took his hand away and swam to the other side of the pool.

"Wait. I do see the walrus now," he called after her.

A few minutes later, he waded out of the crystal blue pool water, stepping onto Abbattista's back lawn and directly into the crisp offshore breezes. The air cooled his body, raising tiny goose pimples on his chest and arms. He welcomed it, even stood against the brunt of the wind, willing his body temperature to drop. He was horny. There was no other way to describe it.

They had played two rounds each on the Petosiris platform, and both Rhona and Star had begun the second game standing on the wooden structure, dripping wet in just their underwear. Half against his will, Bobby had drunk in every curve of their bodies, every line of muscle, every graceful feminine tendon.

There was something smarmy about Abbattista's celebration of all their bodies, something exploitative and indulgent and reckless. But there was something honest about it too. Standing on the lawn now, Bobby could feel the blood and the beer rolling together into deep waves at the base of his skull. He was trying hard not think about what the two women looked like under those thin wisps of cloth. Unfortunately, it turned out that horoscopes weren't the only thing his imagination compensated for when important information was just out of the reach of his senses.

Bobby took a few steps closer to the cliff face and whispered just loud enough to reach his own ears, "God? You made two perfect women, including, of course, the raw materials which went into Rhona's body after her creation. I know I am weak. I know you know I am weak. The truth is, I would really like to . . ." Bobby stopped himself short of explaining to God the conflict going on in his imagination. It was one thing to pray casually but another thing entirely to be profane. There was also the return of Sarah's husband just around the corner, reminding him of the looming cost of moral corruption. "I would appreciate it if you'd help me keep a clear head tonight," he prayed.

Bobby exhaled deeply, and then he turned back toward the small party. Timur, his lower half wrapped in a towel, was talking to Star, celebrating his victory and probably challenging her to a tiebreaker. Terry had an arm around Rhona, plying her with a drink that she did not need. Behind them, the house was full of light and sound. Servants moved through rooms, carrying bundles of wet towels, empty wine glasses, and half-finished hors d'oeuvre trays. They would pass into Bobby's view through lighted windows and then disappear, only to drop back into view again in the window of another room. In the center of the indoor recreation room, Bobby could see the framed one-dollar bill, illuminated by the warm light of a desk lamp.

Bobby walked across the grass, his toes curling around long, soft strands of manicured lawn. He still dripped with water, and his body was slowly cooling down. He slipped through the opening in the wall that separated the indoor and outdoor portions of the pool. When he reached the desk, he fished the Kepler plaque from his pocket, returning it to the place where he'd first seen it. He read the words again. *Mensus eram coelos, nunc terrae metior umbras. Mens coelestis erat, corporis umbra iacet.*

On the wall above the desk, Abbattista had seven framed photographs: One with him standing next to a young Maria Shriver and a slightly less young Ronald Reagan, another with peak-movie-star-era Clint Eastwood. Two were business pictures Bobby had noted on his last visit. The remaining three were of Terry at the Del Mar racetrack. In one, he stood beside a jockey in the winner's circle. Another was the photo finish—a sweaty horse with a thin line of blood running from its nose was edging to victory. The last was a much younger Terry Abbattista in feminine polo-cut riding pants, astride a fine-looking stallion.

While Bobby was looking at the pictures, Rhona approached and put her hand on his elbow. He turned toward her, but she didn't step away, and his body pressed against hers. She was still in her underwear, emboldened by her fifth or sixth drink.

"Hi," Bobby said.

Rhona just smiled at him, her arm cradling his bicep.

"Terry owns horses?"

"It looks like it," Rhona said.

"Where's Timur?" Bobby asked.

"Why do we care?" Rhona said, gesturing with her free hand.

"With you standing this close, it seems like an important question."

She leaned forward and kissed him, her hands moving to his shoulders.

Shocked, he stepped back and broke the embrace. *The problem with women,* Bobby thought, *is their saliva tastes like sweet, wonderful candy.* "I'm going to go talk to Terry," he said.

"Suit yourself," Rhona said, pulling out Abbattista's desk chair and sitting down heavily.

Bobby walked back onto the lawn, but not before leaning down to splash cold pool water onto his face. Abbattista was sitting atop the Petosiris dais swinging his legs. He stared down into the water, watching it be pushed gently by the coastal winds. After a moment, he glanced up and smiled at Bobby.

"What a great night," he said.

"I was looking at your pictures inside. Do you own a horse?"

"Why do you ask?"

"Just curious."

"I own three. Thoroughbreds. Lucy is Lucky placed at Del Mar last summer in early August. She's running again this year. I can send you tickets if you want."

"I used to love the races. It was one of the few memories I have of my father when he was at peace. He quit taking me when I was thirteen though, used to complain quite a bit about doping. He said LASIK pretty much killed the sport in the late sixties."

"Lasix. LASIK is an eye operation," Abbattista corrected him.

"Do you use it on your horses?"

"Everyone does. Your father was being naïve. It's just a diuretic. And it helps prevent internal bleeding when the horses are running."

"My father is a lot of things, many of them unkind, but I wouldn't call him naïve."

"What do you want to hear me say, Bobby? Everybody uses Lasix."

Bobby gave a short bow. "Terry, you've been a great host."

"You're not leaving, are you?"

"I have to finish a story at the paper. About a missing girl. Her name is Stephanie Ambrosino," Bobby lied. He watched Terry's face when he said Stephanie's name. It registered no emotion whatsoever.

"Well, that's a worthy cause, I guess. I'll let you leave under two conditions."

"Name them."

"One, you come back again next week."

"Done."

"Two, you forget about the other girl, your married friend, and you give Star a chance. She's a dynamo."

Somehow, Abbattista had figured out that Star wasn't the married girl Bobby had told him about. "It's a tough circumstance, Terry, but I appreciate your advice."

"When you find a great woman and she gives you her time, you should be joyful for it. You never know what's going to happen next, Bobby. Never. You could eat a bad oyster, get in a car crash, trip, break a leg, and send a blood clot right up to your brain. Something terrible could even happen to one of the girls. Take love where you can find it."

"I'll see you later, Terry," Bobby said.

"I'm happy to have my Kepler plaque back," Abbattista called after him.

Bobby walked across the expanse of lawn to find Star. He knew very well what Lasix was. He knew horses and he knew doping. Lasix wasn't just a diuretic, it was a masking agent, used to cover doping. It would flush all fluids from the horse's system, including PEDs. It was hard to trace illicit chemical enhancement when the animal was pissing like a racehorse.

Timur and Star were sitting on lawn chairs staring out over the expanse of night. She had changed back into her sundress. She was covering her legs with a damp beach towel, and Tamba was beside her, on his hands and knees, struggling to start a small fire in the hearth. Bobby crouched down, positioning his body to block the wind and help Tamba light the logs.

"Ready to go?" he asked Star.

"I can't drive. I've had too much to drink," she said.

"I can drive us."

Star let out a long sigh. "I was just getting comfortable."

"Let the lady stay if she wants to stay," Timur said chivalrously, his hand patting her leg.

"It's a beautiful view," Star said.

Bobby reached for her. "I already thanked Terry for the nice night."

Reluctantly, Star took his hand, and he pulled her to her feet. She walked around to the small table behind her chair and picked up her bra and panties, which she had laid out to dry. She wrung them in her hands trying to get the last of the water out, and then stuffed them into Bobby's front pocket.

"Always a pleasure," Bobby told Timur, flatly. Timur stood up and turned Star toward himself, pulling on her hips. He kissed her once on each cheek, then said, "You are better than he deserves."

"Don't I know that?" Star said, sighing again.

As they walked away, Star became something much closer to sober. She leaned into Bobby's ear. "Was I putting on a show for nothing? I thought we were going to snoop around."

"He's the guy."

"What? Really?"

"Yeah. He's the guy. After the tiger attack, I went to the zoo and walked around in the animal's enclosure. It was covered in piss. Piss on the walls, in the tiger's bed, everywhere."

"So?"

"The tiger was doped up. That's why it was enraged and how it got over the partition. The poor animal was loaded with something

—probably anabolic steroids—and then zapped with Lasix to cover the injections."

"That's ridiculous."

"The tiger's blood was bright pink. You should have seen it contrasted with the blood of the man it killed. I'm an Olympic athlete. I know what doping looks like."

"Bobby, we still don't have motive. Why would Terry do something like that? He seems like such a nice person."

They were back in the recreation room, on the far end, close to the entrance to the foyer.

Bobby looked up from Star and saw Abbattista, still sitting on the Petosiris dais, staring back at them.

Bobby waved and smiled. Abbattista gestured to Star and then pushed his fists together, pantomiming a kiss. Bobby smiled and waved again. Then he and Star walked together out into the darkness of Abbattista's long front lawn.

24

THERESE LAPEYRE SPENT several minutes under water. Diving deep into the freezing murk, she discovered thick concrete blocks surrounding the legs of Dock 44 and tried to cling to one, barnacles digging into her hands, eyes squeezed shut, nose pinched. Every thirty seconds or so she'd float to the surface, to be battered by churning waves. She fought to suck in a mouth of air and dove to the bottom again. During each surface visit, her nose and forehead, naked in the glacial wind, would tingle with danger. On her third dive, the adrenaline was starting to be replaced by bitter cold. Therese let herself rise slowly, and she paddled against the whitewash to stare up at the edge of the dock. Flashlights roved over the surface of the water looking for her. "Hey! Down here!" she yelled, and the closest light zigzagged back toward her, trapping her in its wane circle.

She heard a voice say, "We got her!" and then someone lowered a rope net, barnacled and dirty from being stored outside on the dock. Therese was lifted by a wave. She grabbed the net on her upward trajectory and was pulled toward the top in slow, jerking motions. When she got there, her eyes swept over the pandemonium. Three ambulances were parked on the dock—one more than they'd had at the ready—lights slowly rotating. Paramedics in powder blue were running toward her, first aid kits in their hands. A second set of paramedics was pushing a stretcher into the back of their rig.

Someone was on it, wrapped in a blanket with an oxygen mask pulled over his face. The paramedics reached Therese and she waved them away, but they pushed into her anyway, trying to force her to sit down.

Therese put her hands on the lead paramedic who nervously recoiled at her grip. "Who's on the gurney?" Therese asked.

"We just got called. I'm not sure."

"Did he get shot? Is it Michaels?" Therese squeezed the man harder, shaking him.

"He broke his ankle. We're not sure if he was pursuing someone, or diving for cover. I don't know who it is."

Therese shoved the paramedic aside and knifed through the crowd of gathering police officers, most still disguised as dock workers, to reach the man on the stretcher.

On her way she passed the crates where she had been sitting and she saw Consorte's phone, still resting where she'd left it when the bullets had begun to strike. Therese scooped up the phone, but her clothes were too wet to put it in a pocket, so she just clutched it with her left hand.

The man on the stretcher wasn't Michaels, because Michaels was striding toward Therese, full of confidence and purpose. "Are you all right, Therese?" he asked.

"Who's on the stretcher?"

"One of mine; his name's Bisbas. It's an ankle."

"Did we get the shooter?"

"Not exactly." Michaels held up an evidence bag. Inside was a string of firecrackers, charred black and smelling of sulfur. "We think someone threw them down from the freeway overpass. They almost landed on your head."

Therese's mouth gaped. A police helicopter roared above them, peeling off into the dark ocean. It appeared from nowhere, rising from the east like some great black bird. Therese stripped off her soaking jacket and her fake shoulders, then hooked her hand under her bullet-proof vest.

Tearing apart the Velcro, she tossed it onto the ground. She stood on the dock dripping in her wet undershirt. When she glanced around, she realized that the attention that had been focused on the paramedics had shifted, and now many pairs of eyes were looking back at her. She took two deep breaths, cleared her throat—and then Leslie Consorte's phone began to ring.

BOBBY WAS DRIVING Star down the winding roads of Soledad Mountain. He pulled his iPhone out of his pocket and dialed Leslie Consorte.

"Hello?" a voice said on the other end. "Who is this?"

"Who is this?" Bobby asked back.

"This is Detective Therese Lapeyre," the voice said. "Now who is this?"

"Hey, Detective. This is Bobby Frindley, from the *Register*. I need to speak with Leslie."

"He's not available right now, Bobby. He probably won't be for a while."

"What's going on, Lapeyre? Did he get suspended?"

"I appreciated the way you wrote him up in the fraternity story. You made him sound like a hero," Lapeyre paused for a moment, "despite what happened. You've got a little credit with me, but that doesn't mean I'm going to answer every question you ask."

Bobby let go of the steering wheel to rub his left eye with his bicep. Then he pulled at the gauze on his chin, wet and loose from all the time he'd spent in the pool. "Lapeyre, if Leslie was suspended, I can't think of any good reason you'd be answering his phone. I'm a little worried. What's happened?"

"Thanks for calling, Bobby; I'm sure Leslie's fine. I have to go."

Bobby said, almost as an afterthought, "Wait, Lapeyre, hold up. There's something I need, related to the tiger attack."

Lapeyre was silent for a moment as well. When she finally spoke, she said, "I'm standing on a dock right now, dripping wet. Everyone's staring at me. Talk quick."

"I think you should test the tiger's blood for Lasix."

"You want me to order an autopsy—for the tiger?"

"It's a chemical masking agent for horses."

"My dad is a pretty big gambler. I know Lasix. What makes you think—"

"The appearance of the blood. I noticed how thin and pink it was at the zoo. I also have . . . other reasons for thinking our killer might have had access to Lasix."

"You'll have to tell me more than that if you want my help," Lapeyre said firmly.

Bobby thought about what he knew of Therese Lapeyre. Could he tell her the whole truth as he'd been prepared to tell Leslie? Only a dummy wandered through a dangerous situation trusting everybody. "It's just a hunch," he said.

"Hell, I don't even know where the tiger's body is being stored. If it's even being stored. I imagine the PD left it at the zoo. Also, the ME doesn't run tests on a hunch."

"It's a strong hunch," Bobby said.

———

THEY'D GONE TO Denny's to give Star a chance to sober up. She had ordered a Super Slam which impressed Bobby for some reason.

After they ate, he drove them slowly back to Crown Point. Bobby parked Star's car on his street, scanning for any sign of Sarah's Camry.

"You okay to drive?" he asked.

"I was pretending to be drunk," Star reminded him. "And I just ate two pancakes."

He was starting to wish her goodnight and climb out of the driver's seat when he realized it was after ten.

"We should check the email," he said.

Star turned down the radio as Bobby poked away at the lighted screen of his cell phone.

The first nine predictions were now what Bobby expected. Aries told him he'd have a miscarriage. Taurus predicted he'd cheat successfully in a blackjack game at a local casino run by the Sycuan Band of Indigenous people. Gemini predicted his restaurant would be shuttered for health violations. Cancer indicated he would break his arm roller-skating.

Bobby's eyes scanned each prediction, looking for a sign that Abbattista was behind it all. He reached the Libra prediction, his own sign.

"With today's astral energies, a significant shift will occur in your entire romantic paradigm. Be open to it. Even though you are a seer and can predict futures, this unique skill isn't enough to stop your lover's suicide when she hangs herself in her kitchen."

Bobby froze. He could feel all the blood draining out of his face. *It's talking about me*, he thought. *I'm the "seer." The horoscope writer. My lover is Sarah.*

He glanced over at Star, fearfully. *Or maybe Star.* His hands gripped the wheel. He climbed quickly from the car.

"Are you all right?" Star asked through the window. She had scooted over the center divider and was now in the driver's seat.

Bobby stared at Sarah's darkened apartment complex. He looked back at Star. Crown Point was unusually quiet. It was likely a side effect of the horoscope phenomenon, but it made everything feel even more abnormal, spooky.

Star locked Bobby's eyes with her gaze.

Her face softened a little bit. Maybe he was supposed to kiss her now, but he could only think about making sure everybody was safe.

When the kiss didn't come, crow's feet appeared bunched around Star's eyes. She wasn't smiling, just twisting her mouth upward. She seemed to silently accept his lack of interest, as if she half expected it, regardless of how he'd treated her in the water. She said, "I'm starting to get now why you say your life is so busy. It's been an unbelievable two days. Fun and everything, but . . ." Star let her voice trail off. He could tell she was hurt. He'd missed the moment, screwing up without doing anything at all.

"Star . . . I'm a Libra."

"The seventh sign. The scales. You're supposed to be balanced and collected—" Star began.

"No, Star." Bobby urged her to understand. "That prediction— it's mine. It's Abbattista threatening me. Or you. Or maybe . . ." Bobby glanced over at Sarah's darkened apartment.

Star took the phone from him and read the prediction. "You can't tell who your lover is," she said wryly. "You're also really starting to do the horoscope thing. Your imagination is in overdrive. Even if we're right about Abbattista, this is the moment he'd do something to draw us off his scent, not fully reveal his hand."

"You were at his house with me. He built the Petosiris wheel. He drugged a tiger! He's clearly willing, and able, to go to great lengths to play games."

"He's an old man with knobby knees, decorating for a big party. Without tests, we don't know what really happened to the tiger," Star reminded him.

"Come on. Of all the people, you should be the one who believes me."

Bobby watched Star swallow her romantic resentment. She passed him back his phone, looking thoughtful for a moment. "In order for me to be in any danger, we'd have to be right about Terry Abbattista. You'd have to be this Libra. I'd have to be your lover, which is obviously not a very accurate description." She tapped on her phone screen. "And this would have to be the prediction that comes true."

Bobby had already taken a few steps away from the car. He turned back a moment and leaned into the window. "Just in case, will you go someplace safe?" He leaned into the window farther and gave her a quick kiss on the cheek. It felt collegial. It didn't do anything to change Star's mood. In fact, resentment seemed to pour back into her expression. "Just for one day?"

"I'll stay with my cousin in Ramona. Just to make you happy. Better warn your real lover too." Star nodded to Sarah's apartment.

Bobby didn't say anything, ignoring the irony in Star's voice. He turned to leave.

"Hey, wait!" Star began to rummage around the floor of her car. She found what she was looking for, a book, and handed it to Bobby out the window. "It's about Kepler," she said. "Max Caspar is his foremost biographer."

"Shit, Star. Thank you."

"Forget it ever happened," Star suggested.

Bobby started to stuff the book in his jean pocket and realized he still had her bra and panties. He handed them to her, awkwardly, through the window.

Star revved the car's engine. She drove away with confidence, as if she was doing her best to leave Bobby's life, slipping away from his circle of influence, forever.

25

BOBBY WAITED FOR Star's car to disappear from sight, then he half ran toward Sarah's apartment. On her stoop, he punched Abbattista's phone number into his cell. Abbattista answered the phone, his voice foggy from sleep.

"Terry," Bobby stated firmly.

"Bobby, is that you? What's up? Did you forget something?"

"I just read through the predictions for tomorrow's horoscopes."

Abbattista's voice brightened, interested, "Yes? What do they say?"

"I want you to know that if someone comes after Sarah or Star, I'll kill whatever son of a bitch tries to lay a hand on them. Do you understand? Someone's going to die if they even get near either woman."

"Bobby, I appreciate your passion, but I don't know what you're talking about. I really don't. Who is Sarah? Your married friend? How is Star in danger?"

"Tomorrow's prediction. The Libra promises that my lover will hang herself in her kitchen."

"And you thin—" Abbattista paused a moment. "I wasn't threatening anybody when I said that thing about her being hurt." He exhaled deeply. "There's something I don't talk about very often. Maybe if I explain, things will make more sense. In August of 2017, my wife was diagnosed with non-Hodgkin's lymphoma. She was a fighter, bless her heart, and the five-year survival rate is eighty-four percent. With my money, and the power it brings, we weren't worried. We both went about our normal lives. She checked in to the hospital one Thursday for routine tests and died a day later. I wasn't even by her side. We live in a chaotic world. You can believe in a thousand gods, but there is no order in the universe, except the laws of physics and the inevitability of death. I was thinking of the mistakes I made with my wife when I spoke to you. I'm sorry if it came across as cryptic."

"That's terrible. I'm very sorry."

"Thank you. Please don't lose sight of the fact that these predictions aren't really coming true," Abbattista added. "There was no money under the cross. Nobody disappeared on the way to work today. You haven't met the horoscope killer. I bet hardly anyone has. He's probably a recluse, living in a cabin somewhere like the Unabomber. It's easy to get paranoid when you feel helpless; I do understand that."

"I don't feel hopeless," Bobby told him. "I intend to pursue whoever is doing this with unholy journalistic fury until I've fully exposed their crimes. That's the opposite of helpless."

"Goodnight, Bobby," the other man said, hanging up the phone.

Bobby pounded on Sarah's door. He looked down and found the note he'd left that morning. It was still there, but no longer folded. Someone had retrieved it, read it, then hastily stuffed it back under the mat. *Had Sarah smashed it up out of frustration? Why put it back?*

Bobby unfolded the note and noticed a series of dirt streaks across the edges of the paper. His mind jumped back to the greasy-haired character who had been lurking around this morning. *Had he come back and read the note?*

Bobby pounded on Sarah's door again, waited a few seconds, and then continued to pound until his fist ached. He cupped his hands against her living room window. A drape was slightly askew, and he could see enough of the kitchen to realize it was completely empty.

Bobby yawned as he forced his tired legs down the alley toward Jewell Street. His shoulders were slumped, eyes heavy. He massaged his elbows absentmindedly. When he reached the end of the alley, he could see Pancho Ernesto Bustos flipping the Open sign on Brest Liquor. It was still dark outside.

If he was going to watch over Sarah's apartment all night, he would need supplies.

For some reason, all the liquor stores in Crown Point and Pacific Beach were inadvertently named with double entendres. Brest Liquor. Dick's Liquor. Liquor Box. Liquor Jugs. *Maybe it's just my imagination?* Bobby thought as he bought a ham and cheese sandwich and six energy drinks.

Once he got home, he went immediately to his closet. Bobby didn't have a lot of possessions, but he had still managed to accrue a large box of junk over the years. He pulled open the box and dug around, casting aside his silver medal to grab his binoculars, a gift from his grandmother on his sixteenth birthday, which had also included home plate tickets to see the Padres. He tossed the binoculars onto the couch, then grabbed two of the energy drinks and the sandwich.

He leaned against the couch, facing Sarah's apartment, his knees on the cushion and his armpits hooked over the back. Yawning, he took his first sip of the energy drink.

26

DETECTIVE THERESE LAPEYRE awoke at six a.m. in a cold sweat. She stripped off her pajamas and stepped into the shower. Her body ached. Even though she hadn't been injured in the pandemonium on the dock, the stress of the situation had bunched up all the nerves in her back. The firecrackers had come from the freeway, a bundle of M80s connected by kite string. About the time Therese was plunging into the ocean, the SDPD had scrambled the first of two police helicopters, both state-of-the-art MD 500 Es with twin-mounted infrared cameras. The cameras found nothing but cold, gray ocean.

Three miles south, at the Sassafras exit in the middle of downtown, a CHP officer on a routine sobriety check had arrested three teenagers with a carload of booze and M80 firecrackers. There had been reports of bricks through windshields and more firecrackers going off, from Harbor Island all the way to El Cajon Boulevard. The kids later confessed that they just wanted to be "part of it." Special Agent Bisbas was fitted for an ankle cast.

Despite claiming he couldn't spare her, Therese's leap into the ocean had convinced Grunden to give her the morning off. She had tried to enjoy it by eating a long breakfast and watching TV from her couch. Unfortunately, the news was one hundred percent about the horoscope predictions, including footage of her spiking her bullet-proof vest onto the dock, with the talking heads selling the teaser, "Another horoscope coming true?"

To avoid reliving the disaster of the previous evening, Therese resorted to watching morning shows full of aged celebrities and perky blonde co-hosts. She made it through an interview with a woman whose cat had saved her from a coyote attack in New Mexico and a recap of the previous night's reality show evictions before the morning show switched to coverage of the horoscope situation "in San Diego, California." A splashy, full-color map appeared on screen just as Therese shut off the TV. She forced herself to her feet and ambled outside to pick up the first *San Diego Register* of her brand-new subscription. The cover story was about a San Diego town hall meeting that had been held at the Scottish Rite Center, a Masonic lodge in Mission Valley. *That's who's responsible for all this*, Therese thought to herself. *It's always the masons, isn't it?*

Therese read the article. Citizens from Ocean Beach, Imperial Beach, Pacific Beach, and Del Mar were badgering local city council representatives, demanding information about the horoscope madness. The secondary headline featured the day's horoscopes. Therese skipped to the Scorpio, knowing it would be her team's detail for the evening shift.

It read: "Times have been tough for you since you paroled from prison. You paid your debt to society, but the system won't let you get back on your feet. Mars is ascendant, and its energies push you to make a rash decision. You will unsuccessfully attempt to rob the Wells Fargo of La Jolla by smashing through a window on the south side of the street."

Therese squinted at the paper. She hadn't believed the dock attack was coming, and it hadn't really come. But this prediction seemed even less likely. It revealed everything but the exact timing of the crime. She suspected that her evening shift would amount to staring at the south wall of the bank, lying flat on her belly on a rooftop. All night. She would dress warmly. Therese had five hours before Grunden expected her at the station. She shrugged into her blue jeans, loaded her handgun, and opened the safe in the closet to retrieve her passport. Consorte had been seen crossing the Otay Mesa border. Therese figured, depending on the traffic, she could reach Mexico by ten a.m.

BOBBY AWOKE TO the sound of car doors closing. He scrambled to his feet so quickly that the world flashed in bright circular lights for a few moments. He put his hand on the wall to regain equilibrium. *How long have I been sleeping?* he wondered.

Through the window, he could see that Sarah was outside, healthy and alive. In the faint glow of dawn, he watched her leaning against the driver's door of her Toyota, a bottle of champagne in her left hand. Her right hand was holding the bicep of the biggest sailor Bobby had ever laid eyes on. It was her husband, Eli. He was still dressed in his desert combat fatigues, right down to the laced-up combat boots.

Eli was much larger than he appeared in the picture on Sarah's desk and almost shockingly handsome. Seeing his size settled Bobby down some. If Sarah was in danger, there were few better to have by her side than a military assassin-in-training who was as big as the parking lot in the old Qualcomm Stadium. Eli put his hands on his hips and glanced up and down the block, his eyes eventually stopping on Bobby's apartment.

Bobby felt like a real champ as he tucked himself out of sight beneath the window frame.

Now seated on the floor, sleep crept up on him again, shaking at his brain with odd and incongruent versions of reality. For a moment, Bobby's father was standing outside, hands on hips. Then the image shifted to his old water polo coach, the first he'd had at Mission Bay High, before his dad determined he wasn't driven enough and had begun rattling the chains of various board members and boosters. Next it was Terry Abbattista, then Leslie Consorte. Bobby groped at the end table, finding the cool round aluminum of an energy drink, and raised it to his lips. When he sneaked another look out the window, the street was empty. He pulled his phone and dialed Leslie again. The hurried hello on the other end was the voice of Detective Therese Lapeyre.

"Lapeyre?"

"What do you want?"

"Leslie's missing, isn't he? Why else would you keep answering his cell phone? It's the Leo prediction. He never made it to work."

"You have a wild imagination and a pleasant disregard for facts, Bobby. It's what makes you a good reporter."

Bobby could hear strange music surrounding Lapeyre. He heard whistles blowing, coupled with voices he couldn't distinguish. For a moment he feared he was falling asleep again. "Is that mariachi music?"

"Yeah, I like to listen to the Mexican channels, the Mighty Six Ninety, mostly."

"You're in Mexico, aren't you?"

"What do you want, Bobby?"

"I want to talk to Leslie. If I can't, I want to talk about Leslie."

"Here's what I'm going to do, Bobby. I'm going to do an old policeman's trick for dealing with reporters. I'm going to tell you the truth, off the record. And if you print even a tiny sliver of said truth, I'm going to arrest you for compromising an investigation." Lapeyre was almost growling when she said it.

"I generally leave the legal issues to Milo Maslow."

"You know they let us carry weapons, right?"

"Where's Leslie? I like him, Lapeyre. If he's in trouble and there's some way I can help—"

Bobby could hear the mariachi music grow louder. Lapeyre must have partially covered her mouthpiece because the sound of her voice became muffled and distant. It sounded like she said, "Estacionamiento! Ayundame, por favor!" The music began to fade away. When Lapeyre returned her attention to Bobby she said, "Leslie disappeared yesterday morning. He slid off the grid on his way to work, just like you said, just like the Leo. We spotted his car driving into Mexico on a border camera. It was impossible to tell if he came here of his own volition or was forced. I'm spending my half day off searching every motel, jail, and bar within twenty miles of the crossing. I've flashed his picture to dozens of bartenders and waitresses in town with no luck. Don't forget that you're not going to print any of this, Bobby. You don't want to."

Bobby thought about Leslie's dramatic behavior at the frat house. He smoothed out a discarded receipt on his coffee table and began taking notes.

"Are you writing this down? You don't want to write this. You want to keep your word to me," Lapeyre said. Bobby got the impression Lapeyre was trying to use some kind of Jedi mind control technique.

"I'll list you as a source who does not want to be identified," Bobby said.

"You want that Lasix test run, Bobby?"

Bobby was silent. Finally, he said, "Yeah. And there's something else I need. The photos the frat kids took of the mysterious nude girl. Did your forensic teams manage to recover them?"

"You want me to open my whole case book to you? A reporter? Seems like the best possible way to lose my job and destroy the investigation."

Bobby knew he needed to decide how much it was worth to publish the story about Leslie. It could cause him to lose these conversations with Lapeyre, permanently. He had been flying by the seat of his pants at this point, but pretty soon he'd have to evolve into a real reporter, or the whole situation would spin right out of his control. That meant making tough decisions. Weighing when to burn bridges and when not to. "If there's anything I can do to help you find Consorte . . ." he said.

"There is. Don't write about it." Lapeyre hung up the phone.

Bobby watched the kitchen window of Sarah's apartment for a few minutes, the phone still held in his left hand. Then he dialed Milo Maslow. Jana answered and put him through to Milo immediately.

"Big Bobby Frindley? Outstanding," Milo said with a sort of sinister warmth. "I know you're new to this so let me tell you how it works. You come to the office. Wait at your desk. When I decide what I want you to write about, I send you out to get it. I know I called you a freelancer when you got the job, but that's only in regard to health benefits. I am the editor. Do you understand what that title means?"

"I'm pursuing a scoop."

"Where the hell are you, Bobby?"

"Did you read the Libra this morning?"

Bobby heard Milo shuffling through papers. Finally, he read aloud, "With today's astral energies, a significant shift will occur in your entire romantic paradigm. Be open to it. Even though you are a seer and can predict futures, this unique skill isn't enough to stop your lover's suicide when she hangs herself in her kitchen."

"I'm a Libra, Milo."

"So's one twelfth of the world's population."

"I'm a *seer*. I predict futures. Horoscopes."

Milo began to laugh, long, pealing cackles, somewhere in a pitch above tenor. "I believe you've crossed over from lucky male ingénue to bush-shaking crazycakes. We've had a good run with this thing, and, yes, it's fun to see how true everything seems when you're looking for it, but it's all a bunch of bullshit, Bobby. Please tell me you know that."

"I think someone's going to kill one of my neighbors. I'm kind of in love with her, and—"

"Are you sitting in your window watching her apartment with binoculars right now?"

Bobby lowered the binoculars, self-consciously. He decided he wouldn't tell Milo about Consorte just yet. Unfortunately, that meant he would have a hard time convincing him of the very real danger. He tried a different tactic. "The girl who had the job before mine is missing. There's another mystery girl, who may or may not be the same one, rolling down the canyon by the college. You told me Stephanie Ambrosia was somewhere in Mexico having a good time, but she's been off her social media. She can't be reached by phone. Whether you want to admit it or not, this thing has landed right in our lap."

Milo sighed, but he grew more serious. "I called my police contact. So far there's been no luck with the frat kids' phones. They're trying a private digital forensics company. In the meantime, I would caution you about assuming the worst for Stephanie. I'm not suggesting these aren't wild times, I'm just worried you're buying a little too much into the horoscope phenomenon. We don't know where Stephanie is, but that's not the same as her being dead."

Bobby gulped down another energy drink. They were keeping him awake, but he felt like an animated corpse.

Milo continued, "You sound like you've been up all night. Let me clarify something. A crime is hiding beneath this big mess, a real, individual, motivated crime, and someone is going to extremely elaborate means to disguise it. I've already got Hawkeye running back through the first predictions. I suspect we'll find our answers hidden somewhere there. Probably something to do with Eidelman and the patent case he was presiding over. Hawkeye insists the suicide reads legitimate, but we're going to keep turning over rocks until—"

Against his better judgment, Bobby said, "They're targeting me personally, Milo."

"Bobby that's . . . unlikely."

"Maybe. Or maybe the person behind all this is bored and they think I'm a worthy opponent? Maybe they've invited me, involuntarily, into their little twisted game." Bobby sounded crazy even to Bobby. He rubbed his temples to try to keep hold of himself.

One of Bobby's neighbors pulled up to the curb in a Toyota Prius. Bobby watched her get out of her car and unlock her front door.

"Hello, Bobby? Are you there? Am I talking to myself?" Milo said.

Milo had been talking. Bobby had picked out just a few of his words, some random turns of phrase.

"Right, I'll do it," Bobby said, half blindly.

"Good, I want the story on my desk by seven p.m."

"Thanks, Milo. Goodbye."

Bobby hung up the phone and continued to watch Sarah's house through the binoculars. He had a view of her front door, her living room window, and her back door, but the view to the kitchen was now partially blocked by the neighbor's car. To see over it, he had to climb to his feet and stand on the couch. Bobby was scratching his head, wondering if Milo was right about his paranoia, when he saw something, just to the left of Sarah's front window. He raised the binoculars to his eyes and saw it again, a shadow faintly moving in the larger shadows of Sarah's landscaping.

At first, he thought it was a reflection, maybe even his own reflection, blinking back at him in the low light of the morning. But he held steady on the spot, not flinching, and he caught the movement a third time. He grabbed his phone first, but he held it without dialing. He looked through the binoculars once more, his view still partially obscured by the neighbor's car. He stood up on the couch again, then up higher, both feet perilously balanced on the seat back. He leaned a forearm on the top of the window for balance.

When his binoculars scanned the street from that higher angle, he caught the inside of Sarah's car, and some small part of his brain registered the camouflaged purse he saw there. His father had been very diligent about not leaving anything in a car. *Don't forget your wallet, don't leave money visible, don't leave loose change visible or better yet, you lazy bum, take it into the house and keep it with your keys. Don't leave the door unlocked, don't leave the keys in the visor!*

Bobby was so intent on investigating the motion outside Sarah's window that all these tiny, unpleasant memories crawled from the small recesses of his brain. He wasn't thinking about the purse, yet he had registered its location in some distant way. So, it was not a complete surprise when Eli, the biggest Navy Seabee in San Diego County history, came out of Sarah's apartment, her keys clutched in his bloated, sausage link hands, on a tiny fateful—perhaps even fatal—honey-do errand.

He took two steps toward her car, intent to retrieve the purse, but then his eyes leveled at Bobby, who was so full of concern that he was standing on the back of the couch, fully visible in the window. Bobby lowered the binoculars and stared back. It was like looking into the face of death itself.

If someone is going to be murdered, Bobby realized, his heart racing, *it's most likely going to be me.*

27

ELI CROSSED THE yard in a little bit less than three seconds. He moved with the grace of a trained killer and with the speed of a very, very angry man, a man who had crossed an ocean and several continents to rectify a serious wrong against his family. Though he had started from a walk, his fists were now pumping like a linebacker closing quickly on Bobby's front door. Bobby had to travel only about six feet to get to the door and throw the bolt, but he still barely made it. Eli was there, staring through the sidelights. His eyes were unblinking.

"I can explain," Bobby shouted through the door. "Everything."

Eli picked up the potted plant beside Bobby's welcome rug. It was the remains of a lily of the valley that Bobby had done a fair job of steadily shrinking since he'd purchased it. The lily plopped to the ground as the ceramic pot shattered against the side window. Eli looked around for something else, his chest rising and falling. He spotted a stepping-stone that the previous tenant had left to provide an unobtrusive way to cross into the back garden. Eli dug his fingers into the dirt and pulled the stone free. He threw it against the side window and this time everything gave simultaneously. The stone shattered, taking the glass with it. Bobby dialed the police. The operator came on the line and Bobby huffed his address into the mouthpiece. He watched Eli reach through the window fragments, groping for the deadbolt.

"What's your emergency?" the woman manning dispatch said in a nasally voice. Bobby swatted at Eli's hands, pushing him away from the lock but also trying not to puncture Eli's arm with the jagged glass. His phone clattered to the ground. Eli disregarded the danger, letting the glass tear into his forearms, drawing blood.

In his periphery, Bobby saw movement in Sarah's front yard. A large shadow. *A person?* He thought of the front door Eli had just left open in his unplanned attack. He thought of Sarah, with that rope around her neck, her vertebrae straining, then snapping.

Bobby swatted Eli's hand away from the lock a second time. His phone was lying on the ground face up. "Send help! Now!" he shouted toward the mouthpiece.

Then he raced for the garage door.

He reached the garage and pushed the button to open it. The door creaked and whined, moving upward so slowly Bobby could hardly believe it. When the gap was no more than sixteen inches, Bobby rolled under and was on his feet in a single motion. He raced toward Sarah's house, his own fists pumping. Eli caught up to him in the middle of the street.

The impact of Eli's body sent both men sprawling, and the inertia carried them apart again. Eli must have twisted an ankle, because when he came back up to his feet his stance was irregular, with more pressure placed forward on his left foot than his right. Bobby was back on his feet just as quickly. He feinted left and then sprinted right, dodging just outside of Eli's swiping hands.

Eli caught Bobby again on Sarah's front lawn and threw him to the ground without actually releasing his hold on Bobby's left bicep. Bobby didn't have time to marvel at how fast Eli was. In water, Bobby would have had a significant advantage, but on land Eli was the dominant species.

"I can explain," Bobby said again as Eli lifted him in the air and threw him onto the grass, shaking all the breath out of Bobby's lungs. Bobby tried to jump to his feet a third time, but Eli moved too quickly, punching him hard across the face and forcing Bobby to one knee. Bobby rolled away from Eli's kick, but it still caught him a glancing blow on the shoulder. Eli's combat boots were steel tipped and heavy, and they sent vibrations down Bobby's arm. He didn't think he could raise the arm to defend himself, so he rolled with the next kick, planting his good hand, and taking two thumping steps from a half crouch.

Head down, he leaped off-balance toward Sarah's back fence. He hit the fence, and it gave a little, bowing backward, but it didn't fold like Bobby hoped. Instead, it popped him backward, right into Eli's grasp.

Eli grabbed him by both shoulders and lifted him off the ground. From Eli's perspective, his manic desire to get into Sarah's apartment must have been the final straw on his sick, trespassive behavior. Eli had to be thinking that this boy wasn't going to learn to leave his wife alone any other way than with a severe beating. He had screwed her and now, in the clear light of day, was trying to force his way into her apartment. Eli shook Bobby savagely. "Sarah's in danger," Bobby stammered. "Someone's trying to kill her."

Eli threw Bobby to the ground and spat. Bobby climbed back to his feet, and Eli advanced on him again, swinging a wild haymaker. Bobby blocked it with his forearms. He dropped low and kicked Eli hard in the knee. Eli buckled to the ground.

Bobby let him stand up.

Eli grabbed his knee and massaged it for a moment. He rolled his head and shoulders and for the first time, spoke. His voice was deep, his tone balanced. "I traveled seven thousand, nine hundred and eleven miles for this opportunity. I counted each mile as a way to keep my head together, a way to not completely lose my shit and start crying or break up the inside of the plane. I was counting miles and singing that old boot camp song, 'Ain't no use in callin' home, Bobby's got your telephone. Ain't no use in lookin' back, Bobby's got your Cadillac.' And you know what? Despite that, when I saw Sarah, I completely forgot about you. I didn't need to get straight to it, to race over to your place and sort you out. Instead, I had a perfect morning with my beautiful wife. Then I come out here and see you spying on us, you sick sonuvabitch."

"I was trying to protect her. I wanted to make sure she was safe. There's a killer on the loo—"

Before Bobby could finish completely saying the word *loose*, Eli stepped forward and swung a huge fist at his head. Bobby ducked the blow and punched Eli in the nose. A little-known fact about swimmers is that they can punch like a kicking donkey. Butterflyers and freestylers, and Bobby was both, develop the same bundles of shoulder and arm muscles as professional boxers—heavy, knotty posterior deltoids, medial deltoids, and trapezii. It was probably the strongest punch Eli had ever received and he took it square in the face. He was wobbly, knees like a jib rope, eyes blinking. Bobby cocked his fist again. He had to get into that kitchen even if it meant going through Eli. He stepped forward to hit Eli one more time, high on the crown of his head, but he had a moment of guilt, just a tiny millisecond slowing his swing. Eli hit him instead, square between the eyes.

Bobby's brain bounced off the back of his skull and he fell, stars exploding in the skies around him. He tried to put his good arm down to steady himself, but it slipped, not on the grass or mud, but in his mind; he couldn't find the motor skills to operate this last good limb. Eli stepped forward and clubbed him, hard. Bobby's head bounced into the waiting embrace of the grass. "I-I-I'm sorry," Bobby said.

His mouth wasn't working quite right. Eli was standing right beside him, looking down into his face. "I love her, but—I didn't—have— any ..." Bobby's words trailed off. The rest of the sentence continued to tumble out, bouncing off his bottom lip, but it was gibberish.

Eli stood above Bobby, his hands on his hips. "I appreciate the apology," he said. And then Bobby slipped off into darkness.

28

LYING ALONE ON the grass, consciousness returning, Bobby hears a soft sound from the inside of Sarah's apartment. It's a thumping sound, maybe just Sarah closing a kitchen cabinet with a little enthusiasm, or maybe something much, much worse. Urgency and fear begin to flow back into his addled brain. Somewhere, the neuron receptors that had been kicked into a numb fog start to reboot. Fresh electricity flows between synapses. His brain had shut down to protect itself, but some tiny strand of his conscious mind is still firing, still ticking away with the strong desire to protect Sarah. His eyes flutter open, and he drags a heavy knee under his body.

He follows it with an elbow, and then a second elbow. Now he only needs to push against the grass, raise himself up, follow that motion with an upward driving of the chest. Concentrate on each body part, will it toward the blue sky. He is on his knees now, both palms planted downward on the grass. *Use them. Push yourself up one more tier.* The knee lifts, finding steady purchase for the foot, and then the other knee. He is standing now, staggering toward the door. Something good is happening to him. Instead of growing weary from each step, instead of draining the last of his strength, the motion is making him stronger. He's made it to the doorknob, fighting the impulse to hang from it, to let it catch his weight. Two more steps and he's through the door.

The apartment is small. The kitchen is just ahead.

Sarah is hanging from the ceiling fan; her hands are not bound, but the noose is tight and she's clawing at it with her nails. Eli is beneath her, holding her legs, trying desperately to keep her up, relieve the pressure on her spinal column. Another huge man is beside Eli dressed in all black. Black sweatpants, black shoes, a black hoodie pulled high over a thick, black ski mask. The man is striking Eli in fluid jabs. He is moving like a pugilist, someone trained in martial combat. Eli can do little to stop the attack. His arms and his concentration are dedicated to supporting Sarah, but he's growing weaker with each strike.

The man has his back to Bobby, who struggles to the kitchen table. Bobby looks for something to give him kinetic advantage, an object sharp enough to stab deep into the intruder. Finding nothing, he simply shouts, the words falling out of his mouth in something more like a fierce moan.

The man in black responds. He turns to face Bobby, his masked head doubly terrifying from this perspective. Eli takes the opportunity. He releases Sarah for a moment, and she gags mightily, scratching at the rope and her own neck and chin. Eli makes a single concentrated swing, hammering his fist into the top of the intruder's head, then he quickly grabs Sarah's legs again. The man falls to his knees, his hood knocked back onto his shoulders. But the hit hasn't done the job. He lurches back to his feet and begins to pummel Eli again. Eli is making pained sounds with each punch, desperate, noisy animal sounds.

Bobby tries to move forward, work his way around the kitchen counter separating him from the conflict, but his legs are getting tied up with each other. He sees something. At the back of the man's head, right at the bottom of the ski mask, it's a telltale lock of wavy brown hair. He's seen that hair before, somewhere.

In the backyard of Terry Abbattista's house.

"Charles," Bobby barks, his voice made hoarse from pain.

The ski-masked man turns again to look at him. Through the mask Bobby sees his eyes narrow with something like anger, or perhaps panic. Eli takes the second opportunity and makes the most of it.

He pushes Sarah up high enough that she's sitting, balanced on his broad right shoulder, and he swings a powerful arcing punch right where the man's ear must be. The impact sends him sprawling to the floor.

Bobby can only watch as Charles claws his way to his feet and stumbles out the back door, past the back window and down around the corner, heading west.

WHEN BOBBY WOKE up a second time, he was staring at the bushy eyebrows of a middle-aged paramedic. Bobby tried to speak, but his words were muffled. He was wearing an oxygen mask. He shuffled the mask off his face and said, "Sarah, is she all right?"

A second paramedic, a woman in her late twenties with tired eyes, walked over to his gurney.

"He's talking about the girl."

The first paramedic looked down at Bobby, his eyes as fatigued as his partner's. "She'll live," he said. "The other unit took her to the hospital already. The big guy rode in the ambulance with her. We're taking you to Scripps Green because Point Loma's booked and you're not the same level of emergency."

"You're not taking me anywhere," Bobby said, rolling over on-to his knees. He swung his legs off the side of the gurney. His ribs throbbed and he had a hollow sting in his throat, but his brain seemed to have sorted itself back together. Bobby hopped lightly to his feet and took a few steps on tentative legs.

"You gotta sign a few forms if you're refusing treatment. You're concussed and you've probably broken a few ribs."

Bobby waved over his shoulder and stumbled up his porch. His feet crunched the broken glass as he moved through the door into his apartment.

The first place he looked was the mirror hanging in the hallway. He peeled off his muddy shirt and examined the damage. There were lacerations on both his elbows, on his cheek, a deep bruise on his chin, and his knees were skinned and starting to scab. When he lifted his arms to examine his stomach and back, pain screamed through his ribs. He touched the side of his head gingerly, then walked to the medicine cabinet and took a handful of Advil.

He knew that if a major organ was going to fail, it would be his kidneys. Bobby used to take three Advil before any important water polo game. It would act as a blood thinner, carrying oxygen more quickly to his muscles in a sport so anaerobic that every bit of extra oxygen helped. It was, essentially, over-the-counter blood doping, and he didn't know a high-level athlete who didn't do it. He leaned against the kitchen sink and waited, seeing what effect the medicine would have. Finally, Bobby tentatively made his way back to the living room, scooped his phone off the floor, and popped open another energy drink.

He couldn't believe the police had never arrived.

29

THERESE WAS TIRED from her long day in Mexico, struggling back and forth across the border, dealing with reckless bartenders and desperate merchants, combative, greedy police, and combative, snarky federal soldiers. Mexico was a true land of the free; people were free to suffer or succeed based on their own unique circumstances. There were limited protocols, fewer safeguards, and absolutely no reason for anyone to do any favors for an American police officer. She'd learned zilch about the disappearance of Leslie Consorte.

Lying on the rooftop of the La Jolla Dry Cleaners, a pair of binoculars in her hands, Therese had to fight sleep, her eyes partially closing, little shakes of her head doing nothing to stem the tide of fatigue. She got a small jolt of energy when she realized Leslie's phone was vibrating in her pocket, but the LED screen told her it was Bobby Frindley, and she ignored the call. If that prick was thinking about printing off-the-record information, he could find himself another source. Also lying on the roof was none other than FBI Special Agent Randy Michaels. In the two days they had been working together, Therese was starting to deride Michaels less—

something she had been doing instinctually because Michaels was way up the chain of hierarchy.

They were obviously on a dead-end assignment. The horoscope killer was not going to walk directly into a trap he himself had created. Half the Scorpio team, an SDPD Lieutenant by the name of Sanders, and two federal agents, Branch and Mulgrew, were in the Rubio's across the street eating fish tacos. They were technically triangulating the bank, but what they were really doing was drinking Coronas and swapping stories.

The other half of the team was in position at two separate points: SDPD beat cops Buchanan, Lloyd, and Havermeyer were browsing in a boutique art gallery, probably bitching that they didn't pull the Rubio's detail; and another FBI man, Hendrickson, was dressed as a beach bum.

They didn't technically have homeless in La Jolla. Those who wandered into 92037 were escorted back out by cops like Buchanan, Lloyd, and Havermeyer. But they did get the occasional lifetime surfers, who'd bought homes in the poorest section of La Jolla, called Bird Rock, back in the seventies before the houses shot up to six- and seven-digit values.

Hendrickson had spent the day burning up in a local tanning salon, and he had assembled a reasonable approximation of the right look: corduroy shorts, bracelets, Hawaiian shirt unbuttoned down to a bulging, leathery belly.

But for all his chameleon work, Hendrickson was slouched on the bus stop bench across the street, looking like he'd rather be anywhere else. It was only Randy Michaels who remained steadily fixated on the rear window of the La Jolla Wells Fargo, one hand on his federally issued binoculars, 15x75s with nice Nikon glass, and the other on his 9mm revolver.

"There's really no timetable for this, is there?" Therese asked Michaels.

"Seems the timeline for each set of new horoscopes is a twenty-four hour window between 2200 and 2200, starting the night the prediction was received. It's a little after 1800, so we've got four more hours. I want to rotate the rest of the squad in fifteen. They look listless down there."

Therese squinted down at Hendrickson, who was yawning. The bus pulled up to the stop, idled for a few minutes, and then rumbled away. "They're not listless. They're agitated. They want to be near the action and that action isn't here. You think this whole thing will be over after twelve days? You know since there's twelve horoscopes?"

"I think it's all a scam," Michaels said. "And, it's pretty clever."

"What do you mean?"

"Even with national help, the police force is stretched so thin you haven't done any real proactive investigation. How could you when we're reacting to everything?"

Therese considered what he was saying. "Nobody is even near a crime; we're just camping out on rooftops watching and waiting."

"Is that what sent you diving into the ocean last night? All the waiting?" Michaels chided.

"How'd you like my dive? Was it graceful?" Therese tried hard to stifle a wearied yawn, but it crept out through her folded hand.

"A criminal gets this ball rolling, and they can do pretty much anything they want because the law is too busy and too exhausted to stop them. Not to mention the genius grift at the center: an enticing foundation of mystical . . ." It was Michaels' turn to yawn, "mumbo jumbo." He paused, his eyes scanning the street.

"Mumbo jumbo?"

"Tell me you don't believe in astrology."

"Before all this? I really, really did not," Therese told him. "Lately, I haven't been so sure." She was quiet, thinking about his words. She started to put it together, talking through her thoughts. "But I see what you're saying about the grift. We've got four good leads and ten thousand weak leads. We've got an entire room at police headquarters dedicated just to forensic evidence: endless bags of fiber samples, tissue samples, tiger hair. We still don't have a dental match on the guy dragged to death up in Clairemont. The whole system is strained to the breaking point. Even our phone operators are fatigued. The tip line doesn't stop ringing, not in the morning, not at night, and it's impossible to tell real from fake. I suspect every one of the eight-million-plus of San Diego, San Bernardino, and Riverside counties has a theory on what the hell is going on. And I bet they're all wildly imaginative and totally incorrect. I guess I've always appreciated the tremendous power of lying," she added, "but never something on a scale like this."

Neither of them took the binoculars from their eyes. Therese had worked so many years as a beat cop, and now she was on a roof, passing around ideas with a high-profile federal agent. People were listening to her and doing what she said. She was literally in the seat of power, elevated, armed, and swapping theories with a man who seemed to be taking her seriously. It felt good to be up there, and fatigued or not, she determined not to lose concentration, even so far away from the action.

"I'd give the dive a six, three for form, nine for improvisation," Michaels said.

Therese started to laugh, but then she glimpsed movement on the bus stop bench. It was Hendrickson, patting the back of his head, casually, one of Team Scorpio's nonverbal cues. "Take a look at Hendrickson," Therese said.

Michaels leaned to the right and gazed down at the bus stop.

Therese had to inch backward to give him a direct line of sight. "Is he still doing it?"

"Yeah. Patting the head means look north." Michaels turned his magnified gaze to the north down Girard Avenue. Therese couldn't see anything out of the ordinary, but she pushed the squawk button on her walkie-talkie three times in a staccato sequence. It told the others to look toward position three. She saw the excited faces of Mulgrew and Branch appear at the window of Rubio's Fish Tacos, glancing in Hendrickson's direction. They, too, recognized the head patting and turned their gazes north.

"You see anything?" Therese asked.

"Not yet," Michaels said. "Wait, look now, just left of the electrical box."

Therese looked. A man was walking unsteadily toward the bank, curly brown hair greased back from an unshaven face. Despite the relative heat of the early evening coastal air, he was clad in a long gray trench coat, his hands shoved deep into his pockets.

It must have been his eyes that had caught Hendrickson's attention; they were unfocused and wild. No, unfocused was the wrong word. They were, in fact, intensely focused, but cloudy from anxiety, or some type of manic fervor. His clothes weren't quite dirty enough to be homeless.

"Something's wrong with that guy," Therese whispered.

As the man got closer to the bank, his eyes darted in every direction. He sat down on a short wall beside a recycling bin, then he stood up again and started to cross the street away from the bank. His strides evened out. He pushed his dirty, wavy hair back from his eyes and he looked directly into the reflective glass.

Therese saw his features clearly and it was no less shocking than if someone had slapped her in the face. It was Jack Madrigal. The thick eyebrows. The unusually high, almost gaunt cheekbones. His hair was lightened to a dirty brown, but still in the tumultuous waves he'd had in his original mug shot, and his face was unmistakable. Madrigal was here, at the exact spot the paper had predicted he'd be. Madrigal was the horoscope killer. Therese whipped her walkie-talkie up to her mouth. "That's Jack Madrigal. Grab him. Grab him."

Hendrickson made a small circular motion with his right index finger and Buchanan, Lloyd, and Havermeyer shuffled out of the art gallery, one at a time, each moving toward the bank via a different, but no less direct route. When Madrigal reached the south window, the window the horoscope had predicted someone would break, he glanced around feverishly.

His eyes moved passed Hendrickson, slid right over Lloyd, who had taken the center route, and fell right on Havermeyer, who had her right hand shoved deep in her pocket, an art brochure still clutched in her left.

"Stay back," he yelled at her.

Michaels yanked his handgun out of its holster and then rolled to his right, swinging his legs over the side of the rooftop and then dropping down onto the top of a dumpster. Therese heard him land with a solid *clang*. She stayed in position, working the binoculars and the walkie-talkie to give the whole team an eye in the sky. She watched Michaels close in on Madrigal from north to south, crossing down Girard Avenue and then coming back up the same path Madrigal had traveled moments before.

Havermeyer and Lloyd both stopped in their tracks. Havermeyer raised both her hands, letting the brochure drop and flutter to the ground. She didn't say anything, she just stared at Madrigal with a blank expression.

Buchanan and Michaels reached the man simultaneously, both from his blind side. They grabbed his arms and pinned them behind his back, Michaels pulling the handcuffs free from his own belt.

"Mulgrew, Branch, hold your positions," Therese ordered into the walkie-talkie, "this could be a trick to draw us out."

Therese watched as Mulgrew and Branch disappeared back into Rubio's. Even Hendrickson peeled off and walked straight into a small craft boutique that was in the process of closing up for the night.

Michaels had had one of Madrigal's wrists cuffed, but as he and Buchanan pushed and pulled on the other wrist, Madrigal unexpectedly popped free from both their grasps. Lloyd dove for his feet, but he sidestepped and reached a hand into his pocket.

"Gun," Therese yelled, as much into the walkie-talkie as into the street below. Hendrickson reappeared on the street. Michaels raised his own gun at the brown-haired man, yelling, "Hold it! Hands in the air!"

Madrigal drew his hand out of his jacket, but he didn't have a gun. He was holding a small silver cell phone. "I'm working with the police," he screamed.

"Don't shoot. It's a cell phone," Therese growled into the walkie-talkie. Madrigal raised his phone slightly and Michaels fired in the air. Madrigal shuddered and he took a step backward and then spun slowly in a semicircle before sitting hard on the ground.

Therese rolled to the edge of the roof and dropped down onto the dumpster, drawing her own gun and moving quickly toward the bank.

30

BOBBY FRINDLEY KNEW the identity of the horoscope killer. More precisely, he knew the man who was behind it all. He doubted Terry Abbattista had ever bloodied a single fingernail in all this, but he had certainly coordinated Timur, Charles, Rife, and who knows how many others in the various crimes that had plagued the city. He was bored, power-hungry, and quite certainly sociopathic. He had the manpower, the resources, and the intelligence to orchestrate the whole thing. They had juiced the tiger and dropped the drugged and naked girl on the Theta Rho Kappa doorstep, hell, maybe even picked her up afterward at the bottom of the hillside. They'd dragged a man behind a truck in Clairemont. *How long had Abbattista been planning this, his most elaborate game? What was his motive? Was there still a quarter million dollars hidden in Presidio Park?* Despite his certainty, not everything stacked up in Bobby's new, neat version of reality. *Was the girl Stephanie Ambrosino? If not, where was Stephanie? Where was Leslie Consorte?*

Bobby was lying on the couch, concussed, an energy drink in one hand, the binoculars laid carelessly across his chest, Star's Kepler book in his other hand. He'd tried to read, opening to a random page, but his mind was raw. Kepler was working as the court astrologer in Linz, Germany. His false astrological predictions had backfired, enraging Count Pappenheim. Printing press in flames, he fled to Regensburg and fell ill, his body racked by fever.

The German doctors had bled him, latching leeches to his forearms and thighs. "I get you, Johann," Bobby mumbled. "I'm right there with you."

The Advil were working to a point. Rather than piercing pain from his various injuries, he felt a deep, dull throbbing. He knew he couldn't face Abbattista by himself. Charles would have reported back exactly what had happened, and Abbattista would have his little psychotic army rallied around him, waiting for Bobby's arrival.

Heck, Bobby thought wryly, Abbattista had planned everything up to this point—he'd stayed one step ahead of everybody by anticipating each move before it happened. It was a different and far more effective type of predicting the future. There was no reason not to believe that Bobby wouldn't be walking directly into a well-orchestrated trap.

No, he couldn't face Abbattista head on by himself, so he waited on the couch, as patiently as his tired body and frayed nerves would allow.

Bobby had slipped into a place between waking and sleeping when the knock finally came on his broken front door. His body had simply begun to shut down, overriding the various chemicals he'd forced into it. But the knock sent him back to the forefront of consciousness. He rolled to his feet and jerked the door open. On his darkened porch, eyes burning beneath a sheen of sweat and a military style crew cut, was Sarah's husband, Eli.

"How is she?" Bobby asked.

"She's alive. The ER doctor said two of her vertebrae were stretched. He said it probably happened when she was initially hung and not . . ." Eli stopped talking to swallow. He was doing his best to not let his voice shake. "And not when I let her go to fight off the intruder."

"You saved her life."

Eli said nothing. He looked at Bobby with intensity in his glistening eyes.

"Is the damage permanent?" Bobby asked.

"They wouldn't tell me. They said they had to wait for the swelling to go down to run tests."

Bobby had been keeping himself under control for the past few hours, but when Eli said these words, his hands began to tremble.

"You know who did this, don't you?" Eli said.

Bobby nodded and stepped aside so Eli could come in. Eli was so large that the two men immediately filled the small living room. His arms were twisted knots of tense muscles and bulging veins. If he didn't have a serious steroid habit, and Bobby wasn't sure if that was possible being stationed overseas, then he had a freakishly powerful natural structure.

Bobby's choice of adulterous sexual partners had been impressively poor.

"I shouldn't have attacked you. If I'd known what you were trying to do . . ." Eli said, trailing off, his big hands spread in an expression of frustration and sadness.

"I earned the ass kicking, and I meant it when I said I was sorry."

"We're close to square. You want to be square? You want me to forgive you?"

"I do."

"The man in the kitchen—Charles?"

Bobby put his hands on his hips. "I know him. I know where to find him. But it's not the right move. He works for a very powerful man with a lot of resources. And I'm not even totally sure it was him. He was masked and I had been hit pretty hard. My vision was moving in and out of focus." Bobby had been replaying the fight in his mind again and again. Each time, "Charles" looked a little bit different. "We need to figure out what exactly is going on and start putting together a plan—"

"I've been sitting in the hospital for three hours. I have a plan already," Eli said.

"I want revenge too, just like you."

"Where?"

Bobby was getting frustrated. "What do you mean?"

"Where's Charles? Who does he work for?"

"I'm not telling you."

Eli rubbed his hands together. The huge muscles in his shoulders were starting to contract and roll.

Bobby's head began to pulse. There was a rubbing, scratching feeling behind his ears as the increased blood flow tried to drive its way through the damaged veins. He knew, fundamentally, that he shouldn't take another hit to the head. "I'm not telling you until you promise to proceed with caution," Bobby said again.

Suddenly, Eli's shoulders sagged. He sat on the couch. "I feel helpless. I couldn't protect her from you and your dick—" he trailed off, then he started again. "I know what's been going on out here. Even in the desert we keep an eye on local news, especially those of us who worry constantly about our wives. Did you ever think about how these horoscopes work? Wouldn't the person behind all this want to make sure they finished the job?"

"You think Sarah might still be in danger? Why did you leave her hospital room?"

Eli didn't say anything. He just looked at Bobby. They stared at each other, the crumpled Olympian and the sad Hercules. Finally, Eli said, "My goal is to be a Navy SEAL. That's advanced recon. I've got gear. I've been through the training. You take me to this man's house, and we'll wait and watch. He sends anybody out to get Sarah, and we'll intercept. It'll be passive aggression. Reactive. While we're there, you can tell me the whole story. I'll recon the area, and we'll figure out the smartest way to proceed."

"You're making sense now."

"And we're square. The second we get to the house, we're square. I swear we are."

"You have recon gear?"

"Right across the street. In the garage of my apartment."

"Let's go get it."

31

AN HOUR PREVIOUS, Jack Madrigal had sat in a small interrogation cell deep in the bowels of the San Diego Police Department's headquarters. He had been surrounded by three officers: Police Chief Robert Grunden, FBI Special Agent Randy Michaels, and recently promoted beat cop, Detective Therese Lapeyre. While Michaels prowled theatrically around the interrogation room, Therese had stood in the corner feeling something akin to vertigo. Three days before, she had been handing out speeding tickets and lecturing prostitutes on El Cajon Boulevard. One day ago, a teenage prank had plunged her into the pitch of the wine-dark sea and onto the cover of the *San Diego Register*. Today, she'd ID'd the biggest collar in the history of the San Diego Police Department: Jack Madrigal, the horoscope killer.

All three detectives stood in the room with Madrigal, who was weeping and shaking his head. "I have a daughter," he insisted. "You can't take me away from her again. She's been in foster care. I will do anything to stay close to her. That's what got me into this mess in the first place."

"You'll have to explain that, Jack," Michaels said.

"I just wanted to have enough money to support my daughter. To give her the life she deserves. It's impossible to get real work if you're a convict. Especially one with my story."

"You're an angel. Pure as freshly fallen snow. Why did you say you were working with us?"

"Where is Leslie Consorte?" Grunden cut in. "What did you do to him?"

"I swear I don't know. I-I-I . . . did you say Leslie Consorte?" A fearsome change came over Madrigal. A sense of purpose seemed to pour into his chemically abused body.

"We know you've had a beef with him in the past. You broke into his house, threatened to harm his wife."

"Me—to him?" Madrigal shook his head like a mangy dog. "He's the one who forced me to be there. He's been hounding me since my parole." Madrigal tried to stand up, but his wrist was cuffed to the table. The sound of metal on metal rung through the small interrogation room. "He does this to a lot of different guys," Madrigal insisted. "If we don't play ball, if we don't do exactly what he says, he busts us with some trumped-up charge. Possession of a firearm. Drug paraphernalia. Nobody takes our word over the word of a cop. He's the one who told me I had to be on Girard Street. He forced me to be there. He honestly did."

Grunden stepped in front of Michaels, either out of true anger, or to shut Madrigal up for implicating one of his own detectives. "Don't give us any of that crap, Madrigal. I've read your jacket. Consorte's the one who dragged you down to San Diego Central Court fifteen years ago. Why weren't you telling this story back then? Bet you're just thinking this is a good chance to squeeze him back a little."

"That's not true. Ask Rueben Estevan. Rueben was in the clink with me too. He's just got out and Consorte was all over him. Ask Lenny Garfinkle."

"I put Garfinkle in prison," Grunden said, "and I was at his parole board hearing. If they had listened to me, he'd still be behind bars."

"But Garfinkle's recently paroled?" Michaels asked.

"It doesn't mean anything," Grunden said.

"We've got your cell phone," Therese addressed Madrigal. "Are we going to find calls from Consorte?"

Madrigal was silent, looking down at his own shoes. There was an off-center vibe to Jack Madrigal. His face was rock-like, even when pleading. His voice flat, his eyes almost dead, Madrigal said, "Maybe? But I know he uses a disposable phone."

"Convenient," Therese said, incredulous.

"What is it, Thursday? He came to my house last Monday, said I had to help him out with something—do him a favor. But he was acting strange. He pulled his gun, and he started shouting. He threatened my daughter," Madrigal went on. "And then he promised me money. I was like, 'is this a shakedown or a job,' and Consorte said, 'Both!'"

"You don't have a daughter, Jack. At least, she's not in your file," Therese pointed out.

"He's the guy, isn't he? He's the guy you're after, Consorte is. He's the horoscope killer. He's got an army of violent ex-cons that he forces to do all this illegal shit," Madrigal said.

Could this be possible? Therese started to think of all the times Consorte had been out of her sight during the last seventy-two hours. All the times he'd stepped aside to make a phone call . . .

"Let me check out Madrigal's house," Therese said. "I'll get us some real answers to balance out the nonsense Maddy here is feeding us."

Michaels turned to Therese. "What's the history on this idiot?" he asked.

"I wasn't around the last time they got him, but his file says he's a chronic liar and an attention seeker. The shrinks had a field day sticking labels all over him: Psychopath. Exhibitionist. Narcissist. Likes to be right in the center of big things. He tried to burn down a library. Went after Consorte's wife in Consorte's home," Therese explained.

"None of that is true!" Madrigal said firmly. "None of it. It's Consorte. It always has been, even back then. He wanted a divorce, so he paid me to rough up his wife. Now he's put me up to this horoscope thing. I can show you the money he gave me. A stack of bills this thick." Madrigal held his pointer finger and thumb two inches apart.

"The last time this dumbass was free from jail he was sending messages to the police, and the papers, made from magazine cutouts," Grunden said.

"He's watched a few too many movies, but I'm not sure he's our guy," Michaels said. "He doesn't seem smart enough."

"That's right. I'm not your guy. I'm not."

"Let's look where he lives. No sense in making decisions before we do some information gathering," Therese said.

Madrigal told them his current address. "It's not a secret. I registered there as part of my parole. You could have got me anytime. If I was better at hiding, Consorte would never have found me."

Michaels jotted down the address and flipped the card to Therese. "I'll arrange the warrant. You take the SIDs guys and get a good look."

———

FORTY MINUTES LATER, Therese was riding shotgun in a police van headed south on the 5 Freeway to Imperial Beach. The folks who had named Imperial Beach had had stars in their eyes. Therese watched with indifference as they passed crumbling homes with dirty, unwatered lawns full of unidentifiable wreckage, windows missing windowpanes, cars on blocks.

The farther south you moved in San Diego, the worse you began to feel about the capitalist system. It wasn't an eclectic city like Los Angeles where you could move from areas of affluence to areas of poverty in a blink of an eye. No, San Diego moved north to south like Dante. Therese was riding the spiral and was numbly thankful they would be stopping before they reached the poorest of the poor in North Tijuana.

Madrigal lived on the bottom floor of a tiny triplex that was simultaneously overpainted and underpainted. Heavy layers of thick latex were chipped away from the window frames and peeled in large continent-shaped blotches from the tiny one-car garage doors.

Therese could tell that Madrigal had sealed his garage door shut, which wasn't entirely uncommon in this area. Most of Imperial Beach considered square footage too rare to be wasted on something like a car. Therese knew once they got inside, she would find a mattress in the garage, probably a television, perhaps even a portable stovetop and a makeshift toilet.

The forensics team was right behind her, photographing everything and dusting for prints on every inch of the porch. For the last few years, Therese had a vision of what being a detective was going to be like. She imagined her and her partner pounding on doors, tricking witnesses into revealing their secrets. She'd felt a little of that the first night in Clairemont when Leslie had shaken down the old drunk on her porch. But as Therese waited for the SIDs team to dust, photograph, and slide cotton swabs across the doorknob, she started to understand her true role. She was a chaperone. A thug hired to make sure the lab guys' horn-rimmed glasses didn't get punched in. They, in turn, were the brains, the fact finders, the great detectives.

When they finished with the doorknob and gave her the all clear, Therese kicked the door open and stepped carefully inside, gun drawn. The inside looked like the outside: an overturned coffee table, trash strewn across the floor, beer cans and a bong alongside a television remote on the threadbare sofa. Therese lowered her gun slightly. This wasn't the house of a man who could turn a city on its ear. He probably couldn't remember to take the trash out on Tuesdays. Therese thought of Madrigal's original crime. He'd sent threats to the PD and the *Register*, promising all sorts of spectacular chaos, but he'd been barely able to singe a library.

Therese swept forward, a phalanx of nerds marching behind her. She cleared the kitchen, finding nothing more dangerous than bacteria and tetanus. Madrigal's bedroom was a study in despair. There were piss stains on the bare mattress. Therese found a broken frame with Madrigal hugging a young blonde girl who looked to be about six. Madrigal himself was quite a bit younger in the picture, clean shaven with bright, mischievous eyes.

Flashbulbs moved in behind Therese and she pressed forward, down the dilapidated hallway. The bathroom was dirty with mold and more human waste. A small storage space broke the line between bathroom and garage. Therese looked at the weather-beaten and yellowed boxes stacked high around the garage door. She carefully pulled open the door with a gloved hand and poked her gun out into the darkness. Her left hand groped for the light switch, but flipping it produced nothing—so Therese yanked a small utility flashlight free from her belt. She followed it and the barrel of her pistol through the doorway.

Madrigal had not converted his garage into a living space. Instead of the dirty couch and cast-off TV Therese was expecting to find, the floor of the garage was empty—though far from clean. Therese ran her flashlight along the walls, illuminating exposed power wires and beautiful gobs of spiderweb. Her foot crunched on broken cardboard boxes of the same age and color as the ones stacked outside the door. She had run her light nearly around the entirety of the small, square room when it happened to illuminate a small puddle in the far northeastern corner. At first it seemed like oil—thick, dark, and smeared carelessly across the rough concrete. But some small trigger in her mind brought the light back to the puddle and she saw it incarnadine.

She took a step toward the smear of blood, her gun raised high again, her eyes alert, flashlight bobbing in quick sweeping motions. She was full of both dread and a terrible thrill that had her heart beating hard in her chest. She listened as a new drop of blood struck the ground with a dreadful *plop*.

Therese raised her flashlight upward toward the small wooden rafters. There was something up there, balanced on rotting two-by-fours. It was human sized and shaped, clumsily wrapped in dirty plastic. Through the plastic, Therese could see the object inside was pale pink and naked. Only tresses of blond hair broke up that bundled flesh. Just blond hair, pale pink skin, and zigzagging rivulets of dark red blood.

32

ON THE RIDE up Mount Soledad, Eli disassembled and cleaned and reassembled a set of Bushnell night gear optics, a police-issue Taser, a collapsible baton, and a P266 semiautomatic. He had everything in a black canvas bag, packed in against combat fatigue paint, two black ski masks, and a wicked bone-handled knife. When Bobby saw the gun, he waited until Eli had finished cleaning it, then he pulled the car up to the side of the road.

"No guns," he said.

"It's just part of the pack. I didn't bring it to use. You can hold on to it."

Bobby felt a rush of adrenaline as he tucked the weapon under the driver's seat.

Eli asked Bobby every conceivable question about Terry Abbattista and Bobby recounted each of the times he'd spent with him. He described every conversation, in person and by phone. Before they'd left, Eli had even asked Bobby to draw a rough sketch of what he could remember about Abbattista's triangular home.

When they reached the top of the hill, passing the cell phone towers and rounding onto Abbattista's street, they drove right into an extravaganza. Abbattista's house was lit up like a Roman candle—whatever the hell that was. Cars lined the street, a barrage of Tesla, Porsche, Mercedes, Audi, Maserati, and BMW. Eli pulled Sarah's humble Toyota Camry into one of the last spots available on the street, wedged between a genuine military-grade Humvee and a Land Rover Defender.

Both men looked toward the house.

Couples walked together along the sidewalk, illuminated by candles in thin, but ornate, paper lanterns. Bobby realized that each lantern represented a sign of the zodiac.

The guests themselves were dressed thematically as well. Bobby saw a fish walking to the party holding hands with a bull. He saw a man with ram's horns sticking up from his wavy gray hair. He walked beside a woman in her early twenties, dressed as the blind scales of justice. She had a black headband pulled over one eye, a set of chrome scales in her left hand, and her body was wrapped in a fashionably cut gray toga, Pilates-refined belly exposed to the night air.

"I hate the rich," Eli growled.

"It's a horoscope party," Bobby said. "Terry told me he was planning this. It's in celebration of being mentioned in my newspaper article. The entrance to the house is there." Bobby pointed to the front gate, which was glittering with the afterglow of a five-by-four-foot mirrored zodiac symbol. "We can't go anywhere close now. Not only are there two hundred witnesses with two hundred cell phone cameras..." Bobby glanced down at the black satchel Eli had loaded with his gear.

He was interrupted by a voice from outside.

"Bobby?"

Bobby had parked on the right side of the street, so Eli's window was facing the sidewalk. He glanced toward the sound of the voice, and it was coming from a tall crab: red designer slacks, a matching

red Hollister polo, large red foam claws, crab cheeks, and crab ant-
ennae all attached to the unusual, lanky body of Milo Maslow.

"Bobby Frindley, what are you doing here? Are you all right?
What happened to your face?"

"Hey, Milo."

Milo was silent for a moment. His concerned tone turned cold.
"Didn't I tell you to drop the Abbattista angle?"

"Things have gotten more complex."

"Drop the Abbattista angle. For all our good. I still decide what's
published, Bobby. And what's not published. There are certain
people who are simply . . ." Milo waved his crab claws in a small
circle, searching for the right word, "off limits." His intense gaze was
almost made comic by the crab accoutrement. "I assume if I called
Jana, she'd confirm you turned in the article we talked about. The
one that was due at seven? The one that hadn't yet arrived when I
left the office?"

"I don't think you're going to be disappointed in the story,"
Bobby said. He left out the part about it not being written yet. Or
that it would be about the owner of the paper. "Enjoy the party, Milo.
It's just a coincidence we're on this street."

"There've been a lot of coincidences lately," Milo said. He stood
at the curb, looking into their car for a full minute in silence. Eli
continued to lean across the passenger side, staring back in equal,
rude silence. Bobby waited patiently for the posturing to end.

Milo clicked his tongue against his teeth twice. He leaned farther into the window, his eyes lingering a moment on the black
duffel bag in the back seat. "It makes me nervous, you sitting here,
staking out the home of one of San Diego's top philanthropists. I'll
be honest, it makes me nervous. It really does. You don't want to so
much as point a cell phone camera in Abbattista's direction until
you've investigated this story from every possible angle. Until you've
uncovered every piece of evidence and double and triple sourced

it. And even then, when you're absolutely sure of your information, you still don't act on it until we talk to the legal team." Milo shook his head. "What was it you said on that first day we met? Something about our culture being too full of half-baked information zooming around the world, twisting itself into more and more ridiculous shapes? Isn't that exactly how you'd describe this whole horoscope experience? We made a little money with it, but now we have to do the real investigating. We have to put aside bias, emotion, and imagination and find the real crime hidden in this mess. Journalism is not a business of hunches; it's a business of facts. You were the one who reminded me of that." Milo clicked his tongue on his teeth again. When neither man responded, he nodded to them both. "Go home, gentlemen," he said. Then he walked toward the entrance. The reflection from the giant mirrored zodiac symbol lit up his red crab costume.

"That was very uncomfortable," Bobby admitted once Milo had reached the inside of the front gate. "And, he's not wrong. And, I don't think we're doing much recon work tonight. We should go back to the hospital. If Abbattista is guilty—and the only proof I have is a lock of curly hair sticking out of a ski mask—but if he is guilty, he's outsmarted us again. He's surrounded himself with two hundred witnesses, including my own employer, at the moment he knew our fury would be at its highest point. If we're going to catch the horoscope killer, we have to be just as smart and just as careful . . . and wait."

"We'll wait. See what develops," Eli agreed.

"We can't judge if anyone in his gang is coming and going with this crowd moving around anyway. Let's go home, and I'll get started on the story. Give me a little time to look closer. I'll find the facts I need to expose him, and then he'll die financially, socially, and in other slow, painful ways."

"Didn't I just hear your editor say he'd block the story?"

"Abbattista partially owns the paper," Bobby admitted. "But that won't stop the truth from getting out. Once we have enough evidence. Any other site in the world will publish it."

Bobby pushed himself into a better position in the cramped seat of Sarah's sensible Japanese automobile. By accident, he kicked the P266 with his heel.

"We wait here," Eli said firmly. "Just for a little while."

Bobby took a deep breath and looked toward Abbattista's house. Music had started to play and long, thumping bass was rolling out of the backyard. His head still ached from the concussion, and his ribs felt hollow in his chest. He put his hands over his eyes and scrunched down in the seat.

———

HE AWOKE UNABLE to remember where he was or what he was doing there. The tiny yellow lights on Sarah's car radio blinked 3:14 a.m. The air was quiet. The street was empty of all but one other car. A woman in a slinky dress was helping her drunk date stumble across the street. The seat next to Bobby was empty. He shook his head sharply and looked down at the center console. The canvas bag with the weaponry and the recon gear was still there. He felt under the car seat in a panic. The P226 was still there.

Slightly calmer, he looked up and down the empty street. As he did, the passenger door swung open. Eli crushed out a cigarette and climbed back inside. He picked up a cigarette box on the center console and banged out another. He put it in his mouth and lit the end. Bobby blinked his eyes and straightened up in his chair.

"Sorry. Those energy drinks kicked me in the face," Bobby said.

"I kicked you in the face," Eli said.

"I don't think I'm supposed to be falling asleep with a concussion."

"Yeah."

"You ready to go back to the hospital?"

"That drunk couple stumbling across the street, they're the last. Look."

Bobby stared straight ahead, noting the couple. The young woman wore jewels around her neck and wrists that sparkled even in the dull glow of the streetlamp. On her arm was a big man, nearly as large as Eli. He had brown hair, tight curly locks held back by salon products. It was Charles, tuxedoed, healthy, his long hair pinned down, showing no signs of the fight that had nearly crippled Bobby. He was mildly drunk and proud to be with his beautiful date. He did not seem to be a killer. Bobby said nothing to Eli. Charles and the girl piled into the car, laughing. It pulled unsteadily away from the curb.

"It's time," Eli said, climbing back out of the driver's seat and dragging the canvas bag out with him.

"Hold on a minute," Bobby said. "We had a deal."

"You told me this was the guy. And from everything that happened, it sure as hell seems like it is. Did you think I would keep my word with someone who screwed my wife?" Eli lowered the bag to his feet, yanked at the zipper, and pulled out the collapsible baton. He extended it, checked the weighted end, then snapped it shut again. "If you don't want to come, suit yourself," he said. "Call an Uber. Leave the gun in the glove box."

Eli climbed back out of the car before crossing the street to approach Abbattista's front gate.

Bobby pulled the gun from beneath the seat, feeling extremely foolish, and gently put it in Sarah's glove box.

He climbed out of the car and watched Eli step up onto the mailbox, banging the security camera aside in the exact way Bobby had sneaked in two days before. He was surprised the mailbox could hold such a large man.

Not knowing what else to do, Bobby checked his wrist to see the time. His watch was gone, lost somehow in the fight with Eli, maybe removed by the paramedics.

His phone told him it was 3:17 a.m.

And then it began to ring.

"Is this Bobby?" a familiar voice asked.

"Lapeyre?"

"Why are you awake?"

"I've stopped sleeping entirely," Bobby told the police detective.

"Don't write the story about Consorte," Lapeyre instructed.

"This isn't really the time to talk about it," Bobby said, looking back again at the front of the Abbattista estate.

"I'll give you something, Bobby. Something to take the place of the Consorte copy. The biggest story of your life."

"I'm working on other stuff right now," Bobby said, but he was very curious about Lapeyre's information. "There is something I need from you," Bobby negotiated. "My neighbor was attacked today. It was the Libra prediction, targeted directly at me. I called the cops, but nobody showed up."

"We're stretched pretty thin. We've got backup from Long Beach and Orange County, but they don't know our streets or how to use our gear. They're probably still looking for the address."

"If I squash the story, I want extra protection for my neighbor. She was attacked because of me, and I want to do what I can to keep her safe." Bobby was underselling the situation, but Lapeyre didn't need to know everything.

"Did you see who did it?"

"All I saw was wavy brown hair. But I've—"

Lapeyre cut Bobby off. "That's Jack Madrigal. He's in custody already. I busted him in La Jolla a few hours ago. He's a big guy and his hair is wavy brown. That's what I've been trying to tell you. We caught the zodiac killer, the horoscope killer, whatever you want to call him. He's in police custody. Grunden says the scoop is yours if you'll bury the Consorte lead."

"No," Bobby said. "I think it was—" He stopped again. "Are you absolutely—"

Lapeyre interrupted again. "I searched Madrigal's apartment myself. In the rafters of his garage, I found the remains of a dead, nude girl. We ID'd her from our registry of missing persons. I think you might know her. Her name is Stephanie Ambrosino."

Bobby was silent. His mind was absorbing this new information, rearranging itself around the facts of this new reality.

"The Cybercrimes division finally dug out the pictures from the frat guys' phones and they're a match. There's not much doubt Madrigal is the one who dumped her on the fraternity doorstep and came around with the van afterward to pick her up. If she was a friend of yours from the paper, I'm sorry. I'm sorry for her in every way possible, actually. I'm thinking that if Madrigal came after you and Ambrosino, that means he was focused specifically on the paper, which also adds up. That's his MO. He even has a history of mixing it up with Consorte, who's still missing." A note of sadness crept into Lapeyre's voice. "Madrigal was in prison a long time, lots of chances to dream big. To plan something elaborate like this."

Bobby thought of the strange, muscular homeless man staring at him from the corner of Lamont Avenue. The way that man's eyes had looked out from under his wavy brown hair, lingering on the note Bobby had left under Sarah's doormat. Bobby looked quickly up at Terry Abbattista's perimeter wall. Just a few moments before, he'd caught a last glimpse of Eli's combat boot, slipping over, followed by the heavy canvas bag.

"Oh shit," Bobby said.

33

SPEAKING QUICKLY, BOBBY agreed to drop the Consorte story for an exclusive interview with Madrigal. Lapeyre agreed to post a guard at Sarah's hospital door and let absolutely no one inside. Lapeyre promised she'd even take a shift herself.

After ending the call, Bobby was up and over the wall in a single bound. He landed heavily and had to roll forward to keep from twisting his ankle. The perimeter garden was empty. He'd expected to find guards, possibly armed guards, but it appeared they were away from their post, either drunk or helping clean up after the party. That was his theory, at least, until he inched forward and tripped over a body. It was Rife, eyes closed, tongue lolling, a gun disassembled in the dirt beside him. Bobby placed two fingers on Rife's carotid artery and felt it pulsing with blood. He exhaled and moved forward quickly.

Bobby knew the layout of the house better than Eli, and he figured he had a good chance to beat him to the target if he went directly to Abbattista's bedroom. He wasn't sure exactly where that would be, but it had to be in the southern wing, upstairs, because he'd been just about everywhere else.

Bobby veered south toward the garages. He jumped up onto the branch of a potted avocado tree. From there he was able to extend himself up into a larger tree, resting a moment in the crotch of a thick branch. *Have I been deluding myself the whole time? Was Abbattista just an old, nice guy? A benefactor for the city? Did I create an entire fragile world around a three-inch placard and a single lock of brown hair?*

What had Star said about horoscopes? You only see what you're looking for. The dumber and less disciplined the person, the more likely they would be to self-delude. Sitting in a tree next to Abbattista's roof, he realized that *dumb and undisciplined* pretty much described Bobby Frindley. And now there was a Navy Seabee hunting a potentially innocent man in his own house.

Bobby wasn't more than thirty feet from Terry's front door, so when it opened, the light from inside flashed outward and momentarily killed his night vision. Bobby recognized the silhouette of Tamba, Abbattista's manservant, standing uncomfortably in the doorway. Tamba was saying, ". . . a special treat for you tonight, you little, fat psychotic."

Bobby saw Tamba was addressing a short tank of a pit bull, waddling right toward the tree he was sitting in. Bobby had a rational fear of pit bulls and a passive dislike of anyone who owned them. It seemed the whole point of civilization, with all its humiliations and compromises, was to be safe from things like pit bulls. Abbattista's pit looked particularly vicious, its stubby, powerful legs driving it toward Bobby with a lunatic authority, its beady, brown eyes unicolor with its trimmed, oily coat. When it reached the base of the tree, it let out a low, lazy growl. Its nose sniffed the air, and it walked in a small circle. Bobby could see the inside of its wide mouth, down into its bottom jaw of razor-sharp teeth.

"What have you got out there?" Tamba asked. He left the doorway, walking toward the dog and Bobby's tree. Bobby held as still as death, wishing Leslie Consorte was around to pistol-whip this dog too.

Tamba stood at a safe distance from the dog. "You bite me again and I swear I'll break your stubby legs." He peered up into the tree, seeming to look directly at Bobby. Bobby pinched his eyes into a squint, his mind racing. After a moment, Tamba walked back toward the house. "Come on, killer," he said.

Bobby waited until man and dog were safely back in the house. He lurched forward, grabbing the bottom edge of the roof. He found a foothold for his right foot on the top of a window frame, and inched his way up, like Spiderman. Once he was on the roof, he took off his shoes and walked quickly and lightly to the southwest. He swung onto a balcony, but the door was locked, so he pulled himself over the other side, continuing to pad south.

When he reached the highest point of the second story roof, he looked down into Abbattista's backyard. The view was even more breathtaking, but it gave Bobby a rush of vertigo. There was no sign of Eli or residual violence. Hired Latin American caterers and live-in Latin American staff moved back and forth, over the large swath of grass, putting away tables and packing and loading up food.

Bobby stayed low, the front of his shirt dragging lightly against the dirty wooden shingles. There was a second balcony on the west side of the residence, overlooking the whole of the ocean. It had a separate chimney sticking out of the roof. Bobby realized he'd probably found the master suite. He began to crawl toward the balcony, conscious of the many pairs of eyes working on the grass below.

He put his hand on the railing and was about to vault himself over when he was stopped by the sounds of sex. A girl, moaning in pleasure. A man panting, then groaning, then panting for breath again. Bobby was still trying to figure out what to do when the act was interrupted by a fit of rough coughing. Thirty seconds later, Bobby saw the handle of the balcony door shifting open, and he raced to the far side of the chimney, hoping the creaking of the door would mask the sounds of his rapid ascent. He leaned his back against the squared concrete. There was room for two of him to fit behind the wide, gray chimney, but he still sucked in breath, pinning his arms against his sides. A seagull was resting on the roof, ten feet to his left, eyeing him warily. He waited for a full two minutes, but it felt like an hour.

No sound came from the balcony, so he peeked carefully around the corner. Rhona was standing on the veranda, moonlight reflecting off her dark, naked skin. Bobby could see tensed muscles in her lean arms. She had no tan lines, her dark skin smooth across her entire body, accenting perfectly shaped backbones. Bobby had a little bit of a weakness for backbones and lean, well-muscled shoulders, and naked breasts and legs and beautiful foreign faces with high cheekbones. She had her arms open to the ocean, outstretched, better to feel the ocean breeze against her skin, better to cool herself off after lovemaking.

She put a hand on the balcony railing and then started to turn back into the bedroom.

Bobby must have guessed wrong. He must have found Timur's room instead of the master.

Before she walked through the balcony door, Bobby heard an unmistakable voice say, "Rhona, honey, come on back inside. Your Uncle Terry has one more thing he'd like to try before this whiskey knocks him out cold."

Bobby had not guessed wrong. He crouched on the roof like a gargoyle, thinking.

As he swung down onto the balcony, he tried to decide if a naked Rhona in the room made the situation worse or better. He did know one thing: He wanted to get moving before the lovers had a chance to really get rolling again.

Peering inside, he saw Abbattista stretched lazily across the bed, wearing only his socks. The remains of his zodiac costume were scattered around the room, including a large lion head, crafted from papier-mâché, sitting on an end table facing the bed. The room was large, close to six hundred square feet, with a dresser, a wardrobe, an ornate fireplace along the east wall, mantled with furnished oak, and a brightly lit opening to a master bath, sparkling with silver faucets and finish. It was the kind of room that made just about everybody envious.

There was a tall tumbler full of whiskey and ice in Abbattista's left hand and a very relaxed smile on his face.

The smile disappeared when Bobby strode into the room and said, "Don't panic, but someone's in the house and they want to—" Bobby couldn't quite get to the word *kill*. He had to stop talking to duck the tumbler that Abbattista had hurled at him with all his strength. The glass missed, but whiskey rained down on his hair and a cube of ice grazed his cheek. Abbattista staggered out of bed, gravity shifting his old naked body from wrinkly to droopy. He lunged for the exit. Bobby had no idea if Abbattista had guards, or staff, or a murderous sailor on the other side, so he moved to intercept. He crossed twenty feet of carpet at a dead sprint, hitting Abbattista with a lot of unintended velocity. Both men crashed into the wall.

Abbattista's head struck the oak fireplace mantle. They crumpled to the ground in each other's arms. Abbattista let out a long, low groan, and then he went unconscious. Bobby stood up, attempting to disentangle himself from the other man's sweaty, sticky body. When he got to his feet, Rhona was a step away, and she tore into him with her fingernails, raking a claw across his chest. He gave her a shove on both shoulders, and she backed up a step, swinging another claw in a clumsy arc. Bobby ducked and dodged left, but her long, red fingernails still caught him on the side of the neck, opening another set of jagged red lines.

"Someone's in the house trying to kill Terry," Bobby whispered urgently.

Rhona made a sharp intake of breath, her chest rising. She was about to scream. Bobby grabbed her in a bear hug and twisted her off her feet, clasping a hand over her mouth. She fought back, threw her weight every which way, knocking Bobby off-balance. Both of them crashed their hips against the dresser, sending the lamp teetering off the side to shatter on the carpeted floor. The sound of laughter on the other side of the master door stopped their fight. Abbattista did have a guard stationed outside. His tongue probably loosened by a night of drinking, the man was laughing at what he thought was Abbattista and Rhona's violent lovemaking.

Bobby still clutched Rhona, trying to ignore her naked skin against his bare arms. His head was right next to her left ear, and he again whispered, "Someone is in the house trying to kill Terry. We have to get him to safety."

"Let go of me."

"Only if you promise not to scream."

Rhona relaxed her grip on Bobby's arm and shoulder and stood up straight, her chin lifted proudly.

"I'm going to leave. You need to alert the guard outside this door. Call the police if you have to, though they'll never get here in time."

"And tell them what?"

"Tell them—" Bobby didn't get to finish his sentence. From the other side of the door, they heard a muffled voice cry, "What the fu—" then the sound of a fist striking a skull. Two more deep thumps, a *huff*, and then a body landing heavily on wood flooring.

Bobby looked at Rhona; fear was replacing her anger and pride. "Lock the door," he mouthed to her.

She padded barefoot across the room and threw the latch slowly, trying to make no noise perceptible on the other side.

Bobby wished she would hurry. He gathered Abbattista in his arms and carried him to the balcony. Rhona silently followed, grabbing her underwear from the bedpost.

They both heard the latch of the door wiggle. Eli was working the lock from the other side.

Bobby locked the balcony door from the inside and then pulled it shut behind them. He dropped Abbattista on the roof and then hoisted himself up onto the cold shingles. Rhona was pulling on her underwear when he grabbed her arm and lifted her off her feet. He deposited her on the roof beside him. Bobby picked up Abbattista again and padded quickly up to the chimney, once more placing his back to it, this time with the haggard naked body of an old Italian propped beside him. Rhona came around the chimney and Bobby caught her wrist again, pulling her down into his lap. She opened her mouth to object, but there wasn't enough room to fit three abreast. They held their position on the roof, listening to silence for a long three or four minutes.

Rhona began to shiver, goose bumps forming on her arms and chest. Bobby pressed closely against her, his heart thumping from the confluence of fear, excitement, and her nearly naked body wrapped in his arms.

Bobby's attention veered back to the master bedroom as they heard the balcony door open with the whisper of wood across carpet, and then footsteps on the heavy balcony tile. There were a few more moments of silence. Bobby felt Rhona's heartbeat increase. Her chest stopped rising as they both held their breath. And then the footsteps drifted away.

Rhona exhaled, and her lower jaw started shaking from fear, or cold, or both. Bobby had thought of calling down to Eli and explaining the situation, but he didn't dare. He was afraid Eli wouldn't listen and would pitch Abbattista off the side of the roof.

They heard nothing but silence for a full ten minutes, and Bobby started to let his body relax.

Rhona ran her hand over the scratch on his neck. She felt loose on his lap now, her face buried under his chin. "I'm sorry about this scratch," she whispered in her lovely accent. "Did you just save my life?"

There was a certain evolutionary science involved in what was happening to Bobby on the roof. If a Y chromosome was present, a woman like Rhona could survive by adapting herself to fit just about any situation. Men liked her, and that *like* could be shifted laterally to suit her needs. She had probably been born beautiful, sliding out of the primordial ooze with her high cheekbones and prim, feminine jaw. Around puberty she must have systematically begun rearranging herself to achieve higher and higher levels of appeal, and consequently, socioeconomic standing. How else to escape postwar Serbia? She'd paid for a scalpel to reshape portions of her body and worked in the gym to tighten and emphasize parts the scalpel wouldn't or couldn't fix. She'd learned fashion, mimicked upper-class dress, manner, and form. This same instinct for adaptation must have caused her to accept Abbattista's advances even though she was supposed to be Timur's girlfriend.

Bobby did his best to ignore her purring voice and her soft skin. He glanced down at Abbattista, wrinkled and equally soft, covered in loose skin and wispy gray hairs. He tried to imagine Eli nearby. Eli, who had violently accepted his explanation of the tryst with Sarah but might not be as quick to understand why he was on the rooftop sitting beside the supposed killer with a different, nearly naked woman in his arms.

"The scratch is no problem," he said. "I'm starting a collection."

Rhona kissed him softly on the neck, in the dead center of the long red mark. "I'm sorry anyway," she said, sweetly. Then her smile turned into a grin. "Do you have an erection?"

"No?" Bobby said.

Bobby's hands were on her slender, lean-muscled back. For a moment, their mouths hovered just inches apart, and then Abbattista let out a long, low grown. His eyes began to flutter. Bobby hit him again, hard across the crown of the head. Then he lowered Rhona gently from his lap and stood on wobbly legs.

He carried the two lovers down the roof, one on each shoulder. The old one was groaning and the young one was making small sounds of protest.

Bobby left the house the way he'd come, the lunatic pit bull snoring safely somewhere inside.

34

THE WALK DOWN the mountain was not an easy one. He knew he had a lot of explaining to do to a lot of different people. He wasn't looking forward to it.

He worried about Sarah, and poor dead Stephanie Ambrosino and her father, whose hope for a happy ending was going to be extinguished by police knocking on his door—or worse, with the thump of a newspaper on his driveway the next day. He thought of angry Eli and the missing Leslie Consorte. He thought of how the powerful Terry Abbattista would feel when he woke up the next morning. *Will he be as forgiving as Rhona for my three a.m. interruption? Who is Abbattista? An evil genius or a random, philandering philanthropist?* Tonight's events seemed to imply the latter, but Bobby wasn't fully convinced of either reality. He was uncertain enough to be glad Eli hadn't killed Abbattista, anyway.

He thought about his own father. Maybe he would finally be impressed, simply by the colossal size of the mess Bobby was a part of. Probably not.

"How did I raise such an idiot for a son?"

"Relax, Dad, I managed to be an idiot all on my own."

He counted the wounds on his body; Rhona's scratch on his neck could now be added to Timur's bamboo attack and Eli's steel-toed stomping. It all would have been slightly better if he had been heading home to a nice, comfy bed and lots and lots of pillows, but Bobby's night wasn't over yet.

While he walked, he dialed Therese Lapeyre, who was still awake despite the late hour, her voice high and quick and full of excitement. Bobby listened carefully to all the details of the capture of Madrigal outside the La Jolla bank, the raid on Madrigal's house, the discovery of Stephanie Ambrosino, wrapped in plastic and suspended in dusty old rafters. Madrigal had a history of crossing boundaries. Lapeyre was convinced Madrigal had done something to Leslie and Lapeyre promised Bobby she'd break Madrigal to get that information. It was Madrigal's thing to go after the principals involved in the case. He'd attacked Leslie's wife fifteen years ago. He'd no doubt pursued Sarah because of her relationship with Bobby, the headlining reporter on his case. Lapeyre hung up, breathless.

Exhausted, and a safe distance from Abbattista's estate, Bobby punched at his phone screen to order a rideshare. He was standing in the shadow of the Soledad Mountain cross. The cross was a strange part of the history of San Diego. Being on public land, various groups had attempted to have it removed over the years via the separation of church and state. Others had tried to get equitable religious iconography added to the space, maybe etch in a Star of David and a Muslim crescent? Still others had taken wily and improvised legal steps to preserve it. Eventually the city had shoehorned in a war memorial, laying pictures around the base of the cross and putting the issue, finally, to rest.

Most of the silent majority were happy it was still up. Most felt it represented the history of San Diego more than any one notion of God. Whatever the prevailing wisdom, Bobby was glad it was there now.

The cross shared the same view as Terry Abbattista. It sat cliff-side, overlooking the wide Pacific. Detouring to the foot of the cross, Bobby sat on the brick steps and looked up at the cloudless, starless sky. "God," he said, "I've been counting on you a lot lately. Thanks for being there for me."

With his rideshare creeping closer, Bobby walked away from the cross, down the dirt path that led back to Soledad Mountain Road. He'd only gone fifteen feet or so when he turned and walked back. "Please help me to stop acting irresponsibly. Help me to take care of the people I love, not hurt them. The truth is, God, I don't want anything for myself, other than to impress my dad. I'm sure you know that already."

A half hour later he reached the twenty-four-hour FedEx Office Center on Garnet. It was now a little before four thirty in the morning. He rented two hours on a computer near the front window and sat down to write the strange, tragic story of Jack Madrigal, Therese Lapeyre, and Stephanie Ambrosino. After writing just the first sentence, he called Milo Maslow and told him that he'd better prep the printing plant. They were going to need to run a special edition if they wanted to beat cyberspace to this final, unexpected climax to the odd tale of the horoscope killer.

When he finished the story, he checked the Ask Ambrosia email account. His heart was beating heavily while he watched the little circle flip endlessly, telling him to wait, loading in progress. Finally, the email inbox was open, available. And completely empty.

35

BOBBY WOKE UP the next afternoon a little before three p.m. to heavy knocking on his door. He'd managed only seven hours' sleep. His body creaked with each step he took as he hunted around the floor of his bedroom for his cleanest shirt.

His visitor pounded the door with even more urgency. He could recognize the knock, in all its organized fury, one hundred out of one hundred times. Bobby limped into the front room and jerked the door open. On the welcome mat, fist still clenched in preparation to inflict more damage to the poor, shattered door, was Bobby's father. Standing in her customary spot, a few feet over his left shoulder, eyes twinkling, four or five copies of the *Register* tucked under her arm, his mom smiled a warm greeting.

"Hiya, Mom, Pops, come on inside," Bobby said, moving out of the way. "Watch the broken glass."

They marched inside. His father was wearing a light-green jumpsuit over a white undershirt. His hair was as thick as Bobby's, but a salt-and-pepper gray, combed into a sleek, oily pompadour. His mom was wearing a less obnoxious pair of sweatpants and sweatshirt, and pink running shoes, laced tight.

"What happened to your door? This place wasn't such a dump the last time we visited," his father said. "The landlord will want to hear about this."

"You're the landlord, Dad."

"Which is why I'm concerned about the shape of my property!"

"Oh, Bobby, what happened to your face?" his mother asked.

"The same guy that got to the door. A Navy Seabee." Bobby sat down on the couch, pulling his leg up under him. "It was a misunderstanding, sort of."

"What a terrible mess."

"I think it's pretty much over now. I have a little more explaining to do is all."

"Well, start talking," his father said.

"Not to you. To the guy who broke the door."

"The door doesn't matter to us at all." His mother's face lit up in a smile. "Not after what we read in the paper today. In a special morning edition, no less. I think you're the most famous journalist in America. Your Aunt Brenda called from Indiana, and then my brother Bob in New Mexico. They all read the story. It's gone national. How did you learn to write so well, Bobby, and how did you learn all that interesting stuff?"

"You sent me to good schools, Mom." Bobby looked at his father, who was sitting in his green easy chair, a blank expression on his face. "What did you think of it, Dad?"

"I think the *Register* is a second-class paper. It didn't used to be, but . . . I don't understand why they can't afford to hire a copy editor like all the online rags. You shouldn't have a story going national with that many pronoun-antecedent errors."

"Ron, don't," Bobby's mother said, then she turned to Bobby.

"This morning he was all atwitter when the paper showed up on our door. He's very proud of you. He just has a hard time showing it."

Gruffly, Arthur Frindley said, "You did well." Then in the same breath: "Here's what I don't understand. Where's the motive? Who benefitted from this big mess? What's the point?"

"I haven't had the chance to follow up. A lot happened last night. The police seem to think that Madrigal just wanted to be some kind of supervillain," Bobby suggested. "That he was obsessed with fame."

"Your article says he insists he's innocent."

"That's what Lapeyre told me."

"That belies the supercriminal motive, doesn't it?" Arthur Frindley said.

"I haven't really had time to think about it. I scheduled a follow-up interview with Lapeyre for this evening. I also plan to talk to Madrigal if I can get in to see him. We write those placeholder articles very quickly to make sure we break the story, then we follow up with more information as events warrant."

"It's three in the afternoon, and you're still wearing your pajama bottoms."

Bobby stood up. This felt very familiar. Nothing was ever quite good enough. No rest allowed because there was always more to do. That approach had pushed him all the way to the Olympics. *But when did the relentless push forward ever stop?* Bobby stretched his arms in a long arc. "I'm glad you're so happy for me, Dad. Last week I was unemployed."

"And now you have work to do."

"Then I better get to it. You two can show yourselves out."

Bobby's mom tsked sadly, so he gave her a long hug goodbye. His dad just nodded. His parents resumed their morning walk around the neighborhood. They lived about three miles up the hill on Wilbur Avenue in North Pacific Beach. Bobby himself was in an apartment his grandfather had purchased as an income property back in the 1970s. It was just far enough away to avoid their afternoon walk, but they still made it by occasionally, to remind him that it was unrealistic to expect to live for free, forever.

Bobby had been excited to tell his dad that he could finally pay a little rent, but his father's antagonism had drained his enthusiasm, and as his parents marched back over the broken glass, he'd kept his AP check to himself. He went straight to the shower, letting the water drum against his face. The long sleep had reduced the throbbing in his head to a faint timpani. He got out of the shower, toweled off, and pulled on his jeans and T-shirt.

His father's words echoed around the small apartment. *What's the point?* And more importantly, *Who benefitted?*

Milo was one answer. Subscriptions on the *Register* were through the roof after a steady decline of almost three decades. Therese Lapeyre benefitted too. Bobby had written her as a hero, almost single-handedly apprehending Madrigal and then crusading her way into the tenement apartment to find Stephanie's body. Most of all though, Bobby Frindley benefitted. He had sneaked into a horoscope position and ridden the rocket right up to the paper's regular headline.

Bobby combed his hair with his fingers. He walked into the kitchen and found his cell phone. He dialed Milo Maslow. Jana did everything but blow him kisses through the phone. Her voice was glowing with warmth. Bobby felt pretty unhappy with himself, but apparently other people had other perspectives. She connected him to Milo, whose voice was full of celebration. "Bobby Frindley! You were the best thing to ever walk through my office door, can you believe it? We almost put you in telesales. Instead, we give you horoscopes and you bloom like a summer flower! Outstanding. Why aren't you in the office? Is there something about it you don't like? Bobby, I want to make you a full-timer. Maybe some editorial responsibilities. You've got benefits, now, starting today. Welcome to the lower-middle class. I'll have Jana draw up the paperwork. We need a follow-up. What's going on in San Diego PD's headquarters? What was on Madrigal's mind? Was this revenge? I'm a spectator on all this. I just sit in my office waiting for the email to ding! When I saw you outside Abbattista's last night, I thought—I thought—and all that time, you had the story of the real killer. This is really great. Why don't you ever come into the office? We have paper clips, and Wi-Fi."

Bobby switched the phone to his other ear and poured a bowl of Cheerios. He said, "I promise I'll come by with this next article. I'm calling Lapeyre in two minutes. She owes me a sit-down with Madrigal."

"Bobby, Stephanie Ambrosino's father called. He wants to thank you for putting him at peace. Do you want to call him?"

"I don't think I could bear that."

"Suit yourself. You have a lot to be proud of."

"Thanks, Milo. I'll see you soon."

Bobby hung up the phone and ate his Cheerios standing up. He called Lapeyre's phone, and it went directly to voicemail, so he left a message requesting access to Madrigal and the follow-up interview.

Bobby thought about Eli and Sarah the entire ride to Scripps Mercy Hospital. He glanced around for Sarah's Toyota Camry in the parking lot, but he didn't search too carefully. He had sworn to himself that he would visit her, even if Eli was in the room.

The hospital was fairly empty for the middle of the afternoon. It was an ocean of white, like most hospitals, but with a few nods to its location in swanky La Jolla. The receptionist's desks were solid, varnished, expensive-looking wood. Hand sanitizer was mounted on the walls in every conceivable location. At the front desk, Bobby inquired as to Sarah's room number, nodding yes when the efficient looking woman with thin lips asked if he was family. She sent him to the fourth floor, Med-Surge.

The elevator opened directly into the nurse's station. He was disappointed to find no police protection.

Sarah's room was dark. Bobby pushed silently through the door, not wanting to wake her. When he turned the corner of her small, single room, she was lying prone in the bed in a heavy neck brace, her body curved into a posture held usually only by the heavily medicated. Her eyes were closed and her mouth slightly open. Bobby could hear wisps of soft breath slipping in and out of her throat. He looked at her etherized body. It was minutes before he could look away and he realized, in relief, that Eli wasn't there.

There was plastic everywhere, plastic bags painted with hazard signs, plastic gloves on the wall, more plastic bags dripping fluid into Sarah's veins. Bobby sat in the lounge chair by the bed. The seat was still warm, and he figured Eli would be back soon enough. He waited patiently, thinking about Leslie Consorte, Terry Abbattista, Jack Madrigal, and curly locks of brown hair falling out of the back of ski masks.

36

B OBBY HAD MOVED back out to the parking lot and was sitting near the hospital entrance on his bike when he saw Eli return. Eli was headed to Sarah's room with a stack of paperbacks, a home-made sack lunch, and a large bouquet of flowers. The man could protect democracy, storm a well-guarded beach chalet, and make sandwiches.

Before Bobby fired up his motorcycle, his phone rang.

Milo's voice squawked through the phone line. "Bobby, I haven't stopped drinking since noon, but we're going to do even more cele-brating tonight."

"Tonight, I'm celebrating the beauty of sleep," Bobby said.

"Terry Abbattista has asked—well, demanded, that I bring you to dinner at his house. He says we need to celebrate our circulation numbers. I'm inclined to agree."

"I think we should stay away from Terry Abbattista for a few days."

"Whatever for? Professionally speaking, this is the kind of invita-tion that you don't decline. Since I caught you lurking outside his home just last night, I suspect you don't need directions. Be there at seven."

"Wait, Milo, don't hang up. You shouldn't go to the dinner. I will if one of us has to."

"Why wouldn't I?"

"I hassled Abbattista a little bit last night, after his party. I sort of went into his house, a little bit. He may not be too quick to forgive and forget."

"Jesus, Bobby. I don't want to know the details. Don't tell me. I'll be there, tonight. Someone's got to watch over you. Dress nice."

IN PREPARING FOR Abbattista's dinner, Bobby put on jeans and a cotton button-down shirt. He was four steps up his clothing hierarchy: shirtless, T-shirt, Hawaiian shirt, something not-Hawaiian with buttons. He doubted Abbattista and Maslow would appreciate the effort at formality. In truth, he wasn't sure how he'd be received. The last time Abbattista had seen him it was from the business end of a flying tackle.

If things went south right away, Bobby preferred Milo not be involved, so at six thirty, a full thirty minutes early, Bobby was puttering his motorcycle to a stop outside Abbattista's house on Soledad Mountain Road. The house was still recovering from the party the night before. There was a flatbed semi parked on the street outside, the garish disco ball strapped to the back alongside ten or fifteen plastic rental tables and four stacks of plastic chairs with rounded metal legs—the kind that slide easily together but you have to be Harry Houdini, or Hercules, to get apart.

When Bobby got to the front door, he noticed that someone had removed the mailbox and laid it against the side of the front wall. The security camera had also been shunted back into its proper position. Bobby rang the security system and heard Timur's rough voice over the intercom, "Yeah. Who is it?"

"It's Bobby Frindley."

Timur didn't respond but the gate popped open electronically. Bobby pushed his way through. He checked the spot where he'd found Rife lying unconscious in the grass, but it was repaired, flowers and bushes teased back into place. Bobby heard the distant barking of the pit bull, quartered somewhere on the second floor of the estate. He knocked on the front door.

Rhona answered, biting her lower lip, her lean supranatural body squeezed into a skintight strapless dress. Timur was crossing the foyer to greet Bobby. When he reached the door he put his hand on Rhona's back and said, "You're early. And why is it that I always find you alone with my girlfriend?"

Rhona's eyes narrowed. Bobby absently rubbed the slash on his neck. He opened his mouth to respond but Timur spoke quickly, "I'm just fooling around. It looks like a donkey kicked you in the face recently."

"It's still a beautiful face," Rhona said.

Timur clutched Bobby's arm and led him down to the recreation room. The wooden Petosiris wheel hung, partially deconstructed, over the outdoor section of the pool. Costumes, padded bamboo, and champagne flutes were littered around the edges of the deck.

Abbattista was sitting in the loft above the indoor portion of the pool. He had a book in his hand and reading glasses perched on the end of his nose.

"I read your story this morning. An interesting piece of journalism," Timur said. "Do you think they got the right guy?"

"I sure hope so," Bobby said, looking at Abbattista.

When Abbattista spotted his guest, he waved him over to the couch. As Bobby walked toward Abbattista, Timur and Rhona stayed where they were and spoke to each other in harsh, guttural Serbian. Bobby climbed the stairs to the loft and sat in an easy chair at a ninety-degree angle from his boss.

"You're early," Abbattista said, calmly.

Bobby spoke in a whisper, clasping his hands together, "Listen, Terry, I wanted to explain a little bit about—"

Abbattista shook his head. He arched his eyebrows in Rhona's direction, a huge smile on his face and in the same soft voice Bobby had used he said, "We all have our secrets. Let's share them some other time."

"You don't want to talk about it?"

"It's a conversation for someplace a little more private." Abbattista nodded to Timur. "Timur is one of my best henchmen. I'd rather he not know all the details." Abbattista's face was very serious, until it broke into a crooked smile. "Plus, we have a lot to celebrate. I've invited a few more still."

"Who else?" Bobby said.

"You'll see," Abbattista said in a singsong voice.

Bobby started to laugh but then reality came back down on him. "You're really not mad about last night. You don't want me to explain—"

"I'm sure you had your reasons. And I am curious to know them." Abbattista stared back at Rhona and Timur, still talking rapidly by the pool deck. "It's my understanding that you saved my life. Tommy, the young man who guards my second floor, is still in the hospital."

"So's Sarah," Bobby said.

"Who's that?" Abbattista asked.

"My neighbor. The girl I'm a little bit in love with."

Abbattista's eyes widened in what appeared to be genuine surprise. "What happened to her?"

"So many things."

"How did you know I was in danger? How did you know someone was in my house? How did you get on my roof? These questions must have answers. But I'm already craving the simplicity of your previous visits. How about we have a cordial, pleasant dinner first?"

The security button rang, and Timur stormed off to answer it. Bobby relaxed in the easy chair. He was relieved that he didn't have to explain more. Yet.

Abbattista showed him the back of the book he was reading. "Have you ever read Camus? He's one of the great godless existentialists, though he always rejected that second label." Abbattista thumbed through the book.

Bobby caught the title, *La Chute.*

"I was thinking about your baffling Christianity. I found this . . ." Abbattista began reading from a dog-eared page: "'Sometimes it is easier to see clearly into the liar than into the man who tells the truth. Truth, like light, blinds. Falsehood, on the contrary, is a beautiful twilight that enhances every object.'" He stopped reading and smiled with satisfaction. "It's the notion of the seductive nature of the lie."

"*La Chute,*" Bobby said. "Doesn't that mean the fall?"

Abbattista nodded. "This is a beautiful treatise on man's movement away from the concept of God. I can loan it to you. The fall, in this case, is metaphoric, representing more than just our eviction from the Garden of Eden. It was written a full eighty years after Nietzsche made his famous declaration that God is dead—but then the French have always been a little behind the Germans in all but wine and baked goods." Abbattista was interrupted by the return of Timur, who was walking up the stairs to the loft trailed by none other than Star Lunes.

She waved at Bobby. "Hello, Bobby."

"Star!" Bobby said. He was excited to see her. He stood up to give Star a hug, but before he did, he leaned into Abbattista's ear and said, "What else is there in life other than wine and baked goods?"

Abbattista laughed heartily. "You're the one who believes in God," he said.

Star reached out and took his hand as they walked down to the pool deck. They stood and looked up at the giant wooden Petosiris platform. "I read your article this morning," Star said. "You're a busy man."

"I've been trying to tell you. What did you think?"

"Really good. A few pronoun-antecedent errors, but I'm guessing that's because you were exhausted, and the copy editor was probably fast asleep."

"I don't know what an antecedent is. Sounds like an illness. Or a medicine."

"It can be," Star said, smiling.

Before either of them could say another word, a lanky praying-mantis-of-a-man came sweeping into the pool area from the foyer. He was carrying flowers, and when he moved them away from his face, Bobby saw that it was Milo Maslow. He strode over to where they both stood.

"I was going to present these to you, Bobby, in honor of your journalistic accomplishments, but I find myself enchanted by the beauty of your companion." Milo handed the large bouquet to Star, who returned a shallow curtsy. "Hello, Miss Lunes."

"A pleasure, as always, Milo."

"It's funny because I gave Bobby here your phone number so he could learn astrology, yet I find you together in Terry's house, holding hands. This is typical of Bobby's tendency to overachieve."

"Actually, she pursued me," Bobby said.

"I did not."

"She did."

"Okay, I really, really did. Can you blame me? Look how beautiful he is."

"I prefer *rugged*," Bobby said touching the bruises on his face.

"I'd better go say hello to our host," Milo said, wandering off in the direction of the loft. Star kept Bobby's hand and led him through the sliding glass door opening into Terry's picturesque backyard. Indoors, the ocean was simply a blue blanket stretched out beyond where the eye could see. Once the door opened, they were hit with the wind, the sound of crashing waves, and even the faintest misting of sea spray.

Star put the bouquet down on one of the pool lounges, then pulled Bobby toward her and they strolled along the large retaining wall at the end of the estate. They walked its distance and then sat down on a wooden and ceramic bench. Star finally released Bobby's hand.

"I'm sure you don't want to talk about Stephanie Ambrosino, but when you're ready, I'm a good ear," he told her.

"Jack Madrigal," Star said. "We were right there—at Theta Rho Kappa—just twenty-four hours later. I wish they'd done something to help her. They could have called somebody, anything—" Star couldn't finish her sentence, her voice catching in her throat.

"At least we got to knock them around a little bit."

"I don't really want to talk about it," Star said. "Maybe later."

"Sure," Bobby said. They looked at the ocean for a while. Off in the distance, a parasailor leaped from the cliffs high above Black's Beach. Bobby watched him make a careful arc through the sky. "I thought we weren't going to see each other again. It kind of felt like we were saying goodbye the other night."

"Terry's a hard man to say no to," Star said. "It's funny to think that last time we were here, we were going to snoop around his house. Implicate him in all sorts of madness, and suddenly the criminal ends up being a guy we never even heard of. How do you like that?"

"As Terry Abbattista would say, life is a chaotic mess. We can't expect it to all make sense. Not every gun must be fired, not every virgin gets bedded, and not every dragon gets slain, or something like that. In fact, I suspect the virgin just moves into a duplex in Loma Vista and huddles over horoscopes about 'romantic possibilities,' hymen solidly intact."

"Five or six cats at her feet, meowing for Friskies?" Star gave a small shudder. "That's pretty close to what I said to you the first time we spoke. It sounds so dry and terrible now. Do you really believe all that?"

"Not even for a minute," Bobby said, grinning a wolfish grin. "But do you see how well I was listening?"

"Oh, Bobby," Star said, laying her head on his shoulder. "I'm infatuated with you. I know you're in love with your neighbor. I know you're emotionally distant. You're kind of a slut and you love challenges. And I know you're going to be turned off by this declaration. But there's something so simple about you, and when I'm around it, it makes me simple too, and that's a nice thing to be sometimes. And so, I'm telling you the truth."

Bobby rubbed Star's right arm. She was wearing a pair of capris and a blouse with sleeves ending at her elbows. She had woven yellow and orange beads in her hair. It was an outfit that would have looked silly on ninety-nine percent of American women, but Star had the moxie to pull it off. Bobby ran his hand along her bare forearm and up under the shortened sleeve of her blouse. Her biceps were covered in goosebumps from the wind.

"I think you're a better person than I deserve," Bobby said truthfully.

Star sighed. "I know."

They watched the waves crash far below, then went back inside to the recreation room. Abbattista had gotten off his couch and was walking Milo around, pointing out various items he had on display: a three-foot vase of blown glass, a painting that looked like it was purchased at a Sotheby's auction, an elaborate rug of indeterminate age. Rhona walked in from the kitchen and leaned over Abbattista to whisper in his ear. Abbattista patted her lightly on the rump. He separated himself from Milo and cleared his throat. "Ladies and gentlemen, fine guests of mine, dinner is served."

37

THERE WERE FIVE of them, Bobby, Star, Milo, Timur, and Rhona. They stood up from various points in the sprawling room and followed Abbattista into a large dining area. Timur and Rhona exited through the far door, and Bobby caught just enough of the room on the other side to see they were headed into the kitchen.

The house was huge, but mostly without pretense. The dining room was the most elaborate room Bobby had seen, with a high crafted-glass chandelier and an ornate wooden dining table that comfortably seated twelve. But even this room was not strictly for entertaining guests. There was another five-hundred-square-feet off the west side with a large television, several bookshelves, and three comfortable looking couches. Charles, all knotted muscles and matted hair, was sitting on one of them, barefoot, watching an ESPN replay of a New England Patriots-Denver Broncos playoff game.

Abbattista was already seated at the table. Bobby took the chair next to Star and watched Charles. The big man rubbed the bottom of his left foot, stood up, stretched, and ambled over to the table. He took a seat next to Abbattista as if he were the petulant son at a dysfunctional family dinner, his eyes downcast, his forehead wrinkled with displeasure. Timur and Rhona filed in and out of the dining area carrying plates of delicious smelling cuisine. They had to make three trips each, but when Star stood up to help them, Abbattista insisted she sit back down. Milo let out a small, high-pitched squeak when Rife backed through the kitchen door carrying enough ham to be the whole pig. Rhona followed with various red, yellow, and white dipping sauces.

Bobby saw the ham was basted and rolled in some type of crust.

"Mustard crusted ham," Star said.

Bobby wondered where the servants were tonight; perhaps given the day off following last night's big party. He was getting more comfortable with each passing moment, but still felt Abbattista was an existent threat. You don't tackle a man in his home without repercussions.

Watching Rife, Timur, and Rhona carry the food was concerning. He would have appreciated if more people had been around as witnesses.

Abbattista lifted his wine glass and stood up. "I'd like to offer a toast to the continued success of the *San Diego Register*, the little paper that could. I suppose we owe a debt to everyone over the last one hundred years who has worked hard to keep her afloat, especially those who joined us recently and helped usher in a new era of prosperity. I'd like to toast Bobby in particular."

Bobby nodded, finding himself blushing. It was odd, getting the praise he craved from his own father from this surrogate.

Abbattista lowered his glass. "But let's not toast just yet," he said, turning to Bobby. "The first time you visited me here, I spoke about an ancient poem, *Sir Gawain and the Green Knight*. Do you remember?"

"Yes," Bobby said.

"At the start of that poem, King Arthur sits before a great feast. A feast of this exact meal I have asked be made tonight."

Abbattista continued, "But Arthur won't sit down to eat. He is young, brash, and full of desire to prove his vitality. No one dares partake of the meal before the king does, so all eyes are fixed on him. Arthur stands tall and addresses the whole hall. He yells: '*Vpon such a dere day er hym deuised were. Of sum auenturus þyng an vncouþe tale. Of sum mayn meruayle, þat he my3t trawe. Of alderes, of armes, of oþer auenturus.*' He is demanding an adventure. A game. He will not allow the feast to begin until he is entertained. If you all will indulge an old man, I would do the same now."

A small bell appeared in Terry's left hand. He rang it. Milo slowly lowered his knife and fork.

Rife stood up from the table and moved to stand next to the main exit, near the edge of the wall.

Charles took a position next to the other door on the south wall. He opened it and whistled. The thick pit bull waddled into the room, its eyes half-mast. It reminded Bobby of a three-foot-long shark. Bobby brought his legs back under his chair as much as he could. Charles shut the door but remained next to it.

"This is kind of freaky," Star whispered.

"Maybe we could even take a break from playing games?" Bobby suggested. "We could just enjoy your amazing view and this excellent meal?"

"That sounds nice," Abbattista said. He seemed to be considering Bobby's suggestion. "But, truthfully, I get a little bored when nothing's happening."

Bobby felt the low buzz of his cell phone trembling in his right front pocket. He fished it out of his pants and glanced at it under the table.

Lapeyre: I'm at the hospital with your neighbor. She's beat up pretty badly.

Bobby typed back:

Can't talk now. With Abbattista. Please keep her safe.

He put the phone back in his pocket.

The pit bull rose languidly to its feet and crossed the room to disappear under the table.

"I don't feel very comfortable around these sorts of dogs," Milo admitted.

"What kind of game do you want to play, Terry?" Star asked.

Bobby's phone buzzed in his pocket again. He fished it out and glanced quickly at the screen.

Lapeyre: How'd you know to run the Lasix test on the tiger? ME couldn't believe when it came back positive. Grunden has questions for you.

A chill ran through Bobby's whole body. He looked up from the screen to see Abbattista smiling back at him.

"What do you say, Bobby? Are you willing to play just one more game?"

Behind him, Rhona clutched Timur's hand and leaned in. She put her face into Timur's shoulder, eyes closed.

"I'll play," Bobby said. "Under one condition." Under the table he blind texted what he hoped said, *Danger. Come to Abbattista's now. Bring Eli.*

"Name it."

"Milo and Star sit this one out. They get to go home before the game starts."

Abbattista pursed his lips. He shook his head in a barely perceptible *no* motion. "Games are enjoyed at least as much by the spectator as the participator. Have you seen the price of NBA tickets these days?" Abbattista took a small sip from his wine glass, looking at Bobby intently.

A clock had begun to tick in Bobby's head. Whatever Abbattista's plan was, Bobby needed to keep him talking long enough for Lapeyre to arrive.

"It's okay if they watch, but let's keep the game just between the two of us," Bobby said. "One-on-one. I win, you spend a Sunday in church. You win, I read your Camus." Bobby was purposely setting low stakes. He hoped it would convince Abbattista to keep rolling with his façade of jovial intellectualism.

Star stood up. "Which way is the bathroom?" she asked.

"Sit down, *bitch*," Timur said evenly.

Star gasped, genuinely shocked. It looked for a moment like she might take a run at the door. Bobby gestured for her to sit back down, and she did, warily.

Rhona walked away, visibly upset. She moved into the television room and turned it on. She cranked up the volume and sat down on the couch, staring numbly ahead.

"You'll play one last game, then?" Abbattista said.

"I do think I will be leaving," Milo said, standing up from the table. Speaking to Abbattista, he said, "I have deep respect for you professionally, but this kind of silliness is too much for me. I guess I'm just getting old." Milo's usual clipped speech and manic cadences were gone from his words.

He was weary, or worried.

"Don't leave yet," Bobby said.

"There's no reason to talk to Star like that," Milo said. "We should all leave."

"I don't think he'll let us," Bobby cautioned.

Abbattista smiled a warm, friendly smile. "No one ever walked out on King Arthur! I just want to play a short game, and then everyone can go about their way. I'm sorry if I scared anybody; Timur was just worried about the dog." Abbattista gestured to the dog, which had exited the other side of the long table to curl up next to Charles at the south entrance. It couldn't have been less interested. "It would be a shame to waste all this good food," Abbattista said.

"We're okay. We'll stay and hear more about the game. I've been reading about Kepler," Bobby spoke quickly. "About his time in Linz, Germany . . ."

Milo was still on his feet. He walked around the table and stood next to Abbattista. "Thank you for the invitation and the meal, but I'm really very tired. I had a number of drinks to celebrate the successes we've been having. If I don't get to bed soon, I'm going to fall asleep on my feet."

"Milo, wait just a second," Bobby urged.

"Are you sure you don't want to play?" Terry asked Milo.

Bobby stood up. The movement caused Rife and Charles to tense visibly. The pit raised its head, eyes still half closed. "Milo—" Bobby said.

Milo walked across to the large dining room and stood before the exit. Timur followed, taking longer steps to close the gap between the two men. At the door, Milo turned to Bobby and gave him a short, quick wave. When he turned back again and put his hand on the doorknob, Timur drew a revolver from his belt and clubbed Milo over the back of the head.

A blood vessel broke beneath Milo's thin skin, firing out from the point of contact in a crimson arc. He fell to the ground with a thud.

38

MINUTES HAD PASSED, and Bobby's eyes were still fixed on Milo's limp, bloody body on the floor of the dining room. They'd taken away Bobby's phone, Charles hustling outside after reading what he had texted Lapeyre.

Somewhere over his left shoulder, Star was screaming, then her voice grew muffled and she started to gag. He rolled his gaze over to Abbattista, who was still sitting at the head of the table, mock sorrow unable to hide the smug expression on his face. Timur was placing the revolver in front of Abbattista.

Everything felt distant. As an athlete, Bobby was used to thinking fast in high pressure situations, but this was so much different. Abbattista smiled at him, waved a hand in front of his gaze, and said, "Hello?"

Bobby stood up and steadied himself at the table. "Did you kill him?"

"Probably not," Abbattista looked at Milo on the ground. "Actually, I don't know. He's pretty fragile."

"Why are you doing this? What's the point?" Bobby was still buying time, but also giving his mind a chance to adjust to the new reality. Various emotions were racing for dominance: fear, sadness, outrage. They brought clarity and adrenaline.

Abbattista's mask of calm slipped off his face. "He was trying to leave the game. The game everyone plays. Survival. Or, more pessimistically, we could call it 'who dies first?'" He rose to his feet, and veins appeared in his neck, just for an instant. "Because you can't break into my house, walk into my bedroom when I'm screwing a whore, ATTACK ME, and think that's the end of the story, Bobby. Jesus."

Abbattista sat back down, shaking his head. He took a drink of wine, calm once more. "You don't know it, but a few minutes ago, you finally wrote your first horoscope. It reads: 'Libra—For the last week I have played a big trick on you, but certain people will soon solve my little riddle, including Detective Therese Lapeyre. After I kill her and my insufferable boss, Milo Maslow, I will kill myself in the shadow of the Soledad Cross in La Jolla. The game will be over, and I will be the winner, for I, Bobby Frindley, am the horoscope writer.'"

"Prose is a little clunky," Bobby said. He could see that Rife had a gloved hand clamped over Star's mouth. Tears were rolling down her cheeks. He turned back to Abbattista. "And why? You already framed Madrigal, perfectly. I'm assuming you put Stephanie Ambrosino in his garage sometime after the police got their hands on him."

"There are always complications. Always. The game never really stops. Sit with me."

Timur pushed Bobby back down into the seat.

Abbattista put his hand on Bobby's shoulder and squeezed. "Timur paid Jack Madrigal to say all the things he said. He wanted to be famous. He had some kind of sick fixation about it, so he jumped at the chance. The deal was we just had to take care of his daughter while he went back to prison." Abbattista shook his head. "I don't believe the man has a daughter. He's quite insane."

"It also gave him a chance for a little revenge on Leslie Consorte," Bobby suggested. "Was killing Leslie part of the deal?"

Abbattista shook his head again, more vigorously this time. "We set Detective Consorte up to be framed as Madrigal's accomplice, but he disappeared before we could put it all together. That was the first thing to go wrong. Unless you consider the fact that Stephanie Ambrosino didn't actually get raped. When did frat boys become such pussies?" Abbattista rose to his feet, his hand still on Bobby's shoulder. "Madrigal doesn't even know Consorte is gone. It won't take long for his whole story to fall apart. People like that can't be trusted to improvise, even when their heart is in the right place."

"So, you're going to frame me instead?" Bobby was connecting the dots for Abbattista. "It had to be someone high-profile enough that it redirects everyone's attention off Madrigal. And dead enough to not have to answer any questions."

"It was a pretty easy choice after your call the other night. What was it you promised? Oh yes, to pursue me with unholy journalistic fury until you'd fully exposed my crimes?"

"And I uncovered the truth, just two days later," Bobby said, with as much arrogance as he could muster. He looked at Abbattista and the man rearranged before Bobby's eyes. His kindly expression now seemed hollow. His smile, which an hour ago had appeared warm, was now just a jagged facsimile.

Bobby glanced at Star again. She was struggling against Rife's grip, but she didn't seem to be in immediate danger.

He hoped that time was on his side. He just needed to buy a little more of it. "Your wife died, how many years ago?" he asked Abbattista.

"She was an upstanding woman right until the end," the older man answered with a half smile.

Star smacked Rife hard with the back of her forearm. He didn't let go, instead using his own forearm to pin against her neck, holding her face down on the table. "I always get the worst jobs," he said, ruefully.

It took all of Bobby's resolve to keep up his mask of calm indifference.

"Your wife dies a couple of years ago, and it makes you rethink everything. You realize that all your influence, all your money, all the things you've collected—this fancy house—they're not actually important. Because they couldn't keep her alive. Did you try praying, when you realized she didn't have long to live?"

Abbattista grinned. "The housekeeper prayed for her every night for a month. Prayer could not save her. Of course it couldn't! Don't be ludicrous. My wife was a moralist. She never cheated on me, despite my many indiscretions. She was traditional, modest and loving, and I hated. Every. Bone. In. Her. Body. You're too young to know this, but when you're tied to a person for forty years, you'd rather be anywhere except by their side." Abbattista held his right first clenched triumphantly. "After she died, I couldn't believe how free I felt." Abbattista turned to Rife, who was still standing behind Star. "Cover her ears a minute," he demanded. "I don't want her to hear this part."

Half of Star's head was pinned against the table. Rife covered her upturned ear with his free hand.

"Soulmates? True love? Good? Evil? These concepts aren't any more real than horoscopes," Abbattista whispered to Bobby. "They're just more fancy words for superstition. The only reason society even functions is because we agree to play along in these shared delusions. What my wife's passing made me realize is the way that death can set us free. Not my own death." Abbattista put his hand on his chest. "Other people's deaths. Why did I waste so many years dealing with the inconveniences of her cloying personality? Why did I wait for some tiny cellular misfire to do what I had been desperate to do for so long?"

Abbattista picked up the revolver again. "Contrary to your original point, my money did not fail me when my wife passed. Quite the opposite. While my 'soulmate' died coughing up blood, money stood by me and granted endless opportunities."

"By your logic, it's just green paper," Bobby said.

"If you're going to believe in one shared delusion, definitely pick money," Abbattista said. "It's a physical cipher for power. Not as real as the bullets in this gun, but capable of so much more. Money gave me these men who will take away your life. It bought me this house isolated on a cliff, so no one is around to prevent me from doing whatever I want." Abbattista nodded to Rhona, who was lying on the couch with her forearm over her eyes. "Look there. That's what money looks like when it's molded into flesh. Could anything be more erotic? These last few days, my money has allowed me to indulge my wildest impulses, and when I was done, it paid Madrigal to wash me of my sins." Abbattista lowered the revolver, pointing it casually in Bobby's direction. "And now it's going to protect me again, when your dead body does what Madrigal can't."

39

THERESE LAPEYRE WAS still trying to get over the size of the man in the car next to her. She was driving a standard issue, unmarked Chevy Malibu. Beside her in the passenger seat, Sarah Kohl's husband, Navy Seabee Eli Kohl, was so large that his elbows, forearms, knees, and thighs filled every piece of space, leaving none to spare. Therese estimated that Eli was roughly six foot seven and bumping up against three hundred pounds of pure muscle.

They were driving North on the 5 Freeway, and in a mile they would exit into La Jolla and begin the slow crawl up Soledad Mountain. When Therese had told Eli about Bobby's text, Eli had offered no explanation. He'd simply risen to his feet, kissed Sarah on the forehead, and walked out of the hospital room ahead of Therese. Before he would get into the Malibu, he'd walked to his own car, a curiously small Toyota Camry, and rummaged in the trunk until he found a long canvas bag. He now rode with the bag across his large knees, his thick fingers folded over its top. Rolling onto the freeway off-ramp, Therese had tried to get information from Eli. What was the danger? Should she radio for backup? It certainly felt like it. Eli had remained silent, answering the questions politely but without real effort, his mind clearly elsewhere. In answer to the question about backup, he shook his head a curt no.

Halfway up the mountain, she tried again, deciding she was most likely to succeed if she brought Eli's focus back from the nether and earned his trust. "You're a Navy Seabee; is that right?"

"Yes."

"Stationed where?"

"Yeonpyeong Island. South Korea."

Therese didn't say anything. She hoped Eli would feel socially obligated to fill in the silence. Finally, he did.

"We're expanding the green zone, building trenches and tank traps. A new command combat center. Things have been heating up since New Year's, but it's mostly safe work, which keeps Sarah happy. I'm trying to get into recon."

"The SEALs?"

Eli nodded. "The knock against me is that I'm too big, but I can pass the tests just as well as anyone else. To be honest, my captain is a nice guy, we're close, but I have a feeling he's keeping me back, refusing to let me out of the unit."

"Of course. With your size, you must do the work of two men."

Eli's face drew into a tight smile. They were passing the cellular towers and less than a mile from the Abbattista estate. Therese quickly said, "You know anything about Terry Abbattista?"

"Just that Bobby told me he was the horoscope killer. Then I read in the paper that someone else was."

"We already caught the horoscope killer. Abbattista is a pillar of the community," Therese said, shaking her head. "I hope we're not wasting our time here. Bobby didn't respond to my last two texts, which is ridiculous. Is he prone to dramatic behavior? Can he be trusted?"

Impossibly, Eli's jaw tightened even more. Therese could see a sharp mind moving behind his eyes. "In my experience, Bobby is not an honorable person," Eli said.

At the end of the block, Therese could see a man standing at Abbattista's front gate. She squinted into the gloaming of the evening, noting the man was way too big to be Bobby Frindley. Therese brought the car down to idle speed and hung her police badge out the window. The man, a large fellow with a mop of curly brown hair and a T-shirt several sizes too small for his traps, lats, and biceps, walked slowly around the car and looked down at her.

"Detective Therese Lapeyre. I'm looking for Bobby Frindley."

"He's inside. They're having dinner, but they're expecting you. You wouldn't be interrupting."

"Thanks." Therese started to pull the car forward again, driving past the house to park on the empty street. Before she could, the big man slapped his palm on the hood.

"Use the driveway. Terry says you're to be treated as a guest."

"The VIP treatment," Therese said under her breath. She rolled the steering wheel to her right, while the big man punched a code into the silver press box by the front door. There was a deep metallic clanking, and the gate chugged open, revealing a long driveway spreading out toward a five-car garage and a canopy covering three more parking spaces. She had driven halfway onto the estate grounds before she noticed how tense Eli had become. He was gripping his canvas bag so tightly that his fingers were turning beet red.

Once the gate started to close behind them, Eli said, "I think I've seen this guy before. Turn the car around. Now." Eli had unzipped his bag and was frantically digging through the gear inside.

"The biggest danger we face here is high-powered lawyers wielding lawsuits—" Therese began. She didn't finish her sentence.

The large man was still waving the car forward, indicating a spot on the driveway next to the other cars. When Therese stopped rolling toward him, the man flashed her a confused expression and walked to the hood of the car. Something in his posture had set off a warning bell in Therese Lapeyre's brain. "I think you're right," she told Eli, reaching behind her back for where her firearm was resting against the seat cushion.

The curly-haired man withdrew a pistol from the center of his back, its snout elongated by a wicked looking silencer. Therese had her own weapon free, and she was pulling it under her arm, just past her ribs when the first sickly explosion went off in her chest.

It was fire-hot at the base of her sternum, but there was no pain, she just felt a sudden senility that made holding her gun upright nearly impossible. There was a second thudding sound, like a hammer hitting meat, and her left arm went numb. She felt another explosion in her ribs. Her gun clanged to the floor of the passenger seat, between Eli's legs. Therese tried to reach for the car door handle but was overcome by weakness and her hand kept slipping off the metal grip. Her other hand came to rest on the police CB, but she couldn't push the button. She couldn't remember how to tell her muscles to operate the suddenly, vastly complicated machine. On the third try for the doorknob, her whole body collapsed forward, her cheek coming to rest against the cool glass of the driver's door window. At that moment, pain started to join the hollow fire burning in her chest.

What happened next Therese only experienced from the furthest periphery. Her senses were dulled by the expanding throb in the center of her body. Face sliding down the window, she could hear Eli somewhere in the distance, gurgling and coughing and spitting. Long, low moans emitted simultaneously from a distant place and the seat next to her. Therese could see the fractured front window, the three precise round circles where the bullets had passed through on her side, and three more on Eli's side. Therese could hear the car door open and, still faintly aware of her own location, she expected to spill down on the bloody red concrete driveway. But it wasn't her door that opened, it was on Eli's side.

Therese watched with empty, ancient eyes as the large curly-haired man began rapidly reloading his pistol. The bullets were in the pocket of his jeans, but his jeans were snug, as tight as his formfitting shirt, and he could only roll one or two bullets out at a time. Therese could see Eli at the hood of the car now, lumbering forward, one arm clutching his belly, another dripping with blood and grasping at the hood of the Malibu for balance. The large man got one bullet in the long rectangular clip, but the second and third leaped out of his hands and danced on the ground at his feet. Therese's eyes fell closed for a moment. She opened them at the sound of another shot fired, just a gentle wisp as the bullet whipped out of the silencer.

Eli shivered as the bullet struck him somewhere. His huge body convulsed, and he stopped his progress on the right front fender, leaning heavily there. Therese closed her eyes again. When she forced them open once more, Eli had his huge fingers around the man's throat. The man was hitting him hard in the stomach, raining expertly placed punches again and again on Eli's bloody midsection, but Eli's big hands were fitted tightly around the man's windpipe.

The punches slowly lost force; they came less often. The man lifted his left hand and wrapped it around Eli's wrists. He pulled, pulled with everything he had to free his trachea from Eli's death grip. The man was big. He must have spent hours every day working with weights. His muscles bulged as his body fought against death.

He might as well have been trying to lift a house.

When the man died in Eli's arms, Therese felt a tiny surge of adrenaline. They were only twenty feet or so from the street. Even deeply wounded, Eli could obviously still walk; he was ambulatory. He could drive them to safety. Therese saw Eli glance into the car and their eyes met. Therese mouthed a silent "help me." The words dribbled like spit on her chin.

40

"WHY STEPHANIE?" STAR demanded as Rife took his forearm off her neck. She shook her head and stared hatefully at Abbattista. "What did she do to deserve being brought into your . . ." Star stopped, like she couldn't find the right word for what Abbattista had done.

Abbattista smiled, lowering the gun for a moment. He spread his hands apart, palms up in the pose of a blackjack dealer. "A few weeks ago, I was returning home from a visit to the *Register*. I bumped into Stephanie Ambrosino in the elevator, literally bumped into her; she was exiting, I was getting on.

"My knuckles grazed her butt cheek, and she went crazy, howling about how I'd done it on purpose. I hadn't, and it stung to be accused of something when I wasn't remotely guilty. On the ride home, I was thinking about the whole experience, which I'll admit had me driving slowly.

"Cars were racing past, not bothering to use their turn indicators. A man in a GMC truck drove up on my bumper, honking his horn and extending his middle finger crudely. When he screeched into the passing lane, I heard him call me a 'piece-of-shit old fart.'"

Abbattista enunciated each of the words of the insult as if impressed by the man's creativity. "He was a disgusting man, covered in tattoos with stringy black hair and an unkempt beard. I followed him home and wrote his address on a receipt I had in my glove box. I was fuming with anger. Then I didn't think of the man in the GMC or Stephanie again, for a while.

"I was in my library reading Kepler's *Mysterium Cosmographicum* when an idea occurred to me. Kepler had used horoscopes to rule the Bohemians. A brilliant scientist and mathematician, but the only way he could get the king to pay attention to him was by passing off his advice as astrological 'truths.' A divine message from God! So, I decided to borrow a bit of his magic for my purposes as well. To use Camus's words, I had been languishing in the harsh light of truth instead of enjoying the glory of the lie.

"I walked out to the Caddy and dug through the glove box until I found the receipt with the truck driver's address. I felt a great rush of happiness when he died, screaming. After that, we went to Stephanie's apartment and grabbed her. If you thought she was indignant when I accidentally grazed her ass, you should have seen how she acted when we bound and stashed her in one of my warehouses.

"The next night, I sent Timur out to bury the quarter million dollars below the cross in Presidio. It seemed a reasonable investment to participate in the game of a lifetime." Abbattista took a drink of his wine.

He turned to Star and smiled.

"But the quarter of a million dollars wasn't there," Star said.

"I almost killed Timur when it never surfaced. He swears he buried it, but it's most likely he took it to the post office and mailed it back to some babushka in the motherland. He's been letting Rhona slowly work off the debt," Abbattista explained.

"That's a lot of trouble just to kill two people," Star said.

"I buried the money. I honest to God did," Timur insisted.

"'Honest to God,' what a funny choice of words." Abbattista walk-ed around the table. He lifted a lock of Star's hair in his hand, feeling the texture. "I didn't do it just to kill two people. Though that was satisfying. Mostly I wanted to see how far I could go with a lie. I wanted to test the upper limit of society's blind faith in superstition. I broke all the rules of horoscope writing. My predictions were grand-iose, specific, and utterly ridiculous." Abbattista went back and sat in front of Bobby, his face dropping into mock sorrow. "And yet, people believed. I learned a horrifying lesson from Timur's screw-up. It didn't even matter if the crimes were committed or not! Everybody in the city was already onboard. They were seeing all the predictions as truth, no matter how silly I made them." Abbattista grinned. "Did you hear there are copycats now? In several different cities! My religion is spreading."

Inwardly, Bobby felt terrible. Abbattista had been ahead of him from the start. Despite Bobby's dedication to the higher values of veracity, honesty, and truth, his investigative work had only served to stir up the city and prove the old maniac's point.

Outwardly, Bobby relaxed. "Nobody actually believed in the mysticism. They just liked the spectacle," he lied, stretching his feet onto the table, ankles crossed. "Besides, Timur might have stolen the money—"

"I buried it."

"—but you were making most of the predictions come true. It's not magical thinking when it's really happening. The brush fire near Fashion Valley? Which one of these clowns started that?"

Abbattista smiled, pointing a finger at Rife.

"People died. My friend died. And for what? So you could prove how stupid everyone is? You didn't accomplish anything," Star spat.

"That's fair. It's been a lot of fun though. By far my best game. And I've figured out a system that allows me to kill anyone who pisses me off, without repercussions." Abbattista rolled the chamber on the revolver. He stared menacingly at Bobby. "It sure beats waiting for cancer to do it."

Bobby tried to look as casual and unafraid as possible. "I accepted your challenge to a game. You're not going to back out now, are you?"

"Your conditions included seeing Milo and Star safely home. Obviously, that's no longer possible."

"But there is something you haven't done yet. You haven't shaken my belief in the existence of God. When I threatened you over the phone two nights ago, you said I hadn't ever met the horoscope killer; you said how could I believe that I was that special? But I had met you. I'd even had dinner with you. I'd played your games. I'd seen the pictures of the horses on your wall. I'd had my own experience with performance-enhancing drugs. I'd even recognized their effect on the body of the tiger. Every step of the way, God showed me exactly what I needed to see. God brought me to this moment for the purpose of stopping you."

"I wish you could hear how ridiculous that sounds."

Bobby just smiled his most satisfied smile, saying nothing.

"It's crazy, Bobby. By every definition of the word. You got lucky. You played it smart. You were tenacious. Those were your qualities, the results of life experience, schooling, genetics. There is no God, Bobby. None. Not even one."

"Prove it."

"How the fu—" Abbattista stood up midsentence and paced around the room. He addressed Rife, who still had his left hand on Star's shoulder. "Bobby here believes in an organized, just universe. I don't. We could argue about it all night, I suppose. Or, if we want to be a little more interesting, we could settle the disagreement with a simple game of chance."

Rife just nodded. "You want me to go outside and make sure Charles took care of that cop?"

"No, but clean up the blood on the floor before it dries, please." Abbattista seemed annoyed that Rife had broken his rhythm. He opened the chamber of the revolver and emptied the bullets. He spread them on the table, paying close attention to the way each looked. He chose one, held it closer to his face for another inspection, then loaded it back into the cylinder of the revolver.

Bobby could feel a hollow despair growing in the pit of his stomach. Each minute passed without rescue even though Lapeyre had now had plenty of time to leave the hospital and make it up Mount Soledad. Bobby kept waiting for an insistent knock on the door. It was fair to say that his life depended on it. But the house was dreadfully silent. *Did Lapeyre ignore my message?* he thought desperately. *Or have I already led her and Eli to their own deaths?*

"This gun is a—what? Timur?" Abbattista asked.

"Smith and Wesson."

"Let's pretend together that God really did want you in this situation. He led you to me with the sole intention of stopping me. It seems then that God would want you to survive dinner, right? In fact, by your logic, he would cause it to happen, wouldn't he? Show me." Abbattista put the gun down on the table.

Bobby stood up and reached for it and Abbattista snatched it away again. "Timur, you have another gun, I suppose? Bring it over here and put it on Bobby's temple. If he points this revolver anywhere but his own skull, kill him for me."

Timur walked over to the table, spread his legs in a catcher's stance, and pushed another gun against Bobby's left temple.

Abbattista touched the long steel barrel of the Smith and Wesson with his fingertips, then he spun the chamber and held it to Bobby's temple. He lifted Bobby's right hand and wrapped it around the hilt.

Timur stood tensely at Bobby's shoulder, the other gun held high and ready.

"Go on now," Abbattista urged. "It's time to pull the trigger."

Bobby's hand was shaking. Abbattista had been arrogant enough to give him a gun, but could Bobby get it turned around in time? And what if he did and the chamber didn't have a bullet?

As calmly as he could, he considered the percentages.

Before the Olympics, Bobby was always climbing up the five- and seven-meter diving platforms at the Olympic-class pool where he trained in Orange County. Once in a while, some jackass teammate would convince him to try the ten-meter. He'd get all the way up and if he looked over the side, he wouldn't be able to jump. The only way to do it was to run from the back and get himself moving too fast to stop once he'd made it to the end of the platform and saw the eminent danger far, far below.

Bobby pulled the trigger.

Click.

Abbattista let out a hoot of pleasure. He fell back into his chair, delighted.

Star sobbed.

Timur said, "He did it! I can't believe he did it." He stood, his eyes wide. "If he'd gotten the bullet, would it have hit me? Wouldn't it have gone straight through his brain and right into my face? Why didn't someone warn me he was really going to pull the trigger?"

"He's a man of faith. Daniel in the lion's den! You should always stand behind him," Abbattista offered.

Timur took the advice, placing the gun back on Bobby's temple and then sliding it along his hairline until the barrel settled into the tiny groove at the apex of Bobby's skull.

"You just beat twenty-percent odds," Abbattista told Bobby. "An accomplishment, but hardly proof of a divine entity." Abbattista nodded to the revolver. "Do it again," he said.

Bobby returned the gun to his own right temple. His knees and arms were shaking. He had to shove the barrel tightly against his own head just to keep the gun from dancing all around.

Star watched, blinking through tear shrouded eyes. "Don't pull the trigger again," she pleaded. "Just let him do what he is going to do."

There was a scraping sound, and Bobby glanced left to see Rife was dragging Milo over to the couch. The pit bull followed, lapping at the blood running down Milo's neck. Rife had fetched a bucket full of sudsy water. After a moment, he picked up the mop and tried to gently nudge the dog away from Milo's head.

Bobby bit his lower lip until he tasted blood and pulled the trigger.

Click.

"You remember to put a bullet in this thing?" he asked Abbattista.

Abbattista responded with appreciative laughter. Timur's chest huffed up and down with happiness.

Bobby lowered the gun to the table, hoping that Timur wouldn't consider the action threatening enough to follow Abbattista's orders and shoot him. His whole body wanted to go limp. He felt like he'd just run a marathon.

He had managed to dramatically improve the chances that the gun in his hand would fire a live round. Now he just needed to get it pointed in the right direction.

He turned in his chair to face Timur. The motion caused Timur's pistol to slide back around to his forehead. Bobby looked up the long gunmetal barrel. "You're okay with him and Rhona, huh? I interrupted them screwing just last night."

"It wouldn't happen if it bothered me," Timur said.

"That true, Terry?" Bobby said.

Abbattista waved away the question. He made a few noncommittal grunting noises. "Don't try to talk your way out of this, Bobby. Only God can save you now."

Bobby continued, "It's funny that a great Olympian, a pinnacle of physical control like yourself, lets a guy play around with your girlfriend anytime he wants. I'm not going to be judgmental here, but—"

Before Bobby could finish, Timur swung the pistol in a vicious arc, smashing it down against Bobby's cheek. The skin split where the hammer connected, and Bobby felt the sting of blood flowing down his chin and neck. It disoriented him more than he expected. He only got the Smith and Wesson raised six inches off the table before the blow to his head sent the gun skipping out of his hand, bouncing to a stop on the tabletop.

"That's distasteful, Bobby," Abbattista said. "You shouldn't be trying to provoke him. He's very loyal."

"Now that he has your quarter of a million dollars, sure," Bobby said, dabbing at his bloody cheek. "That's two I owe you now, Timur."

Abbattista lifted the gun back up to Bobby's temple and once more wrapped Bobby's fingers around the hilt. "It's time for your next chamber."

"What'd you do with Leslie Consorte?"

"I'm going to count to five. If he hasn't pulled the trigger by the time I say five, I want you to shoot him, okay, Timur?"

"My pleasure," Timur grunted.

Bobby took a deep breath and prayed, "God, we both know that it's not good to test you. But please let Star, Milo, and me live through this, and if Milo is dead, please accept his soul up into heaven."

Abbattista started to respond, but instead his mouth lapsed into a broad, condescending smile. "One."

Bobby reset his grip on the revolver. Timur was already angry. Bobby might be able to rile him up again and take a blind shot by turning his wrist just slightly. He tried not to notice how snug the barrel of Timur's weapon was against his skull.

"Two."

There were three chambers left. He was still facing thirty-three percent odds his gun wouldn't fire, even if he got it turned onto Timur. Sweat dripped down Bobby's forehead, making it even harder to hold the gun steady.

"Three."

God? Are you up there?

"Four."

Bobby pulled the trigger. A gun exploded in light and sound and fire. Bobby toppled back in his chair, his nerves twitching and spasming every inch of his body. When he hit the floor, he saw Rife fall to the ground six feet away at the same time and with the same velocity. Rife's body thumped against Milo's, bouncing off, lifeless.

The gun discharged again. The glass serving vase on the table shattered, and water ran free across the hard wood. Abbattista dove for the ground. Eli stepped through the door, smoking pistol raised in Abbattista's direction. Actually, stepped was the wrong description. He stumbled forward, his right arm clutching his stomach, blood seeping out over his wrist and hand.

Timur dove beneath the table, and Bobby immediately threw himself onto the Serbian Olympian. He grabbed at Timur's right wrist with both hands and slammed the gun free. He hit Timur hard on the crown of his head, and the other man's body went limp.

Eli fired again. The bullet sent Rhona scuttling away from the couch. She leaped behind the TV, drawing her feet out of sight. There was suddenly silence, broken by the long low growl of the pit bull. Eli turned toward the danger too slowly. He was too badly injured, his mind numbed by pain and loss of blood. He did manage to fire one last shot, but the pit was too close, lunging through empty air right for his throat. Eli brought his gun arm up just in time for the dog to latch its jaws tightly around his elbow.

Two thousand years ago, the dog's ancestors had marched into battle beside ancient Greek warriors. For the next two millennia the breed would be dragged through Europe, baited, lowered into fighting pits, then carted across the ocean to the American frontier, for another century or two of savage gaming. The dog was ready for this fight. Eli fell to his knees, screaming and shaking his arm back and forth. The dog clung to his elbow joint, a shark dangling on a fisherman's line. Eli clawed at its face with his free hand, his eyes awash in pain.

"Hold the dog out," Bobby shouted. "Hold it away from your body." He scrambled around for Timur's gun, but it had fallen under his heavy body. Bobby saw instead the Smith and Wesson. He dove for it, came up out of a roll and fired at the dangling animal.

Click.

He fired again. The bullet sliced through the dog's neck and it fell to the ground with a thud.

Eli remained on his knees, pawing at his lacerated elbow.

Abbattista moved much more quickly. The old man bolted upright and raced through a door on the west side of the dining room and out into the backyard.

When the bullets started flying around, Star had taken refuge behind the couch. She popped her head out. "I'll help Eli," she told Bobby. "Cut through the rec room and see if you can catch Terry on the other side of the lawn."

"Tell me you recorded the confession," Bobby said, remembering her trick at the frat house.

"Every second," Star said, holding her phone up, the screen alive and recording. She ran toward Eli. When she reached him, she tried to support his weight. They stumbled together toward the western door.

"Where's Lapeyre?" Bobby said.

"She's outside, shot, maybe dead," Eli said.

Eli and Star went out the door and across the lawn in the same direction Abbattista had run.

41

B OBBY PATTED RIFE'S pockets until he found Rife's cell phone. Blood was running in tiny rivers across Rife's chest and right shoulder. Bobby held the phone to Rife's face to unlock it, then dialed the police. When the dispatcher answered he yelled into the phone, "We need an ambulance. Terry Abbattista's house on top of Soledad Mountain. Officer Therese Lapeyre's been shot. Please hurry!" He didn't know the address so he just laid the phone down, hoping they could trace it.

Bobby ran toward the exit worried that he was now too late to catch Abbattista. He was almost out of the room when a bullet spit through the wood frame of the door. He dove forward into the next room, grasping the first thing he could find, a long cue from the pool table.

He waited, crouched. Two more shots came through the door, the wood shattering in Bobby's direction but well out of danger of hitting him.

Bobby could hear his own ragged breath. The splintered door swung open. Bobby knifed back through, following the pool stick into the dining room, swinging it in a downward arc. Timur was standing next to the table, still a little off-balance, the gun held loosely in his hand. The stick caught him directly on the left wrist. Bobby smacked the gun out of his right hand with an open palm. To do so he had to drop the pool cue. It tangled in their legs, sending both men into a clumsy somersault.

Timur was up first, grabbing the cue. He bashed Bobby on the shoulder.

Bobby scrambled to his feet, dancing backward, favoring his right side. He backed through the door into the rec room, his eyes locked tight on the pool cue in Timur's hands.

Timur ignored the fallen gun, moving toward Bobby with the cue. "Just like the first time we met, eh?" Timur said. "You made fun of me that day for making the Olympics in two sports." Timur dodged forward and swung the cue low. It caught Bobby in the left thigh, sending a bolt of pain through his leg. "Do you remember what sports they were, Bobby?"

"I remember they were lady sports." Bobby kept shuffling backward.

Timur's eyes bulged. He stepped forward in a fencer's riposte, swinging the cue in a small arc and bringing it down on Bobby's left ear.

Bobby felt a rush of nausea as his eardrum exploded in four different numbing tones. Timur said something else, a bemused smirk on his face, but Bobby could not understand. He had to shut his eyes to regain his focus. Timur hit him again, hard, across the top of the head. Bobby stumbled to his left, aiming for the railing, aiming especially for the unfinished piece of railing damaged during the assembly of the Petosiris platform.

Bobby held his hands up to Timur. He was in pain from so many different places. "Gymnastics and fencing. Games of balance, violence, and control. I got you pretty good a few minutes ago, didn't I?"

"I was faking."

"You were counting Serbian sheep. I said I owed you two. You've still got one more coming."

"Doesn't seem that way to me," Timur said, swinging the cue from behind his head.

Bobby stood up straight, his arms lowered to expose his upper body.

Timur took the wild swing, throwing all his force behind it, trying to take Bobby's head off his shoulders.

Bobby rolled backward, accepting the weight of the weapon against his upper chest. He felt more ribs fracture, a hot, blinding pain searing through his body. Before Timur could pull away from him he locked his elbows, pinning the cue against his armpit. Bobby dug in his heels, pushing himself back through the broken railing, moving with the force of the swing. The weight of Bobby's body dragged both men backward, toppling through the air, once more enmeshed in a tangle of limbs. They landed with a splash in the deep end of Abbattista's indoor-outdoor pool.

Bobby let his old instincts take over. If he'd had time to think about it, he would have acknowledged the pain in his chest, the deep hum in his shattered ear, the throbbing of his shoulder and the crown of his head. But Bobby didn't have to think about anything at all; his legs started to kick outward, his arms moved through the water to steady his equilibrium. He began to egg-beat, his chest level with the water, then above it. Timur bobbed to the surface, gasping for air, and Bobby punched him in the face, never losing his posture. Timur came up a second time, lunging for Bobby and grasping for Bobby's throat. Bobby treaded backward, pushing the top of Timur's head down and clubbing him back underwater again. Each time he rose to the surface, gasping, Bobby treaded high and beat him back down with his forearm.

On the fourth blow, Timur's body went slack and he rolled onto his stomach, face down in the water. Bobby pushed him under, counting to thirty to make sure he wasn't playing possum again. When Bobby reached twenty-two, Timur began to thrash around, flinging his elbows, kicking his feet, clawing at Bobby's arms, anything to get his head back above water.

When he'd finally kicked his last kick, completely limp in the water, Bobby again counted to twenty. Then he dragged Timur's wet, top-heavy body to the shallow end and began CPR.

42

TIMUR COUGHED OUT the water, spitting and vomiting on his side, great heaving gasps for air racking his chest.

Bobby climbed back to his feet. He was soaked, head to toe, but he was in one piece. His heart was beating in short, controlled bursts. There was a light on the end table next to Abbattista's desk. He yanked its electrical cord free and hog-tied Timur's arms and legs. Then he walked out the door separating the rec room from the backyard.

The wind was blowing off the ocean, strong enough to create a choppy break and thick clouds of white water. A waterskiing boat, moored alone twenty feet off the coast of Black's Beach, rocked and kicked with the pitch of the tide. Bobby scanned the backyard for signs of Abbattista, Eli, or Star. He couldn't see anybody, so he limped along the long green lawn in the direction where the backyard curved left and out of sight.

He hadn't taken more than a few steps when the ocean winds brought the tenor of desperate voices to his humming ears. Bobby ran, following the ghostly sounds to the east, along the tall retaining wall. When he reached the edge of the backyard, he saw Star standing a few feet away from Eli, her back to him. Eli stood stoic, at the very end of the wall, looking down over the edge of the backyard. They hadn't found Abbattista, Bobby realized. His fight with Timur had allowed Abbattista to slip through their fingers.

But as Bobby got closer to his two friends, he realized he had misjudged the situation. Star ran toward Bobby and threw her arms around his neck. Her body was shivering.

"Eli threw him over. He was begging for his life. Screaming in such a terrible way—"

Bobby disentangled himself from Star's arms and walked cautiously over to the edge of the retaining wall. He stood next to Eli and looked down. Bobby could see into the backyards of the other multimillion-dollar estates along the edge of the cliff. Abbattista's retaining wall stood close to thirty feet high, and beyond that there was another twenty-foot drop, created by the natural curve of the mountain.

At the very bottom, fifty feet down, Bobby could make out the crumpled corpse of Terry Abbattista. He'd fallen through the sky, probably screaming for his life, unable to comprehend that it had ended the moment Eli had let him go. He must have landed on his feet because both femur bones were jutting out from the bottom half of his legs, pointing up at Bobby.

La Chute, Bobby said to himself.

Bobby realized that Eli was swaying, standing beside him, elbow bitten down to the bone. He was still looking over the cliff at Abbattista's broken body. He made a grunting noise and Bobby saw that his face was ashen. Blood from bullet wounds on his chest, ribs, and thigh soaked his clothes.

Eli pitched slightly forward, in the direction he'd sent Abbattista, and Bobby caught him by the T-shirt, lowering him safely onto his back, with some difficulty. Star grabbed his left arm, and they dragged the big man well clear of the edge.

Then came the sounds of sirens, and Bobby saw flashlights illuminating darkened rooms of the house, and he heard the urgent shouting of policemen. He wondered if Rhona had had time to escape. Time to scuttle off to the gym and refine one more perfect body part before laying the trap for another man of means.

Bobby touched his ear gingerly. "I've got to lie down," he told Star.

So he did, and she joined him, face down in the wet grass. Star edged forward and kissed him on the cheek. "Once we get clear of this, let's go look for the money in Presidio Park," she whispered.

"We're too late," Bobby grunted. "Somebody already has it."

Weapons drawn, the police busted out onto the backyard, swarming like flies, barking like angry dogs. They yelled and pointed their weapons and dragged Bobby back to his feet. It looked like a dance, all the blue uniforms and yellow lights and shiny golden badges weaving back and forth in frenetic electric synchronicity.

When I write the next article, Bobby thought to himself, *I think I'll end with this image.*

EPILOGUE

E X-LIEUTENANT DETECTIVE LESLIE Consorte really liked hammocks. The problem was, once you were cradled in one, swinging between palm trees in the warm breeze of a tropical shoreline, it was kind of hard to stay awake.

The wind blew across his cheeks and pushed the hammock gently back and forth. Leslie propped his eyes open long enough to look down over the white sand beach of Manuntel. A small village on the Oaxacan coast, Manuntel didn't get many tourists, and those who did arrive would stay for a day of Instagramming, then move on. Even the least transient gringo couldn't make it more than three or four weeks before an odd form of island fever would send them scuttling off in pursuit of a different type of perfection. No, strangers rarely stuck around Manuntel very long, despite its warm blue waters, rich biodiversity, and untouched sands. There just wasn't much to do in the tiny coastal town of five hundred with its spattering of beach shacks and single open-windowed, thatched-roofed tavern.

So it was with some curiosity that the inhabitants of the small Mexican beach town treated Leslie Consorte. He'd arrived rigid, paunched, and pallid. But as the months passed and the strange white man lingered around town, the locals had gotten used to seeing him lying on the sand or relaxing in a hand stitched hammock in the arms of the town's only *prostituta*. In the two months that had passed, they'd watched him slim down, losing his excess weight, gaining lean muscle and a dark, bronze complexion. From the start, he'd pitched in around town without being asked. He'd helped Ana Claudia repair her roof. He'd cleared rocks from the land for Moises to expand his marijuana farm, taking only a small bushel of weed for payment, which he would roll by hand and share liberally with the locals.

On this day in late October, Leslie was lying on his back, running his toes through the sand. A pack of local kids were splashing in the water. The tropical beach had just started to cool, as the fall months came and went. When Leslie would catch the eye of one of the children, they would smile and gesture in his direction.

"Unete," they'd yell.

Leslie was trying to learn Spanish. Even without the language, he knew that they were asking him to join them in the waves. Leslie simply smiled back and shook his head. He slid smoothly out of the hammock and pulled a ripe pouteria caimito from a tree growing at the edge of the sea. The yellow fruit was about the size of a tennis ball with an end nippled like a lemon. The first time he'd tried to peel one, months ago, he'd found his hands covered in soupy mess. After that he knew to bite directly into the fruit's soft flesh.

When Leslie walked away from the tree back toward his hammock, he strode with erect posture. His back hadn't been hurting him since the last week of August. It seemed obvious now what the real cause of his back pain had been: The United States of America.

Leslie lowered himself into the hammock, the juice of the caimito running down his cheek. He had his right hand digging deep into his pocket for a joint when he spotted another white person, picking his way along the long, soft sand beach.

Leslie sat up, at least the best you can in a hammock, and tracked the lone figure as he moved north to south, toward where Leslie himself was swinging lightly in the warm breeze. The Mexican kids spotted the new gringo just after Leslie, and they abandoned their play in the ocean to run at his heels, shouting questions that the man didn't seem to understand. As he drew closer, Leslie recognized something in his posture. This was a person he'd seen before, somewhere in his seventeen aborted years of police work. Leslie climbed out of the hammock, swinging his legs to the ground, the caimito dropping and gathering sand as it rolled away from his feet.

Leslie squinted his eyes, peering at the approaching figure.

"Oh, no," he whispered.

The man continued walking toward him, and now some of the kids were laughing and pointing at Leslie as if they understood the stranger's intentions at the same moment Leslie did. It seemed undignified to run, so Leslie Consorte simply waited in his hammock while Bobby Frindley picked his way along the long sand beach toward him. Leslie recognized Bobby from a distance, but as he drew closer, he was aware of subtle shifts in the way the young man carried himself. Like Leslie, the last few months had served Bobby well. He moved with assurance and strength, a man in full.

When Bobby reached the hammock, Leslie had managed to get the joint out of his pocket and was holding a long drag of smoke in his lungs. The boys nipping at Bobby's heels peeled away, an awareness of the gravity of the situation drawing them to a safe distance. Leslie exhaled and looked at Bobby as Bobby appraised the changes that had come over Leslie's own body.

"You look good, Leslie."

"Thanks, Bobby. You too."

"Last time I saw you, you were a zombie. All loose flesh and cheeseburger." Bobby leaned down and picked up the caimito, dusting it off.

"Mexico is a better place."

Bobby didn't say anything for a few moments. He stood, back slightly turned, arms crossed over his chest. His expression was unreadable. Leslie got up slowly from the hammock, inching his bathing suit back down from where it had crept up high on his waist. "I suppose I owe you an explanation," he said.

"You do. But let me tell you what I've spent the last few months learning first."

The two men walked together down to the edge of the shore. The pack of boys, not finding the drama they were hoping for, had returned to the water to play. They were leaping, from a full sprint, over the small waves as they crashed just past the reef.

Bobby picked up a stone and skipped it along the water. Then he said, "The reason you asked me to come back to the Theta Rho Kappa house is you truly believed the rape had happened. The reason you believed that was because the night before, you had discovered a quarter million dollars, buried under the cross on Presidio. Once you had all that money, the horoscopes must have suddenly seemed pretty realistic."

"We'd seen the tiger attack, and the dragging, when I found the cash—I mean, I didn't go looking for it. Lapeyre and I were there in anticipation of a crowd, and once Lapeyre started digging around her cross, I just figured—It was barely hidden. The dirt had been recently turned over, fresh . . ."

"So, you found the quarter million, stashed it somewhere, probably the trunk of your car, and then stuck around and worked the rest of your shift."

There was a large cropping of rocks, wet from high tide. Bobby sat on one. Leslie stood next to him watching the sea.

"I give you credit. Some people would have left right then and there, but you wanted to see justice done to the 'rapists.' Unfortunately, your newfound riches made you reckless. You not only burst into the house, but you clubbed the dog and shot the ceiling. Stephanie Ambrosino died at the bottom of that hill, but it's been impossible to prosecute the boys for even a misdemeanor—"

Leslie wanted to explain to Bobby that wasn't really his problem. He'd been dealing with weaknesses in the American judicial system for most of his adult life. But Leslie had felt a tiny sensation in the base of his spine for the last three months—ever since he'd arrived on the shores of Manuntel and realized he could be happy there. It had taken him a while to isolate exactly what that sensation was, but as his back pain had eased, the little mental itch had grown more and more real. One morning while the pretty Mexican prostitute had been snoring peacefully in his arms, he realized at last what it was. Guilt. His decampment had been a reflex, like a young boy fleeing imagined monsters in a darkened garage, with the difference being that Leslie's garage had actually held all sorts of real creatures, from chronic pain, to grubbing ex-wives, to serial killers and high cholesterol, and it had held the worst monster of all; it had held obsolescence.

"What do you want, Bobby?"

"We stopped him. We stopped the horoscope killer. It was Terry Abbattista."

"Even down here, I saw the news. I read your article in an internet café in Mexico City. I'm really sorry for what happened to Milo and Lapeyre."

"Milo's still in physical therapy. As sharp and mean as ever, even though he lost some control of the muscles in his face. I'll give the blame for Milo to Terry Abbattista, one hundred percent. But we could have stopped him sooner if we'd done our jobs better. Investigative Reporter. Detective." Bobby threw another skipping stone across the water. Leslie put his hands on his hips.

"I wasn't a detective anymore, Bobby. I was a babysitter. Didn't you notice how we handled each crime scene? The last three years of my life I spent waiting for the SIDs, with their rubber gloves and their baggies and their microscopes. Their team is steadily growing while the rest of the department shrinks. Lapeyre got the promotion to homicide on that first night in Clairemont, but I couldn't celebrate with her. She'd put so much into making detective, but there's really no job left. We just secure the crime scene and wait for the scientists. The clues that juries want aren't visible anymore. They're not a telling twitch of the eye or a tiny contradiction in motive or alibi. They're microscopic. Bugs. Or a follicle of hair. I have old eyes and an old mind, Bobby. I can't do what the scientists and the technicians can do. Lapeyre got a promotion to manager in a buggy whip factory."

"Milo told me the same thing about journalism when I started at the *Register*. Abbattista told me the same thing about God."

"The newspapers will be gone soon, just like the real detectives."

"Yeah, maybe. Maybe it's not so necessary to always be moving forward." Bobby watched the tanned, slender boys splashing in the break, then he lifted his right foot to avoid the last of a rolling wave. "I do think you're going to be wishing the detectives were gone pretty soon. You've got three tailing you right now. Nakamura and Pierce are in Acapulco pursuing a lead. Detective Lieutenant Therese Lapeyre is much closer. She's in Tuxiua. Thirty miles east of here."

"Did you say Detective Lieutenant?"

"Lapeyre's going to own the whole buggy whip factory soon. Her month-long stay in the hospital helped catch the attention of the higher-ups. My article didn't hurt either. But she paid a high price for a six percent pay increase. She lost a kidney and was in surgery for eighteen hours. They had to remove three bullets from her stomach and legs. If her partner had been around and had cautioned her not to trust Abbattista's men—"

Leslie felt that tiny circle of guilt in his brain widen. He decided that he wanted Bobby Frindley to leave. But he was curious about one thing.

"What sent Nakamura and Pierce to Acapulco? I've never been there."

"I did. I didn't want them to scoop me."

"You're here in pursuit of a story? A last follow-up to a larger story that you've ridden like a prized horse. How about letting this part go? I've found a good life here. I found a person in me that's better than the person I was."

"You found a quarter million dollars."

"Bobby, please. Forget about finding me."

"In the last six months, I've met three men I considered father figures. One's dead. One can't move the right side of his face. The last one's here on the beach. Do you remember what he told me before he disappeared, almost without a trace?"

Leslie didn't answer. He picked another caimito, bending a branch down to bring it into reach. Then he patted Bobby on the shoulder and started to walk toward the long dirt road that led to the small handful of shacks and shanties the natives called Manuntel. He would wish Ana Claudia goodbye. He would warn Moises and his pot plants that soon the police and a lot of media would be swarming the small Oaxacan town. Leslie would pack his few things and keep moving south. He'd heard Costa Rica was nice.

Before he reached the edge of the beach, he turned back and saw Bobby Frindley, still sitting on the rock, right at the high-water mark. The waves were crashing at his feet, pulled up by the invisible gravity of the moon, only to roll back to the deep blue sea. At that moment he remembered the answer to Bobby's last question. "I told him to write the whole story," Leslie realized. "Looks like that's exactly what he intends to do."

As Leslie crested the hill, Bobby stood up from his rock seat and smiled, waving goodbye without malice.

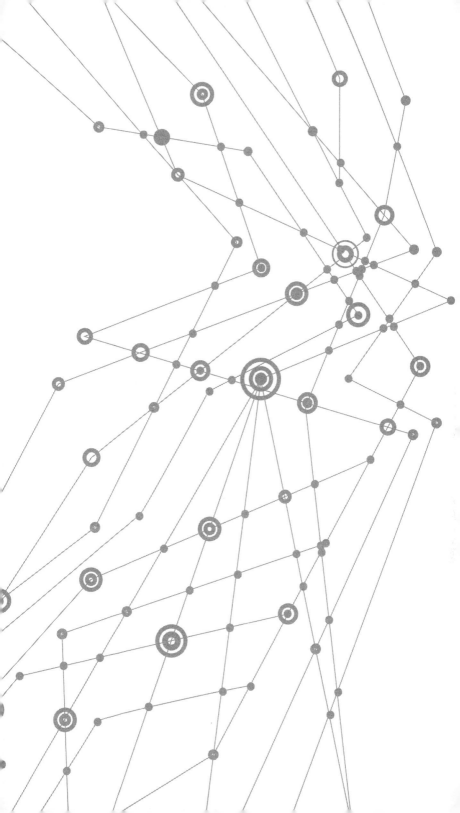

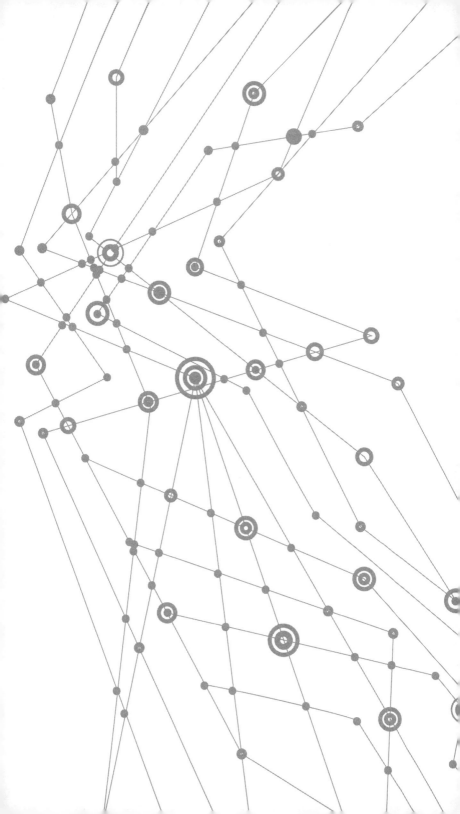

ABOUT THE AUTHOR

ASH BISHOP WAS born in Bloomington, Indiana, where his dad taught at Indiana University. His family moved to Orange County, California when he was very young, and he spent his formative years on the mean streets of Irvine. He attended college at UCSB, then the National University of Ireland, Galway. Ash is also a graduate of San Diego State University with an MFA in Creative Writing. He's married to a wonderful wife with two wonderful children. He is also the author of *Intergalactic Exterminators, Inc.*

He spent a good number of years as a high school English teacher, but he's also done a few less important, though slightly more glamorous, things. He worked in the video game industry for Sammy Studios and in educational app development; he even used to fetch coffee for Quentin Tarantino during the production of *Jackie Brown*. He currently assists military service members transitioning into the civilian workforce with the non-profit organization Hire Heroes USA. When he was young, he worked as a lifeguard because he may or may not have grown up without ever missing an episode of *Baywatch*.

Ash is a lifetime reader. He especially loves the mystery, science fiction, and fantasy genres. He grew up reading Chandler, Hammett, Gregory Mcdonald, and Robert B. Parker. His favorite author of all time is John D. MacDonald, and Ash recently visited Slip F-18 in Bahia Mar, Fort Lauderdale in MacDonald's honor.

ACKNOWLEDGMENTS

HEARTFELT THANKS TO Elana Gibson, Eric Wheeler, and Marissa Holzer for their help in making this novel so much better than it would have been otherwise. Thanks also to my parents, Ash and Sue Bishop, for raising me to believe that anything is possible. Thank you to the late, great Joe Rascoff, an early *Horoscope Writer* champion. And a special thanks to Jennifer: companion, confidant, inspiration, ace PR manager, and loving wife.

If you enjoyed
Ash Bishop's *The Horoscope Writer*,
we hope you will consider leaving a review
to help our authors.

Also check out
Lest She Forget by Lisa Malice.

1

MY HEARTBEAT IS racing, almost synchronized to the windshield wipers slapping furiously at the snow alighting on the car. The frantic rhythm draws me in, leaving me staring ahead, into the darkening night and the thick snowflakes swirling in the beams of the car's headlights. The effect is almost mesmerizing. My eyelids start to droop. I want nothing more than to let sleep come, let my mind shut off.

Under slumber's spell, the ache in my heart would subside, the guilt in my soul would vanish, and, if I was lucky, I'd wake up to find that the four little words I heard earlier today were just part of a gruesome dream, an awful nightmare.

Your sister is dead.

The words echo in my mind. Though I try, I can't get them out of my head. My stomach lurches as my thoughts are pulled toward my last moments with her. Fraught with suspicion, accusations, anger. *It's my fault, her death. I didn't step up, didn't protect her. I left her to take her chances against a ruthless man, one I suspected of murder. How could I have been so stupid, so naïve to have fallen for that man's lies, his manipulations?*

If I could go back in time and change everything, fix my mistakes, right a host of wrongs, I would. Things would have turned out differently. Two—no three—people would still be alive. But I can't. There's no going back, no path forward, at least not one I can live with, not without a clear conscience or, at least, forgetting everything that has happened.

Please, God, have mercy on me. Make this all go away.

My gaze is drawn to the rearview mirror. The hazy pair of headlights I see fill me with a sense of dread, a foreboding sense of fate.

Will I be next? Is he coming for me? *Is my fate tied to those headlights behind me now?*

A shiver courses through me, even as a bead of sweat trickles down the side of my face. My heart races, my chest tightens. My fingers, clenched atop the steering wheel, go numb as my foot presses down on the accelerator.

Calm down. Don't let fear trick you into imagining what is not there. I squeeze my eyes shut for a brief moment, then open them again and glance into the driver's side mirror. They're still there, those headlights, keeping pace with me and the car. I force my gaze ahead, take a deep breath, and let it go slowly. "Get a grip on yourself," I say to myself out loud. "If he wanted me dead, I'd be dead by now."

Staring ahead, a forest of pines engulfs the road. Its trees block out much of the remaining daylight, casting a gloominess all around that grows blacker and grimmer with each passing moment.

But I can't go back. I'd have to face the truth, accept my own culpability, surrender myself, my life, my future . . . and never look back.

I turn on the radio and flip through the channels, a distraction to keep my thoughts, my anxiety at bay. I pause when I hear a woman talking.

" . . . it's time for a quick station break, after which we'll go to a weather update with WCVA's meteorologist, Alec Bohanan. Our meteorology team says the blizzard hitting Virginia and much of the

East Coast is a bad one. It could be a killer, so sit tight at home and keep your radio dial tuned to this station . . ."

She's right. The snow is getting worse. Coming down thicker, heavier with each passing mile. The roads will only get worse. But I have to press on. I need to get home. I can think better there. Figure out what options I have left, if any.

My attention is pulled back to the voice on the radio. "When the last segment of the June Jeffries Show returns, we'll join the Virginia State Police press conference with breaking news on the missing person case of—"

Your sister is dead. The words reverberate in my ears, pulsing louder and faster with each echo, drowning out the woman's voice. I slam my fist down on the radio's power button.

It's your fault. The words echo in my head.

Suddenly, flashes of light bounce off the rearview mirror into my eyes. The muscles in my jaw tighten. My neck stiffens. My hands, locked in a death grip on the steering wheel, grow cold, numb.

The light intensifies inside my car. My gaze darts to the rearview mirror. I'm unable to look away from the vehicle approaching me from behind, even as the bright beams reflect directly into my eyes. I hear myself scream, a cry no one can hear. I throw my left arm up to block the intense light, causing the steering wheel to jerk to the right. The passenger-side wheels pitch off the road. I clutch the steering wheel with both hands and pull to the left, but overcorrect. The car careens across the snow-swept blacktop, skids beyond the centerline. When I finally pull the car into the right lane, my body is trembling, my heart is racing, my grip on the steering wheel is weak.

"Calm down. Breathe," I say to myself. I breathe in and out, deep breaths, counting down with each exhale. "One . . . Two . . . Three . . . Four . . ."

The headlights explode again inside my car. The rumble of a powerful engine pierces my ears. I can feel my chest tightening, my throat closing. Just as quickly, the light dims inside my car. I hazard a glance in the rearview mirror. The reflection of a large truck, its silver grill inches from my back window, sends my heart racing. *I've seen that truck grill before...*

My car lurches, slapping my head backward against my seat's headrest. After a stunned moment, I punch the gas pedal to the floor. The car accelerates, my heart races with it. Sweat bleeds into my eyes, burning and blurring my sight. I clear my vision with a few blinks and realize I'm on the wrong side of the road. My heart leaps inside my chest as I veer back into the right lane. The headlights glowing inside my car tell me the fiend is still on my tail.

A glimmer of light in my left mirror catches my attention— another pair of headlights drawing near in the distant blackness. *I'm not alone.* The sight sends blood surging through me. "Hurry up!" I try to shout, but the words catch in my throat.

The monster truck bolts into the left lane and accelerates. I force my gaze to the road ahead, but from the corner of my eye, I see the dark beast pull up alongside me. The roar of its ferocious engine penetrates my car and vibrates through my bones. My hands begin to shake. My body follows. Up ahead, I see a narrow bridge, too narrow for our two speeding vehicles to cross side-by-side.

With dread, I turn my head toward the truck. Its dark passenger-side window begins to slide down. I hold my breath and strain for a glimpse of the driver. In the shadows, a man's profile comes into view. He turns to me. My blood runs cold. A gun appears, aimed at my head.

My chest seems ready to explode. "What are you waiting for?" I shout. "Just shoot me and put me out of my misery already."

From the corner of my eye, I see the bridge looming. Closer. Closer. I return my gaze to the road ahead and realize his plan.

"God, please deliver me from this Hell!"

CamCat
Books

VISIT US ONLINE FOR MORE BOOKS TO LIVE IN:
CAMCATBOOKS.COM

SIGN UP FOR CAMCAT'S FICTION NEWSLETTER FOR
COVER REVEALS, EBOOK DEALS, AND MORE EXCLUSIVE CONTENT.

CamCatBooks   @CamCatBooks   @CamCat_Books   @CamCatBooks